One
August
Night

By Victoria Hislop

The Island
The Return
The Thread
The Sunrise
Cartes Postales from Greece
Those Who Are Loved
One August Night

The Last Dance and Other Stories

South Lanarkshire Libraries

This book is to be returned on
or before the last date stamped
below or may be renewed by
telephone or online.

SOUTH LANARKSHIRE
Leisure & Culture
www.library.southlanarkshire.gov.uk

Delivering services for South Lanarkshire

JT12344/Dec13

REVIEW

First published in 2020 by
HEADLINE REVIEW
An imprint of HEADLINE PUBLISHING GROUP

4

Cataloguing in Publication Data is available from the British Library

ISBN 978 1 4722 7840 1 (Hardback)
ISBN 978 1 4722 7841 8 (Trade Paperback)

Typeset in Bembo by Palimpsest Book Production Limited, Falkirk, Stirlingshire
Printed and bound in Great Britain by Clays Ltd, Elcograf S.p.A.

Headline's policy is to use papers that are natural, renewable and
recyclable products and made from wood grown in sustainable forests.
The logging and manufacturing processes are expected to conform
to the environmental regulations of the country of origin.

HEADLINE PUBLISHING GROUP
An Hachette UK Company
Carmelite House
50 Victoria Embankment
London EC4Y 0DZ

www.headline.co.uk
www.hachette.co.uk

One
August
Night

For my beloved mother
Mary Hamson
to whom *The Island* was also dedicated
28 May 1927 – 17 March 2020

Chapter One

FOR SOME WOMEN, pregnancy is a period of good health and joyful expectation, but for Anna Vandoulakis it was a time of misery and nausea. The doctors insisted that she was confined to her bed for the first three months, telling her that it was the only way to save the baby. During these interminable weeks, she lost her vitality along with her porcelain-smooth complexion and her long, glossy curls, which fell out in handfuls.

Once the obstetrician had confirmed that the pregnancy was stable, Anna's husband, Andreas, invited all the estate workers to enjoy a glass of his best wine. More than a hundred of them gathered in front of the house in the Elounda hills to toast the forthcoming baby. Everyone was aware that the arrival of an heir was long overdue and the continuing health and prosperity of such a vast estate as owned by the Vandoulakis family was dependent on the continuation of the line. It was a matter of concern to them all that Andreas and Anna Vandoulakis should produce some offspring.

Anna did not make an appearance. Instead she watched through the fine gauze of her bedroom curtains, noting that her husband's cousin Manolis was the first to arrive and the last to leave. She could not take her eyes off him even for a moment and was certain that he regularly glanced up towards her. Even this did not allay her greatest fear: that he had forgotten her.

Except for those glimpses from an upstairs window, Anna had not seen Manolis even once during the pregnancy. How could she be seen by someone she wanted to impress when she looked so plain? She resented all that the baby was taking away, even before it arrived.

In the final few weeks she became ill again and was confined to bed. The baby was lying the wrong way round in the womb, her back against Anna's spine, and the birth itself was painful and traumatic. The scrawny infant did not make herself any more welcome when she screamed, almost without pause, throughout the day and into the night. The exhausted Anna then declared that she found breastfeeding repellent, and a wet nurse had to be found.

The birth brought Anna no relief from her self-loathing. Almost overnight, she went from being bulky to looking gaunt, and she could not bear the sight of herself in the mirror. For someone who had previously spent several hours a day admiring herself in one, this was a significant change. Anna was unrecognisable from the radiant and beautiful woman she used to be. Andreas was dismayed by what had happened to her, and when he asked his mother, Eleftheria, whether this catatonic state of depression was normal after pregnancy, she had to admit it was not. It was not so long since Andreas's two sisters had given birth, and both of them had been immediately caught up in the joys of motherhood. Eleftheria had expected Anna to be the same. She was particularly surprised that her daughter-in-law had turned down the idea of inviting her father to come and see the new arrival. Although they had never really extended any hospitality to him, Eleftheria found it strange that Giorgos Petrakis was not being given the opportunity to see his first grandchild. Surely, she thought, he deserved a little happiness, given that his other daughter, Maria, was a leprosy patient on Spinalonga, the island where his wife had died some years before. It was Anna's choice, however, and she was not going to intervene.

When the baby was around ten days old, Andreas came in one evening a little later than normal. As usual, Anna turned her head away when he leant to peck her on the cheek.

'I went to see the priest,' he announced. 'To fix the date of the baptism.'

Anna could not object. She had been refusing to leave the house, so Andreas had been obliged to make the arrangements alone. In the Vandoulakis family, a child was always baptised within a few weeks of birth. Any later than that broke with tradition.

'I have also been considering who should be her godparent,' he said bluntly. 'I think we should ask Manolis. He's already part of the family and I can't think of anyone else who will always be there for our daughter.'

Manolis was the obvious choice for *nonós*, given that neither Anna nor Andreas had any close friends, but Anna had been reluctant to suggest it herself. She could scarcely suppress her joy.

'That's a lovely idea,' she said. 'Will you ask him tomorrow?'

It was the first time Andreas had seen his wife smile for many months.

That night, she steeled herself to look in the mirror. She recoiled. Her skin was dry and sallow and the shadows under her eyes were purple. The hair that she had once been so proud of was thin and matted, and her body had lost its contours. It was a shock, but now that she had an incentive, she resolved to regain the looks that she had prized so much, the looks that had made her such a prize. The baptism would be the first time she would encounter Manolis after many months, and also the first time that she would be seen by other acquaintances and family members.

It was more than enough to motivate her. She began to eat better, to take fresh air, to apply the best face creams, to massage olive oil into her hair until it gleamed again, and quickly summoned the dressmaker to make her a new outfit for the occasion.

As soon as she began once again to pause in front of mirrors rather than avoid them, her vanity returned in full. Although she was still slightly slimmer than she had been in previous years, her breasts became plump again and she enjoyed the contrast with her new, smaller waistline.

She threw herself into the practical preparations for the baptism, organising the feast, the flowers, the music, the various robes for the child and favours for the guests. It was to be a grand event, with as many people as could be crammed into the Elounda church for the service and hundreds more invited to the festivities afterwards.

When the date finally came in late September, Anna felt ready. She was renewed and excited about the day. The dress she had had made accentuated her hourglass figure and flattered her regained curves. It was made of crimson silk.

She and Andreas arrived with the baby to an already full church. In the front rows sat all the members of the Vandoulakis family. The patriarch, Alexandros, upright and dignified; Eleftheria, his wife, elegant and expressionless, determined not to betray the slightest emotion, even on this special day for her granddaughter. Olga, the elder of the two sisters, and her husband, Lefteris, sat with their four unruly children between them. Eirini, the other sister, sat with her two-year-old daughter on her lap, nervously looking around for her husband, who eventually arrived halfway through the service.

The others at the front of the church were the numerous lawyers who serviced the needs of this wealthy family, the bankers who managed their riches, and the mayors and town councillors of Elounda, Agios Nikolaos and Neapoli, effectively the capital of the region. This contingent was formally dressed, the men in suits and the women in tailored dresses. Behind them were those who worked on the estate, the land managers, the suppliers of agricultural equipment and livestock and so on. There was an almost visible line to be drawn between the two groups. They were differentiated by the quality of cloth, the fineness of the fabrics worn by those in the front rows being in stark contrast to the rougher weaves at the back.

The only member of the family who was talking animatedly to various guests was the *nonós* himself. Unlike other members of the family, Manolis was as happy chatting with the bankers' wives as to the workers on the farm.

As soon as Anna entered the church, all eyes turned to look at her.

'*Panagía mou*, what *is* she wearing?' Olga whispered behind her hand to her sister.

Eirini was equally aghast. 'I don't believe it,' she murmured.

'It's so *vulgar* for such an event, don't you think? Bright red?' continued Olga.

'I agree entirely,' said Eirini. 'But not exactly out of character . . .'

Anna had chosen scarlet because it suited her perfectly. She had never looked more beautiful and she knew it. The rich colour was a daring contrast with her pale skin and chocolate-dark hair, and the cherry lipstick was a bold touch that few women could have worn as well.

She saw no one but Manolis. It was so long since they had met, and even from a distance this reunion was having an effect on them both. He stared at her, transfixed.

Andreas wanted to hand the baby to its mother.

'Anna, I think it's customary . . .' he said, holding out the little white bundle to her.

His wife was distracted for a moment and did not respond.

'Anna?'

She was gazing into the distance.

'Anna!' insisted Andreas, irritated by her lack of response now.

Flustered, she took her daughter and cradled her in her arms, her legs shaking so much she could scarcely stand. Manolis was approaching, ready to play his central role in the most important spiritual moment of this child's life.

He touched Anna lightly on the arm and leaned in to kiss the baby's cheek.

She breathed in, inhaling his scent. Soap? The fields? The brand of sweet tobacco he favoured? If her arms had not been full, it would have been impossible to resist touching his hair, but feeling the sensation of his jacket on her bare arm was enough for now, as they paused before their walk down the aisle.

Out of the corner of her eye she saw Manolis take a sideways glance, and knew it was a look of admiration.

'I think it's time,' said Andreas impatiently. 'They're waiting.'

Clad in ornate gilded robes and a tall hat embellished with elaborate stitching, a priest stood waiting at the font. He had a beard that almost reached his waist and held a golden crook. His two assistant priests, more modestly dressed, flanked him. They were dwarfed by his majestic height and imposing presence.

The trio began to process down the aisle, Anna in the middle as exquisite as a rose in full bloom, on each side of her a man, handsome, almost aristocratic, in a dark suit. Dressed in this way Andreas and Manolis were even more disconcertingly alike than usual.

Tucked up in Anna's arms and swathed in white lace, the baby was sleeping, blissfully unaware of the trauma shortly to come. It began soon enough: the stripping-off of her clothes, repeated plunges into the font, the coating with oil, the cutting of her hair, before she was dressed again and carried round and round with candles flickering close by. Being passed from parent to priest to *nonós* accompanied by the constant sound of unfamiliar chants and wafts of strange smells was enough to terrify the child, even without the additional rituals.

Sofia, as she was baptised, screamed loudly for the first part of the ceremony, with only the occasional phrase of the liturgy audible above her wails. The first moment of respite was when Manolis fastened a pretty gold cross around her neck, his official gift to her as godfather.

Anna smiled. Perhaps she likes pretty jewellery, she reflected, just like her mother. She hoped that Manolis had noticed she was wearing the earrings he had given her for her saint's day.

For much of the latter part of the ceremony, Manolis held the baby in his arms. She was much quieter then and gazed up at her *nonós* as the priest unfurled a white ribbon to encircle them both. After ninety minutes, it was finally all over and the great crowd filed outside and milled around noisily in the sunshine, happy to be out of the stuffy church and looking forward to the socialising that was to follow. For many it was the first time they had seen Sofia, and the women in particular wanted to get a closer look. They clustered around Manolis, who held the now tranquil bundle with enormous pride.

'Lovely brown eyes, just like her father,' several of them said.

'And she's definitely going to have her mother's luxuriant hair,' said one.

'Yes, look at the curls she has already!' agreed another.

'She's beautiful!'

'So pretty!'

'What a perfect baby!'

'*Ftou, ftou, ftou!*' responded Manolis. Any kind of compliment might attract the Devil's attention, and pretending to spit was the customary way to deflect it.

From a short distance away, Anna watched him. At the same time, she was talking to her father, Giorgos, trying to encourage him to come to the party planned for the evening. He was reluctant, given that he always felt uncomfortable in the presence of the Vandoulakis family. It was not merely his status as a humble fisherman. The far greater issue was the taint of leprosy. The death of his wife on Spinalonga had been hidden from Anna's in-laws at first, but his younger daughter's diagnosis and departure to live there could not be concealed. Even if they had managed to bury their prejudice where Anna was concerned, this grand family made no effort to conceal their disdain for her father. It was only sensible to keep him at arm's length, they agreed.

Once Giorgos had agreed to join the celebration for a short while, Anna seemed happy and moved away. She was ready to leave now.

There was a brief pause while a photographer corralled the parents and godfather to be photographed on the steps of the church. Anna stood in the middle holding Sofia, Andreas and Manolis on either side. It was a formal shot, the one needed to mark the day. Immediately afterwards, Andreas drove Anna and the baby back to their home high in the hills of Elounda. It was a spacious and airy property, set in the middle of olive groves, with a view over some of the few thousand acres that belonged to the family. This was only a small proportion of what they owned.

Since moving in, Anna had made significant changes, not only with interior decoration, but to the exterior too. At the front of the house she had flattened an area to create a terrace. This was where the party was to take place. Trestle tables strewn with flowers were set out in long rows, with bottles of wine and raki running down the centre of each one. Under nearby trees, goats were being turned on spits by a team of chefs.

Guests were arriving in their hundreds. They stood about in groups and helped themselves to wine and copious quantities of food already cooked and waiting in dishes on a buffet. Many showed no restraint and ate greedily. Most had some kind of commercial relationship with the Vandoulakis family, and there was a sense that such a rich feast was their entitlement.

As soon as they had returned from church, Anna had handed the baby to her nursemaid. The child was already asleep and there was no need for her presence during this part of the day.

Giorgos was among the last to arrive and nervously surveyed the throng for anyone he knew. Maria's best friend, Fotini, noticed him standing alone and hurried over with her brother Antonis. The two families were closely intertwined. Giorgos's face lit up when he spotted them. He regularly saw Fotini in the family taverna in Plaka, but it was a while since he had seen Antonis.

'How are you?' he asked affectionately. 'Even more handsome than ever!'

'Yes,' said Fotini, poking her brother's arm, 'he's too handsome for his own good.'

It was not a matter of opinion that Antonis was the best-looking man at the gathering. Even from childhood, his huge brown eyes had held the attention of anyone who looked at him. They were the shape of almonds and the colour of chestnuts.

'And too fussy!' she teased. 'We should be baptising a child of his by now. But he won't even look at the girls.'

'Fotini . . .' protested Antonis good-naturedly. 'That's not true. I just haven't found the right one yet, that's all.'

'You're waiting for her, aren't you?' said Giorgos supportively. 'Marry in a day and you'll regret it for life.'

A few minutes passed with Giorgos asking the younger man all sorts of questions about his work on the estate. It was a demanding job but clearly one that suited Antonis. He had fought with huge bravery for the resistance during the German occupation and returned with extraordinary powers of endurance and physical strength. Manual labour was almost effortless for him and, as Giorgos observed, made him seem more god-like than ever.

Manolis sauntered across to chat with them. Over the past few years, he and Antonis had become best friends. Antonis had been wary of him at first, but the two men had eventually found that they had much in common, not least a great passion for music. They often played together, Antonis on his *thiáboli*, a wooden flute, and Manolis on his lyra.

Giorgos congratulated Manolis on being the *nonós*. Like everyone who saw them together, he was always struck by the similarity between Andreas and his cousin. At just under two metres, the two men were both taller than the average Cretan. They had the same thick brown hair and high cheekbones. The only physical difference was that Andreas was slightly heavier about the jawline, but it was their contrasting demeanour that allowed even a stranger to tell them apart. Manolis had deep creases around his eyes, the result of constant smiling and laughter, whereas

Andreas was dour, his seriousness showing even in the hunch of his shoulders.

The musicians were striking up now, and the first tune was for the stately *siganós*, an eight-step dance that everyone could join. On Anna's terrace there was an area big enough for a hundred people to form a circle, and this was what they began to do. Once the space was filled, a second circle was formed inside the first, and then another, until there were four concentric rings. There were ten musicians: two bowing on lyra, three strumming on *laoúto*, two on guitar, one on a fiddle, one drumming on a tabor and one on mandolin. They made a full and rich sound. Everyone knew the complex step pattern even for the next dance, with its fifteen beats, and small children who had been running amok until now slotted between the adults and confidently blended into the ebb and flow of the movements, never putting a foot wrong, as though they had learned these dances in the womb.

Giorgos felt it was a good time for him to leave. After observing the dancing for a short while, he exchanged a few formal words with Anna's in-laws, then slipped away unnoticed to make his way home.

At one point, encouraged by Antonis, Manolis went to his truck to fetch his lyra. He took a seat, held the delicate three-stringed instrument in his left hand and drew the bow across the strings with his right. It looked so small in his large hands, but out of it he conjured an immense sound, skilfully sustaining the melody against the insistent strumming of the *laoúto*. The notes came tumbling out, faster and faster, and for an hour or more he played without pause.

There was no end to the musicians' stamina. The music flowed over the guests as if it was seeking escape into the hills around them. Manolis gazed into the middle distance. Though his seat was at the end of the row, he was at the heart of the music and the centre of attention.

A well-known singer joined them around ten o'clock. It was the moment that ignited the evening and brought the spirit of *kéfi*, of almost frenzied celebration, to the occasion.

Later, Manolis danced the solo *zeibékiko*. The audience gathered to admire his display of acrobatic turns and pirouettes, and it was clear that he was showing off rather than expressing the anguish that the dance usually conveyed.

Andreas spent most of the evening moving between groups of guests to thank them for being there and for their gifts for Sofia. From time to time he caught a glimpse of his wife and noticed that she was smiling. It was the first time in almost a year that he had seen her looking happy and relaxed. At last, he thought, she is back to her old self.

Once the dancing began, he lost track of her, but occasionally he spotted a flash of red. As the great circle revolved, he could see her face more clearly. She seemed enraptured, held captive by the spirit of the dance.

It took many days to recover from such a *gléndi*. Autumn was coming and there was much work to be done on the estate, but all the workers were a little sluggish.

'The boss only has himself to blame,' Antonis commented to Manolis. 'There was more raki than water.'

'I think we drank every drop there was,' laughed Manolis. 'It'll be time to make this year's supply soon.'

The grape harvest was starting in a few weeks and would eventually be followed by the distillation process, which would create the firewater that fuelled so much merrymaking on the island.

The two friends were at the *kafeneío* in Plaka. The day's work was over and Manolis had gone there to rehang his lyra on the wall behind the bar. This was where it lived. He often played it spontaneously and by popular demand from his friends in Plaka.

'She is my only love,' he often joked.

Dancing next to Manolis at the baptism had fired Anna's longing to be with him again. His lithe figure and the energy with which he danced and played his lyra filled her with lust. She set about constructing an opportunity for them to be alone, and two days later her desire was fulfilled in all ways.

The nursemaid who cared for Sofia throughout the day had taken her for a long walk. The child was a restless creature, even more so during the days following the baptism, and only the motion and vibration of her pram lulled her to sleep.

Anna was unrestrained in her pleasure that afternoon. The day was hot and the windows wide and Manolis clamped his hand over her mouth to muffle her groans. In ecstasy, and in the spirit of near-violence that sometimes characterised their lovemaking, she bit down on his fingers.

'Anna!'

He moaned with pleasure as she let out a final uncontained gasp.

For a while they both lay still, the sheets damp and twisted beneath them.

Manolis played with a strand of Anna's dark hair that lay fanned out across the pillows and wound it round his finger.

She turned her head towards him.

'I can't live without you,' she whispered, only just loudly enough for him to hear.

'You don't have to, *agápi mou*,' he said quietly.

Chapter Two

OVER THE FOLLOWING year, Anna and Manolis fell into a
pattern of seeing each other several times a week. As godfather, Manolis now had even more reason than usual to call in
at the house. Sofia created the ideal pretext, though he always
timed his lunchtime visits with the child being taken out for a
walk. He also had the advantage of knowing when Andreas had
to visit customers in Sitia or Iraklion.

Anna lived for the present. At the very most she thought two or
three days ahead, or to when Manolis's next visit was going to be.
She did not want to be bothered by thoughts of the following month
or year. All she knew was that she had never felt happier than now.

One morning she was sitting contentedly flicking through a
magazine as the housekeeper, Kyría Vasilakis, polished the furniture around the edges of the room. Anna was humming. The
glossy pages featured fashions for autumn, and her dressmaker was
scheduled to come that afternoon to measure her for some new
gowns. There was a shape with a cinched-in waist and exagger-
atedly full skirt coming into vogue, and she knew that it would
flatter her, especially now that her figure was filling out again.
The dressmaker would be bringing fabric swatches, and Anna had
already planned to order three in the same style.

She leaned over the back of her seat to show Kyría Vasilakis
one of the images.

'That will suit you perfectly, Kyría Anna!' cried the housekeeper, giving the appropriate response. 'And you're looking better and better by the day!'

Everyone had noticed the recent transformation. There was colour in Anna's cheeks again, and her hair shone. She looked even more beautiful now than before her pregnancy.

'Doctors can do plenty for us, but if you ask me, I think you've had the eye.'

Anna often found her housekeeper's home-grown wisdom and superstitions mildly annoying. Kyría Vasilakis was a great believer in the power of one person to cast a spell on another, usually on account of jealousy, by giving them 'the eye'. In her view, everyone needed protection from the *máti*, the evil eye. She never ventured outside her own home without wearing her blue glass talisman, believing that it protected her from all kinds of woes and illnesses.

On the subject of health in general, Kyría Vasilakis was in her element, and not to be deterred.

'Ordinary medicine can't treat everything, you know,' she continued.

Anna resumed her perusal of the magazine. She did not want to hear her housekeeper's views on herbal cures and the human body. In order to be prepared for this afternoon, she needed to study pleats and gathers and necklines, and was becoming irritated by this intrusion into her concentration.

'But there's something those doctors never lose patience with,' Kyría Vasilakis went on, 'and that's leprosy. They just keep trying and trying.'

Anna sighed audibly. If only the woman would just go away.

'And they say they might be making progress with it! Who would have thought? People have been dying of it for thousands of years and now they're talking of a *cure*!'

For a moment, Anna could hardly breathe. Her chest had tightened and she sat motionless, her sweating hands clutching the magazine until its pages crumpled within them.

'You see, with some diseases, even I agree there's no place for herbal remedies. They've been trying those for centuries – snake oil, cactus extract, all sorts. Nothing has ever worked. But it's so nice that those wonderful doctors never gave up, isn't? They just kept on and on . . .'

The surfaces were thoroughly beeswaxed now. Kyría Vasilakis was never happy until she could see her reflection in them. She finished off by flicking her feather duster over an ornate clock, straightening the lace cloth on the dresser and plumping up some cushions. Anna sat frozen.

'Can I bring you something, Kyría Anna?' the housekeeper asked. 'If there is nothing more you need doing in here, I'll start the lunch. I can shake the rugs out later.'

Anna shook her head. She just wanted the infernal woman out of the room. She had heard enough. Slamming the magazine down on the table in front of her, she tried to control her trembling.

Kyría Vasilakis's casual comment had thrown her into turmoil. The discovery of a cure for leprosy was her worst nightmare. It would mean the return of her sister Maria from Spinalonga.

The man Anna loved with her whole being had once been engaged to Maria, and she was seized with terror that her own relationship with Manolis was now in jeopardy.

When the dressmaker arrived with his assistant – it had taken them since early morning to travel by bus from Iraklion – he was told that the client was indisposed. Anna had announced to Kyría Vasilakis that she had a migraine, and had withdrawn to her room and closed the curtains.

For the next twenty-four hours, she stayed in bed, tortured by the housekeeper's words, but late the following morning, she remembered that Manolis had promised to visit. The thought of his arrival drove her to get up and into one of her favourite dresses.

With her make-up carefully applied and a favourite necklace and matching earrings clipped in place, she dabbed some perfume onto her neck and went downstairs. The house was silent except for the sound of a ticking clock. Sofia had been taken out for a walk by the nursemaid, and Kyría Vasilakis had the afternoon off.

Anna sat down at the kitchen table and read the front page of the daily newspaper. It was waiting there for Andreas to read when he returned from the estate. It was the first thing he did each evening. He was a creature of habit. There was little in it to interest her. A rise in the cost of fuel. The death of some politician of whom she had never heard. A tremor on some islands further north.

She put a jug of lemonade, freshly made by Kyría Vasilakis, and two glasses on the table, and sat waiting. What seemed an age after the clock struck two, she heard the sound of the latch. Annoyed that Manolis was seven minutes later than she had expected him, she remained sitting, stiff and upright. Instead of a smile and her open arms, it was her back that greeted him.

Manolis was familiar with Anna's sulks. They never bothered him, because he usually found a way to dispel them.

'*Kaliméra, agápi mou*,' he said breezily. There was no reply.

He saw that Anna was pretending to read the headlines, and stealthily pulled a flower from a vase on the sideboard.

She felt a tickling on the back of her neck, but stayed stubbornly still. Manolis then leant forward and caressed her neck with his fingers, at the same time taking the flower and sliding it into her cleavage. Anna spun round, her resolve to remain angry melting away.

As Manolis made love to her that afternoon, Anna reacted to his touch with great passion. Thoughts of her sister's return made her responses even more explosive than normal, and she ran her fingernails hard down his back, feeling them penetrate the skin.

For a short while afterwards they lay still, and Anna rested a hand on his chest. It was only a few minutes, though, before her fears rose once again. In very few ways was she capable of restraining herself, and she told her lover what the housekeeper had said.

'So you think nothing will change?' she persisted. Rumours of the cure had created an unease in her that she could not allay.

'What do you mean, *moró mou*?'

'You must know what I mean! Nothing would be the same if they . . . if they came back.'

Manolis realised what was on her mind. What Anna really meant was 'she', not 'they'. Rumours that a cure for leprosy might be closer had begun to circulate more widely, and he had heard the gossip that even the most deformed might soon be back and living among them. But Anna was thinking only of one person. Maria had been on his mind too, but he had suppressed any thoughts of her reappearance and how it might affect his life. He was reasonably certain that he and Anna's sister had each relinquished any hold on the other when she left for Spinalonga, though there had never been a formal end to their engagement.

Almost roughly, he pulled Anna towards him and gave her a lingering kiss on the lips. He could feel her relax beneath him.

'Promise me you'll stop worrying,' he said softly. 'Nothing is going to change between us. The little one's *nonós* isn't going anywhere.'

'The little one's father . . .?' Anna responded.

'Who knows?' Manolis cut in. 'She is my little *vaftistíra*, my little baptised girl. I am her spiritual father. That's what matters.'

Although they had tried to be cautious in their lovemaking, both Anna and Manolis knew that the question of paternity could not be absolutely certain. The child bore a resemblance to both the men in her life, and given the cousins' strong likeness to each other, this was no surprise. Manolis had occasionally wondered, but preferred to put this doubt to the back of his mind. Anna, on the other hand, seemed to relish the idea that her lover was the father of her child.

Manolis wanted to reassure Anna, however, that if Maria ever did return, it would not end their relationship. There was no possibility of him marrying a former leprosy patient.

He kissed her again, and for the second time that afternoon they made love, this time more wildly than before. It was only the sound of Sofia's loud, insistent crying at being lifted out of her pram downstairs that disturbed them.

Manolis leapt from the bed and dressed hastily. He listened at the door for a moment and then, glancing back over his shoulder, smiled at the flawless naked form of his lover on the bed.

Languidly Anna raised a hand to her lips and blew him a kiss.

Then Manolis turned, picked up his dusty boots and padded down the back staircase out of the house.

Anna lay for a few moments before she got up, washed herself at the corner basin and chose something fresh from her wardrobe. Everyone knew that Kyría Vandoulakis always had a sleep in the afternoon, so the maid would not expect to see her for a while. She did her best to straighten the sheets, and as she was plumping the pillows, she noticed a tiny speck of red, a trace of Manolis's blood, on one of them. She removed the pillowslip, dropped it into the laundry basket and found a fresh one in the linen drawer.

The months passed. Anna was demanding and passionate and emotional, a combination that Manolis could not resist. Her mood was intensified by an ever-deepening terror: the possibility of a cure for leprosy. Whatever Manolis said to reassure her, her dread about what Maria's return could mean gnawed away at her. Fear and fury grew, making her mood febrile and her behaviour less rational. When Manolis visited, she was careless about whether the windows were open or closed, or whether she straightened the sheets after he had gone. It was almost as if she wanted their affair to be discovered.

What would happen if − and it was still no more than this − Maria came back? She constantly circled back to the same question and it was impossible for Manolis to make her understand his position. How many times did he have to promise her that he would never exchange her for her sister? The very notion of it was preposterous. But the idea was like a grub burrowing into her skin, laying its eggs and breeding more.

Manolis resigned himself to Anna incessantly pressing him on the subject. Normally he exerted something close to magic over his lover, but on this subject he was powerless.

Chapter Three

ONE EVENING THAT summer, Manolis was enjoying a second carafe of raki outside the *kafeneío* in Plaka. He loved the view of the bay and in general scarcely gave the sight of Spinalonga a second thought.

Giorgos was coming across the water towards the village. The boat glided over the surface of the sea, leaving behind it a mesmerising pattern of ripples, as even as the lines of a ploughed field.

Manolis watched the old man tether his boat below and make his way up from the jetty. He often bought Giorgos a drink after he had made a delivery to the island, and the two men always chatted for a while. Giorgos was a man restrained in speech and emotion, but today he looked happier than usual. It was evident even in the spring in his step.

'You've heard the rumour?' he asked simply.

Manolis nodded and the two men clinked their glasses together.

Manolis thought of a particular moment a few years earlier when Giorgos had appeared in the bar. He remembered the pallor of his skin, the stoop of his shoulders and the way he had avoided Manolis's eye as he told him the terrible news about Maria. When Manolis thought about it now, his overriding emotion had been sorrow for the old man. He had felt little else. It was Giorgos he had pitied, not himself.

Manolis had always maintained that he had loved Maria once,

but in recent months there had been plenty of time to reflect on this. Beyond question she had been very different from anyone he had ever met before, but her purity had been little more than a tease for him. The idea of her virginity had been alluring because he had enjoyed the anticipation of taking it from her, but when she disappeared from his life, it was sadness he had felt, rather than grief. He believed that the fates had played a role in removing her from his life.

Now that he thought about it, he recalled also feeling something close to relief. He had never been able to imagine himself waking up next to the same person day after day, knowing that this beginning would be some kind of end too.

Even if it was hard to admit to himself, at the core of his relationship with Maria had been another pleasure: that of stirring her sister to a fury. The idea of Anna's jealousy gently but constantly simmering always sweetened his day, and made their eventual coming together all the more ferocious in its passion.

The two men had a brief conversation now about the news of a possible cure.

'Let's hope it comes to something,' said Giorgos before getting up. It was a typical pattern. He never stayed long.

The evening held onto the heat of the day, and as he often did, Manolis stripped to swim off the rocks before heading home. He drove back with his hair still damp and a fine layer of salt on his skin.

Over the ensuing days, the temperature began to climb. There was not even the slightest hint of a breeze. Sea and sky merged into a single mirrored surface and the trees were motionless.

Later that week, Andreas invited Manolis to have dinner at their home. The whole family, including his sisters Olga and Eirini and their husbands and children, were there to celebrate Olga's saint's day. It was a noisy event.

Before dinner, while the grown-ups had a drink, Olga's three boys, who were all under seven, tore up and down the stairs and

along corridors, unrestrained by their parents. The oldest pretended
to be a Turk and chased the younger two, brandishing a wooden
sword he had brought with him, until he felled them one by one,
and then the game began all over again. The only fact of history
that had stuck in his head so far was that his country had once
been liberated from four hundred years of Turkish rule after a
number of battles. It provided endless potential for violent games
with his brothers.

Olga and Eirini's daughters played happily together on a rug.
They were both four years old, and as well as being entertained
by their toys, they were allowed to play with Sofia and plait her
hair.

A real-life doll was even more fun than the ones with moulded
faces and strange staring eyes, and they both got carried away
while their parents were not looking. Suddenly the real one started
crying, which made both of them grizzle, and Sofia was taken
off to bed by the nursemaid. Both girls got a smack on the hand,
which sparked a new wave of tears.

Even with the chaos created by the children, Manolis relished
the opportunity to see Anna in front of the rest of the family. He
knew she found the situation awkward and enjoyed that.

Everyone was uncomfortably overdressed that night, Alexandros
and his two sons-in-law wearing jackets and the women their best
evening dresses. Manolis had put on a clean white shirt, and his
eyes frequently strayed across to look at Anna, who was in emerald-
green silk. The colour of jealousy suited her well.

By the time they sat down to dinner and the children had
calmed down, Anna's nerves were frayed. It was not only the
snivelling of the girls and the squeals of the boys that had caused
this. It was her usual disquiet over the rumours of leprosy treatment.

If Anna was on edge, Manolis too was a little uneasy that night.
The workers were often conduits of the latest – and usually accurate – news, and he knew that Andreas had heard the same

21

information from them as he had. Nothing travelled faster than word of mouth, and as ever, by the time events were printed in the local newspaper, they were already well known.

Even as Andreas was unfurling his napkin and spreading it across his lap, Manolis held his breath. He knew what his cousin was going to say.

'It seems they have made progress at last!' Andreas announced. 'They're going to start sending the lepers home. A few of them have been cured.'

Although she had not yet touched her food, Anna began to choke. It gave her the perfect excuse to leave the table.

Andreas followed his wife from the room and was gone for ten minutes.

'She'll be fine,' he reassured everyone when he eventually strode back in. He vainly attempted a smile.

'It must be quite a shock to find out your sister is coming home after all this time,' said Alexandros.

'A nice surprise, you mean?' queried Kyría Eleftheria. 'Surely she's pleased, Andreas?'

'I am sure their reunion will be a very happy occasion,' Manolis chipped in blandly.

'Just imagine how their father must be feeling,' Eleftheria continued, clasping her hands together with pleasure.

Eleftheria had always felt mildly ashamed that they had not been more welcoming to Giorgos Petrakis at Sofia's baptism, but fear of her husband's disapproval had been enough to deter her from being overfriendly. Alexandros Vandoulakis's concern at the distant family connection to Spinalonga was as strong as it had ever been. Now perhaps things would start to change.

When Andreas returned from checking on his wife again, he told everyone that she was feeling better now and would be downstairs again in a moment. As soon as the *gliká tou koutalioú*, sweet spoon desserts, were set on the table and there had been another chorus of '*Xrónia Pollá*' to toast Olga, Manolis made an excuse to leave. He claimed a touch of heat stroke and exhaustion from a long day in the fields, but the real reason was that he had no wish to stay around if Anna was not in the room. He would need to see her again very soon, to press upon her once more that Maria's return would *not* affect his love for her.

By the next day, the heat had intensified and a lethargy settled over the Vandoulakis estate. Everyone worked at half-pace, and for three hours, when the temperature was at its highest, the men dozed beneath the trees. There was no point making them return to work when both limbs and lids were heavy with heat. These were important weeks of preparation for the beginning of the grape harvest, and Andreas demanded that everyone work long hours, *and* after the sun went down, but he could not ban their siesta.

Manolis knew Anna was expecting him that afternoon, but he sat down for a moment and sleep seduced him just as it had the others. He worked as hard as any of them. He played an indispensable role on the estate these days, acting as a bridge between the owner of these vast and productive acreages of vineyards, olive groves and agricultural land and everyone who worked on them.

He had arrived six years earlier, after a decade of wandering about in Europe squandering a huge sum left to him by his grandfather. Manolis's late father had been the eldest of two brothers and the heir to the great estate, but he had died young and the land had passed to Alexandros Vandoulakis instead. In due course, it would pass to Andreas. Manolis harboured no resentment, and in any case he loved his life just as it was.

'If the gods had wished it, history would be different,' he once said to his friend Antonis. Antonis found Manolis's acceptance of his lot and his lack of bitterness about it incomprehensible.

It had been Manolis's own choice to spend the previous years travelling and womanising and exploring the very lengths and depths of hedonism. He did not regret a single moment. In fact, he pitied anyone who had never lived in Paris, Rome or Barcelona as he had done.

He had returned to Crete with nothing but a lyra that he had treasured since childhood. During his travels, this precious possession had not only been used to entertain, but had often earned him enough to survive. In many cities in France and Austria, no one had ever heard such a pure singing voice as his, nor the mellow tones of an instrument so puzzlingly like, and yet unlike, a violin. Along with the language that few even recognised, people were enthralled by the music he made.

Although he had not a single drachma in his pocket, he did bring back with him a skill that was lacking in the rest of the Vandoulakis family: an ability to engage with anyone, regardless of age, wealth or education. People loved this man. Even animals were drawn to him. It was said that wild goats gathered round him if he whistled, and there was often a trail of eager stray dogs behind him.

Manolis's mother had died in childbirth, and after his father's death when he was five, Alexandros and Eleftheria Vandoulakis had brought him up as their own son. Despite this, when he first arrived back on the estate, Alexandros had decided to test his seriousness about wanting to work there. In his view, the family name alone did not automatically entitle him to a role. He set his nephew the same tasks as he would for any new employee. Manolis must prove himself.

He was shown a piece of neglected land – and on this sprawling estate there were still plenty of uncultivated corners – and told to make what he could of it. Within the space of a few days, he had demonstrated his physical strength and stamina in clearing it. What impressed his uncle most, though, was the way in which he recruited others to assist him. People willingly did him favours. There was no monetary value that could be put on such rare charisma.

Within a short time, Manolis was managing the workforce on the estate. He engaged in hard physical labour alongside them, not only because it motivated them, but because he enjoyed it too.

Anna did not understand why he insisted on working the same long hours as his men. Surely he was their boss? That day she did not care to excuse him for his non-appearance. He should be there with *her*. She was becoming increasingly irrational, and as the days went by and Manolis missed more of their usual lunch-time meetings, she did not hide her anger.

The atmosphere in the Elounda home was tense. Even though the simple explanation was Andreas's instruction for everyone to work overtime, Manolis's continued absence unhinged her. Nothing tempted her to dress or to eat, and she could not even be coaxed into taking an interest in her little daughter. Naturally she offered no explanation to her husband, and increasingly took to her bed.

Andreas telephoned his mother to cancel a dinner engagement with his parents, and Eleftheria Vandoulakis shared her suspicions with her husband.

'Don't you remember how off-colour she was the first time?'

Alexandros was only half listening.

'Is she ill?'

'A *baby*, Alexandros!' Eleftheria cried in frustration. 'I think she might be *pregnant*!'

'Oh!' responded Alexandros, with more interest now. 'I do hope it's a boy this time.'

Eleftheria shook her head despairingly.

'I am sure she'll tell us when she's ready,' she said. 'But at least it would explain her behaviour.'

Manolis had a few late nights with Antonis in the *kafeneío* that week. The two men lost themselves in games of *távli* and carafe after carafe of raki, and one evening they played music until the sun came up. When Manolis picked up his lyra, time lost all meaning. With the encouragement of an appreciative audience, Antonis on the *thiáboli* and very often the company of a *laoúto*, he could play and sing for hours.

One evening, planning just to stay for a short time, he called in for a cold beer. The previous night he had been playing until dawn and had gone straight to the fields without sleep. Normally he knew everyone in the *kafeneío*, but tonight there was a pair of unfamiliar faces. Two men, clearly friends, sat together in the corner. It was unusual in such a small place for strangers not to be integrated into the general conversation, but these men did not seem uncomfortable with being ostracised. They had chosen to sit in the shadows.

Grigoris, the *kafetzís*, approached Manolis with his beer and put it down. Even though Manolis had his back to the strangers, Grigoris knew his customer well enough to interpret his glance.

'They were let out early,' he said, under his breath.

The phrase immediately made Manolis think of prison.

'They took the medicine before the others,' continued Grigoris. 'They're cured.'

The men overheard, and one of them quietly got up and approached Manolis. His proximity was not intended to be threatening, but Manolis found himself momentarily afraid of the presence looming over him. He sprang to his feet and turned around to face him.

'Vandoulakis!' said the man.

The voice seemed familiar to Manolis, but nothing much else did. It was an involuntary reaction, but he stepped back, unable to conceal his revulsion.

'Panagiotis Apostolakis.'

Getting little more than a blank look from his old acquaintance, Panagiotis Apostolakis repeated himself.

Manolis now recalled that someone with the name Apostolakis used to own a taverna in Elounda. He had been there many times.

The man was holding out his hand, and Manolis saw that it lacked several fingers. He had not anticipated that he would feel so repelled. He thrust his own hands into his trouser pockets and took another step back.

Though his thick stature was unchanged, Panagiotis Apostolakis was facially unrecognisable. He had been a handsome man with a moustache that had impressed even Manolis. Now he was bald, with not a single hair on his head or his face.

Manolis looked over Apostolakis's shoulder and caught sight of his companion. The other man was more seriously disfigured, his face deeply scarred, his ears distended. From his vacant stare, Manolis deduced that he was also blind.

He tried to overcome his revulsion but failed to reach out. Apostolakis had dropped his hand to his side now in any case.

'So . . .' was all Manolis could manage to say. Words dried in his mouth.

'We're the first to be . . .'

Grigoris passed them on his way to serve another table.

'They're the first to have tried the drugs!' said the *kafetzís* with enthusiasm. 'Almost the first to come home!'

Manolis managed a smile.

'Yes. It's great news!' he said unconvincingly, reaching for the dregs of his beer that still sat on the table.

He drained the glass and left hastily.

As he climbed into his truck, he found his hands shaking so much that he struggled to put the key in the ignition. As the engine eventually fired into life, he caught sight of Giorgos in the distance. He swung the truck round to avoid having to pass him and roared off.

As he drove, he asked himself the same questions, over and over again. Would Maria look like that now? Would she be without a nose? Without hands? Without hair? He struggled in vain to stop his mind from imagining her this way.

The following day, knowing that Andreas was in Iraklion, he paid Anna a surprise visit. For the first hour or so, she sustained a furious sulk with him for having neglected her for so many days. They sat opposite one another in the drawing room and she would not look him in the eye.

'Don't be angry with me,' he pleaded.

He got up and went over to her, kneeling at her feet like a supplicant and taking her hand. She snatched it back immediately.

'You know how much I love you,' he persisted.

She said nothing for a moment, and then a playful smile crept across her lips.

'You'll have to prove it,' she said coquettishly.

Sofia had been taken out by the nursemaid, so for the next hour at least they knew that the house was theirs.

Even with the windows wide open, they did not hear the sound of Andreas's car arriving and then leaving again.

Anna was happy and chatty that evening over dinner. Andreas, on the other hand, snapped at everything she said.

'Why are you being so disagreeable?' she asked.

Sofia came into the room just as they were finishing dessert and ran towards her father, expecting to be lifted onto his lap. She was finding it difficult to sleep during these hot nights, and often came downstairs while her parents were eating.

'Go back to bed!' snapped Andreas, pushing the child away. 'Now!'

'*Babá!*' Sofia cried out, dropping to the floor. '*Babáaaaaa!*' Anguished by the rebuff, she began to wail.

'Andreas!' exclaimed Anna. 'What the *hell* is the matter with you?'

She picked Sofia up and cuddled her, but the child was inconsolable, and the sound of her sobs filled the house.

Andreas left the room and slammed the door behind him. It took another few hours before Sofia calmed down, and that night she slept in her mother's bed. Andreas had gone to sleep in another room at the far end of the house.

For the rest of that week, he was mostly absent from the house, and on the estate he was particularly bad-tempered with the workers. Manolis had several encounters with him when he was castigated for not meeting targets and for not tending some of the olive groves diligently enough, and he was stung by the harshness of his cousin's criticisms. Clearly he should keep out of his way for a while, but the reason for this change in attitude preyed on his mind.

Andreas's rudeness, combined with the lurking unease over Maria's return, made Manolis unusually withdrawn. All the workers on the estate noticed it and teased him. In spite of his kinship with the boss, he had always been considered one of them.

'Not coming out with us, Manolis?' Antonis asked towards the end of the afternoon.

'He's quenching his thirst elsewhere!' joshed one of the men.

'Aah . . . a woman,' said another man under his breath.

'Love . . . he's in *love*,' whispered yet another.

Manolis's silence was not denial. Of course he was in love, but even Antonis, who was closer to him than anyone, did not know the identity of the woman. Years back, rumours of a liaison with Anna had been rife, but if they had ever been true in the first place, Antonis imagined the relationship must now be a thing of the past.

They all thought they knew Manolis. Most Saturday evenings he would join friends and fellow workers in Elounda, where there were more than a dozen bars and as many tavernas. It was a sprawling fishing village and a very lively place to pass the time, and Manolis flirted with the local girls as enthusiastically as the rest.

The Manolis they saw today was not the one they recognised. It was not the Manolis who shared their happy banter, and they all knew to leave him alone.

He turned his back on them and continued banging in a new fence post, applying more force than needed. The others carried on with their labours.

During recent days, it had been impossible to avoid hearing the words 'lepers', 'cure', 'drugs', 'Spinalonga' endlessly repeated. They filled the summer air as densely as the honey bees. The final plans for the evacuation of the island were unrolling, and in the towns and villages of Lassithi there was talk of little else.

At dinner one night in their grand Neapoli house, Eleftheria and Alexandros Vandoulakis raised the subject with their son and his wife.

'We don't feel it necessary for us to go to the . . . er . . . the event,' said Alexandros tentatively. 'But you should be there to represent the family.' He was referring to the celebration that was going to take place in Plaka.

'And with the family connection especially . . .' said Eleftheria supportively.

Anna sat in silence.

'Yes. Of course we'll attend,' said Andreas curtly. 'Won't we, Anna?'

His wife stared vacantly at her plate of untouched food and managed a nod. She did not look up, so nobody could read her expression, but her taut shoulders said everything about her state of mind.

Chapter Four

AFTER FIFTY YEARS of being bystanders to the tribulations of the sick, 25 August would be a historic moment for the villagers of Plaka. Almost everyone wished to mark it. There had been fear during those decades, but there had also been empathy and even economic gain from the existence of the leper colony opposite. The whole region of Lassithi, a substantial area of eastern Crete, had both benefited and suffered from the proximity of the island. They willingly sold goods to the patients while at the same time fearing potential contamination from them, sometimes wondering whether infection could be carried across the sea.

Giorgos was not the only local person who had been personally connected with Spinalonga. There were many others whose lives had been altered by the diagnosis of a relative, and the dreaded words that would change their lives: 'We regret that . . .'

In Plaka itself, the brothers of Dimitris Limonias, who had gone to Spinalonga at the same time as Giorgos's wife Eleni, waited anxiously. It was almost twenty years since his departure, and their own lives had steadily progressed and improved since then, with wives, children and a successful local business. They were nervous about how Dimitris would fit into their lives.

There was a couple in the village whose only child had been diagnosed with the disease fifteen years before. She had been nine years old at the time and her parents now waited to meet her.

Not only would she be a fully grown woman, but she might be facially disfigured. Time and disease would have transformed her into a virtual stranger.

Other families, such as Apostolakis's, lived in Elounda, and there were plenty in Neapoli too, the biggest and most important town of the region. For patients with families from faraway towns such as Iraklion and Chania, and even Athens, there might be no one waiting for them. There were some who had been disowned by everyone who knew them on the day they were diagnosed, and in many other cases, leprosy patients had outlived their relations.

Whether it was fear or joy, as the day approached there was nobody whose feelings were not stirred by the impending event. This *panegýri* was going to be the biggest the area had ever seen, marking a moment that would never be repeated. For everyone who was there, it was to be an evening of celebration, reunion, repatriation.

As preparations for the mass return of the patients from Spinalonga were under way, Manolis, in spite of everything he had told himself, was having some moments of disquiet. How did he actually know that Maria was not expecting him to be there for her?

He knew that Antonis's sister, Fotini, had been brave enough to visit Spinalonga from time to time, and wondered if Maria might have said something to her. Shortly before the day of evacuation, when they were inspecting the vines together, he tentatively mentioned the subject to Antonis. He hoped his voice did not betray the anxiety he felt.

'Apparently she is excited about leaving,' said Antonis.

'She must be,' responded Manolis blandly.

'Fotini says that she has hardly changed at all. It sounds as if she's had only the mildest form of leprosy.'

'That's good to hear,' Manolis replied with nonchalance. The information did nothing to allay his nagging fear. If Maria was unchanged, there was all the more reason that she might imagine they could resume their engagement.

He drove through the village on the morning of the celebration and saw men hanging lights in the trees and trailing bright flags between them. Children were carrying chairs from the school to the square and women were laying long tables and tying flowers into posies. He saw Fotini and her husband struggling along the street with huge dishes of cooked food, and others with armfuls of *hórta*, picked fresh from the hillside. The baker was unloading trays of golden loaves from his van.

When the day's work was done, Manolis had a quick drink in Plaka. He had missed the spectacle of the flotilla that had sailed across from the island during the afternoon, but he could see all the boats now, crammed into the small harbour, vessels of all different shapes and states of seaworthiness, moored side by side, almost too many to count.

By the time he had gone home to shower and returned to the village several hours later, he had to park some distance away, as many other vehicles had arrived. It was around nine. He had not hurried. It was curiosity that brought him there, rather than enthusiasm.

He had never seen so many people in Plaka. Everyone was oriented in the same direction, watching the dancing that had already begun. The music was loud and joyful and those who did not dance clapped the rhythm. Nobody noticed Manolis. Normally he was the centre of attention — and wanted to be — but tonight he stayed in the background.

He spotted the friend of Apostolakis whom he had met in the *kafeneío* and saw that an elderly woman took the stump of his hand without hesitation and led him to the dance.

There were many strangers there. Some were lame and others were disfigured, but they were outnumbered by those who were whole. Children weaved in and out between the dancers and ran about on the edge of the circle, which moved first one way and then the other. It was a scene of great joy and serenity.

Manolis had a flask of raki in his pocket and sipped it as he observed. The well and the newly well mingled and merged until it was hard to tell which was which. During any other *panegýri*, he would have grabbed his lyra from the wall of the nearby *kafeneío* and played. Tonight his blood was stirred by the music but he had no desire to move forward to join the party.

All the while, he was looking out for one person. It did not take him long to find her. First he made out Antonis, then he saw Fotini and knew that Maria would not be far away. Finally, amongst the hundreds of faces, he spotted her. There was no mistaking her. She was totally unaltered and yet there was some-thing about her that he did not recognise. Every few moments, as the dance completed a circle, she was illuminated by a light that was brighter than the rest and he could see her more clearly. He did not remember ever noticing her smile in this way. It was both broad and radiant.

After a while, there was a break in the dancing. Manolis kept watching. Maria sat down on the far side of the square, and above the heads of the crowd he could see that she was sitting between her father and a man in a smart suit with neatly cut grey hair. Manolis remembered spotting him on a few occasions in Giorgos's boat. The old man had mentioned that he was a doctor. He and Maria were engaged in conversation, heads bent inwards. Something then happened that he did not expect. The grey-haired man got up and, followed by Maria, disappeared from the square.

Noticing the direction they were taking, Manolis skirted round the alleyways behind the square and glimpsed them passing along the street that led up towards the church. They stopped inside its entrance.

He crept closer, but remained carefully hidden behind some trucks, fifty metres or so away. The music had struck up again, and even from this distance it was enough to muffle the sound of their voices. He saw the man reach out, put his hands on Maria's shoulders and draw her close. Then he kissed her.

Manolis felt a shiver go down his spine. Only the day before,

Maria had been on Spinalonga. A leprosy patient. And now a man — a doctor! — was touching her lips with his own.

The kiss was brief but enough to fill him with a mixture of shock and disgust. Soon the couple were retracing their steps to the square.

For a while Manolis stayed where he was. He was almost overcome with a sense of relief, knowing for certain now that Maria had no expectations of him. Leaning against a tyre hub to roll some tobacco, he was careful to ensure that nobody would spot the flame as he lit it, or the glow as he smoked.

The knowledge that Maria might have found love gave him courage. Once he had finished his cigarette, he would make an appearance at the *panegýri* to welcome her back, and perhaps he would then fetch his lyra and play through the night.

Taking a swig of raki from the flask in his pocket, he stood up. He was ready to celebrate now. At last Anna would have to believe that her sister was no threat.

Suddenly the sky was bright with fireworks and everyone was looking upwards. It was the perfect moment to blend unnoticed into the crowd.

As he stepped out of his hiding place, he saw a familiar black car approaching.

Manolis was astonished. He had never imagined that Anna and Andreas would come. He knew Anna well. Taking the hand of a stranger to join a dance was the last thing in the world his haughty lover would ever do, and it was even less likely when that hand was misshapen by leprosy. What he had expected was that she would make an appearance to greet her sister in a day or two. That would be more her style.

As the polished limousine passed, he caught a glimpse of dark hair, pale skin and red lips. Anna was laughing, her head tilted back. He saw an open mouth and the flash of white teeth. Even though it had been a fleeting moment, this was not an expression of Anna's that he knew. There was something ghoulish about her rictus smile. She looked like a second-rate actress feigning happiness, and he felt a stab of unease. It was clear that neither she nor Andreas had noticed him.

Andreas was driving past the square to park, so Manolis strolled slowly towards the crowd. Every face was still turned skywards. Beyond them, out to sea, a deserted Spinalonga was illuminated by a million sparks that brightly lit the sky.

He stayed back in the shadows. It was perverse, but he wanted to be a spectator at the reunion of Anna and her sister. From where he stood, he could see the *panegýri* as well as the back of his cousin's glossy car. He waited for the passenger door to open.

Rockets went off into the sky, one after the other. Then there was a pause, and what seemed like an almost supernatural silence after the huge barrage of sound. A few *laoútos* struck up again. Everyone gathered around to recommence the dancing.

A moment later, two bangs cracked through the air. They were short and sharp. People looked up into the sky, expecting the light show to resume, but there was nothing. Some gunshots had been fired into the air earlier to mark the beginning of this happy occasion, just as happened for weddings and baptisms, but those made a different, duller sound. A few people recognised the latest ones as pistol shots and left the crowd to search for the source.

The musicians could only hear the sound of themselves playing, and for a few macabre moments, they continued. Eventually there was frantic nudging, but one of them, an old chap deaf and oblivious to what was happening, carried on strumming. Finally someone pulled the *laoúto* out of his hands.

Manolis had heard the sound too. He hastened forward, still keeping in the shadows, and when he was less than twenty metres away, he saw Andreas scramble out of the car and run in the opposite direction, away from the village. In less than a second, he was out of sight.

Manolis froze.

People began to converge on the car. Someone opened the

passenger door, but Anna did not emerge, smiling her vain, pretty smile and patting down her dress as he had pictured. There were shouts and gasps, and screams from some of the women. Then the dense mass parted. They were letting someone through to the front. It was the silver-headed man he had seen with Maria. A space was cleared around the Cadillac as people shrank away, some of them turning their eyes from the sight of a body being lifted from the vehicle.

Manolis was taller than most of the men, so he could see over their heads. As people crowded towards the car, Manolis saw six men, Antonis among them, running away from the crowd and down the street. One of them must have spotted Andreas and observed the direction he had taken. In this small village it would only be a matter of time before they found him.

Many of the women dispersed, sobbing quietly in huddles, their arms wrapped around each other for comfort. It was the children who remained curious, ghoulishly interested in what they were watching, craning their necks to find out who was being laid out on the blanket.

Anna.

Manolis watched Maria approach, and then her father, who dropped to his knees next to his daughter's body.

He saw a pale blue dress stained crimson with blood, and dishevelled dark hair. Maria was kneeling next to her, holding one of her sister's hands and stroking it. She was muttering something under her breath. Giorgos was being supported by two men as he rocked back and forth.

'*Theé mou . . . Theé mou . . .* Oh my God,' he repeated loudly over and over, crossing himself.

The man with the silver hair held his fingers over Anna's eyelids and gently closed them. Manolis was incensed. Who was this man to touch her?

He was desperate to get close. Every bone in his body yearned to grab hold of her and take her into the mountains, away from this place, away from these people. Anna was his woman. How many times had she told him that she was his and only his? Anna, his beautiful Anna. He had never felt more possessive of her.

For a moment he pictured himself running forward to seize her in his arms and give her the kiss that would restore her to life. What he was seeing could not be real. It could not have happened. Only a moment before, she had been breathing. He had seen her. That motionless body lying in the street could not be Anna's. It could not.

Manolis retreated a few metres from the scene and for a moment, in a dark doorway, found himself gasping for breath. Sobs now convulsed him, his whole body heaving and shuddering. The cacophony that had resumed in the village was more than enough to cover the noises he made, sounds that were more animal than human.

Crouched down, he buried his head deep in his hands. When he eventually looked up, he saw Anna's body being carefully wrapped in the blanket and carried away. He was numb. With loss, with grief, with shock. Unused to any such emotions, all he registered was a feeling of icy coldness from his head to his feet.

A nip of raki warmed him a little, but he still shivered violently as if it was a cold December dawn. He did not know how long he remained concealed in the shadows, waiting for the streets to empty.

When he was certain that no one would see him, he emerged from his doorway hiding place and began to walk. Against his better judgement, he paused to survey the space where Anna had been laid out. There was nothing there now. Not a trace of blood, not a mark in the dust. The merry flags that hung between the trees seemed to mock him. The tables were still in place, strewn with the debris of the evening.

It must have seemed disrespectful to clear them so soon after such a terrible event, but in due course the men and women of the village would be stirring themselves to get up and set everything straight.

The sun was just coming up now, and in a shaft of low light, something glinted. Manolis took a few steps forward, glancing behind him to make sure that nobody was about. Then he stooped down. There, unmistakable on the cobbles, was an earring. It was one of a pair that he had given Anna on her saint's day a few years ago. They had bright aquamarine stones in an ornate pendulum setting, and although they were worth less than any jewellery she had ever received from Andreas, she had been thrilled with them and wore them on special occasions.

He picked it up and quickly put it in his trouser pocket before hurrying to his truck, parked some way up the road. He had a plan now.

As he drove up the hill towards his home, he could not stop himself thinking of Anna's final moments. Only God and Andreas knew what she had said, but there was no doubt in his mind that he, Manolis, had been the subject. He was the reason that Anna had died and now he had to live without her. The anguish was unbearable.

Although he had not pulled the trigger, he felt responsible, the one to blame. He would not be the one put on trial, but he knew that rumours spread like hill fires in a drought. Suddenly he felt sympathy for those who had left Spinalonga the previous day. Like them, he would always carry a stigma.

The life he had enjoyed in Elounda was over.

Back in his house, he ran upstairs, threw a few clothes into a bag, and then paused for a second, remembering a roll of drachmas tucked into his top drawer. Taking a final look at his bedroom, he caught sight of two framed photographs sitting on a shelf. He ran his fingernail round the seal on the back of one, pulled out the faded image of his parents and dropped it on top of his bag. Next to it was a baptism photograph: Andreas, Anna in the middle, holding Sofia, and himself. He tore it out of the frame and slid it into his shirt pocket.

★

Moments after Manolis left his house, a truck came from the other direction. It was Antonis.

The night before, it was he who had led the search party to find Andreas. Antonis still held close the memories of his years as an *andarte* captain and readily commanded the respect of his contemporaries. He also knew the places where men hid and how to find them. He had split the group of six into three pairs and sent each in a different direction. The men were all young and fast, and within ten minutes they had closed the circle and found their man.

Andreas was cowering in the doorway of the church, still holding the pistol in his hand, but he looked more likely to turn it on himself than use it against anyone else. He was curled into a foetal position, shaking and terrified, and immediately responded to Antonis's command to put down the gun. He willingly allowed two men to lead him back towards the village square.

It was Antonis who picked up the weapon. For a moment he contemplated firing it into Andreas's back as he was escorted away. But death would be no punishment for a man who had murdered his own wife in cold blood. Antonis hated his boss. This past decade he had resented the man he worked for, not for a single day forgetting that Andreas Vandoulakis had stolen the woman he loved.

Anna had been part of his life for as long as he could remember. Their families had been interconnected and they had seen each other almost every day from childhood through to adolescence. While he was fighting in the resistance, he found himself thinking of her endlessly, spurred to acts of courage not only by patriotism but by the hope that she might admire him when he returned. Each night, as he laid his head on stony ground, he imagined the moment when Anna would learn of his selfless bravery. He returned bruised in body and mind, and at the *gléndi* to celebrate the return of all those who had taken part in the resistance against the Germans, he finally held her in his arms. The pair of them had crept away from the party in Plaka to steal their first kiss.

On that same night, Andreas Vandoulakis had appeared in the village. If he was looking for the most beautiful woman in Elounda, he had come to the right place. Anna was there, flushed and beautiful from the dancing and from the touch of Antonis's lips.

The situation had been further exacerbated by Andreas's order to Antonis the following day to take a letter to Anna. Antonis could not refuse, even though he knew that he was hastening the end of his own chances with her. With the exception of Fotini, who was sworn to secrecy, he had never mentioned to another soul the way his hopes had been raised and dashed. It would only deepen his humiliation.

Andreas had been Antonis's boss then, and more than a decade later, he still was. There were few better places to work. The Vandoulakis estate paid well and it caused him no difficulty to take his salary from a man he resented. He enjoyed the physical demands of working with the land, spending all day with men he had known since boyhood, and the company of Manolis, who was now his best friend, someone who had brought so much life and gaiety to their small society. But his anger towards Andreas Vandoulakis had never gone away, and he sensed that Anna knew this. Occasionally when the workers were invited to the boss's house to celebrate the end of the grape harvest or the making of the raki, Anna would be there, and Antonis had enjoyed seeing her discomfort at his presence.

Anna had known that Antonis had never married. For years Fotini had been doing her best to matchmake her brother with friends and cousins of friends. He was extremely good-looking, with chiselled cheekbones and long lashes around unfathomably dark eyes. Potential matches were even impressed by the scar from the German bullet that had grazed his neck during the occupation. All of them found this war hero attractive physically, but there was something that deterred them: his gruff manner, and perhaps his honesty too. He did not conceal his lack of interest and made it very clear that marriage was the last thing on his mind. Most of these girls did not have time to waste so quickly gave up on him.

'Come on, Antonis. There are plenty of women around who want a husband. And need one,' Fotini would say.

'Well I don't need a wife,' he would retort.

He tolerated and was sometimes amused by his sister's efforts, but they both knew that there was nobody in Plaka or in any of the villages around to match Anna.

'You need to stop being so fussy!' were Fotini's usual words to end the conversation.

That morning, after a few snatched hours of sleep, Antonis had woken up with one thought in his head: he had not seen Manolis at all the previous evening. His friend had said that he was going to the celebration in Plaka and it seemed strange that he had not been there with the rest. It was unlike him to miss such an event.

After they had handed Andreas over to the authorities and Antonis had made a call to Alexandros Vandoulakis to tell him that his son had been arrested, the men of the search party had sat in the bar until the early hours of the morning, speculating over what had happened. Now, the words of one of the men suddenly came back to him:

'Hope he didn't kill his cousin too.'

They had seemed absurd at the time, but now they nagged him. He would go immediately to Manolis's place and check on him.

Manolis's truck was not there, so clearly he was out. Antonis tried the latch and the door opened.

He had never been inside the house before so had no idea what kind of state his friend normally lived in, but he was unsurprised to see the messy kitchen with its crumbs strewn across the table and an open bottle of wine, half empty. The state of the bedroom upstairs was more revealing. It looked ransacked, with clothes pulled from the wardrobe left lying on the bed and all the drawers open and empty.

Antonis approached the chest of drawers and picked up a frame that had been put face down on the surface. It was empty, the photograph removed, and it was the same for another. The blank frames were like darkened windows. It was clear that Manolis had gone.

Antonis sat for a moment on the edge of the unmade bed. The notion that Andreas had killed Manolis did not appear to be correct, but he now accepted that Manolis's disappearances at midday had probably been to see Anna. He had always hoped that their liaison was nothing more than a rumour, but he had known Anna long enough to realise that she was perfectly capable of behaving this way.

Shortly afterwards, he left the house and drove to Plaka. He did not recognise what he was feeling, but realised that it was not grief for Anna. It was almost as if a burden had been removed from him. There was no one to mock him now. Perhaps his pride could finally mend.

Manolis had driven down the long hill towards the main road to Iraklion. With virtually everything he owned on the seat beside him, he suddenly thought of his precious lyra. It was still hanging on the wall of the *kafeneío*. It had been his constant companion for so many years and his most beloved possession, and when he reached the junction where he might have turned left to reach Plaka, he hesitated. Perhaps he would go and retrieve it.

On every level the idea was absurd, and with reluctance, he dismissed it. His priority now was to catch a boat.

The ferry for Athens left Iraklion in the early afternoon, and it was already ten. He put his foot down on the accelerator and took the bends like a man with nothing to lose.

Chapter Five

M ANOLIS CAUGHT THE ferry with just a moment to spare, having dumped his truck in an alleyway. He left the key in the ignition. Someone could help themselves to it. He did not care who.

The boat was very crowded, with many people returning to Athens after a few days on Crete for the August holiday. Manolis noticed a group of former leprosy patients. He was now familiar enough with such disfigurements. He knew that they would have been in Plaka the previous night and would have been witnesses to what happened.

Among the group were Papadimitriou, the former island leader, Solomonides, the editor of the newspaper, and Kouris, the engineer. They sat in a huddle talking quietly as if trying not to be noticed. All of them had been instrumental in transforming Spinalonga into a thriving community. Now they were returning to Athens to try and resume the careers at which they had excelled almost two decades before. It was obvious that other passengers on the ferry were keeping clear of them, as though there was an invisible barrier around them.

Manolis spent most of the passage on deck. He had not slept for more than twenty-four hours, but he wanted to think, and the fresh air and the throb of the engine helped keep him awake. Anna was constantly on his mind, in every breath, in every thought.

His time in Elounda had been the longest he had spent in one place during his adult life. Anna had held him there, a willing captive. He did not care what happened next. It had simply been instinct to flee.

The ferry stopped at several small islands on its journey north, and a handful of new passengers shuffled on at each one. Some waited on deck to wave goodbye to people, but the smell of diesel was overpowering and eventually drove most of them inside. Manolis remained alone, staring down at the rolling waves as the day turned to night. The sky was black and the waves were dark. They were one vast continuous expanse. Beneath him was a void that seemed to be inviting him in. Nobody would see, nobody would know. He would simply slip beneath the surface. Now that Anna had gone, he would be a loss to no one. Perhaps Antonis and their *paréa*, their gang, would miss him. But not for long.

At that moment, he saw a slight glow on the horizon. A chink in the blackness. The chink grew and began to let in the light, and after a while the light glowed orange.

Day was breaking. Slowly and surely, the flat line of the sea's surface was replaced by the contours and shadows of land. As the boat made its steady progress north, the irregular shapes of Attica's mountains began to emerge through the early-morning haze, and eventually the grand buildings on the seafront came into view. Piraeus was close to the city of Athens, but had its own identity.

A while later, the huge vessel was steered into port. There were thirty minutes of intense activity and noise: the roar of the engine going into reverse, the deafening grinding sound of the anchor chain being lowered, shouts, instructions, swearing. There was a sense of panic and urgency, but this was just another day's work for the men running this way and that bearing ropes as thick as their arms.

A crowd of people waited for the boat to dock, and Manolis observed that many passengers were now on deck waving enthusiastically to friends and family below.

45

It reminded him that there would be no one to greet him. Nobody even knew his name here. It was six years since he had left the mainland for Crete. He had fallen under the spell of the island's exceptional beauty, enjoying everything it gave him, from mountains to plateaus to crystal seas. During that period, he had not hankered after his former, more urban existence, and was more than satisfied by the limited social life of Elounda. He had only visited Iraklion, the capital city, a handful of times, and then it was just when Andreas sent him on errands.

The thriving and bustling city of Piraeus was spread out before him now, teeming with activity and probably opportunities too. He would think about his plans later, but for now, weak with fatigue, he just needed somewhere to lay his head.

It would be easy to find somewhere to stay. As well as those greeting loved ones, there were others who stood ready to ensnare the disembarking passengers, holding up clumsily written notices: *Rooms for Rent*; *Lodgings for Ladies Only*; *Pension — Clean Sheets!*

Manolis tried to bargain with one or two of them, but they would not budge on price. He knew how many notes he had in his pocket and had a strict limit.

Knowing that the best way to negotiate was to feign disinterest, he began to walk. Out of the corner of his eye he saw that a woman had fallen into step with him. She had red-tinted hair and reeked of cheap perfume and hair lacquer, but there was something about her that he liked. In her younger years she would have been his type, with her full lips and rouge overenthusiastically applied.

'If you want an easy-going landlady,' she said cheerfully, as though they had already started a conversation, 'that's me.'

'Are you close to the docks?' he asked.

'Couldn't be closer,' she laughed, revealing a missing tooth. 'Unless you were on board ship.'

'How much is it?' enquired Manolis casually.

'Four hundred and eighty a week,' she answered. It sounded as if she had just made up a figure.

Manolis did not respond but continued to walk with her along the waterfront. He would need to see the place before he agreed.

It was already midday when they finally reached the woman's pension, but in the dim light, he noted a well-kept entrance and a vase of silk flowers on a table in the hallway. It seemed clean enough too.

A girl hurried past them on her way out.

'See you later, *Theía,*' she said in a sing-song voice.

'That's Elli,' said the landlady. 'My niece.'

Manolis registered long dark hair and a waif-like frame.

'She works at that grand *zacharoplasteío* on the seafront,' added the woman proudly, referring to a huge pastry shop that Manolis had noticed when he walked by.

This girl, with her pale pink complexion, even looked as if she was made from sugar, he reflected.

The landlady took a bunch of keys from her pocket and jangled them.

'What's your lucky number, *agápi mou?*' she asked.

Since childhood, Manolis had always felt that good fortune watched over him. But today, he no longer believed it. Luck had deserted him and its loss made him feel empty.

'Well, if you can't think of one,' said the landlady cheerily, 'we'll put you in Room 9. It's a nice one. View of the alleyway. And close to the bathroom. I think you'll be happy.'

Anna had been born on the ninth of the month. It would have been the number he chose.

Another woman passed them on the stairs.

'*Kalispéra*, Kyría Agathi,' she said breathlessly, giving Manolis a cursory glance before continuing on her way.

'We have one or two like her here,' whispered the landlady when she was out of earshot. 'But they don't bring rough types back. And they mostly only work in the day. So don't worry, it's quiet at night.'

It was what Manolis would have expected for the price, and

he had no objections. In the past, he had spent plenty of time in the company of prostitutes and did not doubt he would do so again.

The landlady unlocked a door at the end of the corridor and threw it open. The mattress was covered in stained ticking and there was a blanket hanging over the bedstead. In the corner stood a dark mahogany chest of drawers, and a jug and basin sat on the floor beneath the window. There was a broken wooden chair. It was just a place to throw some clothes. Manolis had stayed in many places worse than this, and it was no more spartan than his home in Elounda, even if his bedroom there had been bigger. He did not seek luxury.

'So, five hundred and sixty drachmas a week including laundry and lighting. Any other extras are . . . extra. Payment is due at the end of each week. I know what happens when you men get your wages. You have none left by Sunday morning,' she laughed. 'So, you give me what I am owed first, and then you go out on the town!'

This Kyría Agathi was no fool. The cost had already risen, but Manolis forgave her. He had enough.

'I'll make sure to do that,' he reassured her.

'I don't want to know anything about you except your name,' she said.

'Manolis,' he answered plainly, not imagining for a moment that she meant what she said. Within a day or so, the name Vandoulakis might be in the newspapers even here on the other side of the Aegean, and he had no wish to be asked questions by this kind-hearted but no doubt gossipy type.

'Manolis,' she repeated with a smile. 'I suppose you did just step off the boat from Crete.'

Manolis nodded.

'No women in your room. And no animals – I had someone in here with a monkey last year and it stank. So I'm strict about that.'

'What about those?' Manolis had just spotted a small creature dart across the room. It was now quivering in the corner.

'Oh yes. You *are* allowed a pet mouse. I make an exception for them.'

Manolis laughed good-naturedly. He liked this woman. She was quick-witted and clearly happy that he appreciated her joke.

'Well, I'll just find you some bed linen. Then we'll be done for now.'

She returned five minutes later, singing under her breath, with some grey-looking sheets and a second, even rougher-looking woollen blanket, and made up his bed. While she was busy, Manolis gazed down into the alleyway below. It was empty but for some stray dogs.

As soon as she had done her work, she fiddled with her bunch of keys and handed over the one for Manolis's room. Then she gave the rather lifeless pillow a final plumping and straightened the blanket now lying across the bed. However uninviting it looked, he could hardly wait to be in it. Fatigue was beginning to overwhelm him.

'Thank you, Kyría Agathi,' he said politely.

'No doubt I'll see you in a few days,' she said, standing by the open door. 'I sweep your room once a week.'

Manolis nodded. His landlady left.

He sat down on the bed, pulled off his boots and then stood up again to remove his clothes. As he took off his trousers, he heard the tinkling of something falling to the floor. He stooped to retrieve Anna's earring and rested it in his palm for a moment. The photograph was still in his shirt pocket, and only now did he allow himself to take it out and gaze at the face of the woman he had loved.

With his hand closed around the aquamarines, he slid the photograph under his pillow and climbed, exhausted, into bed.

Sleep overwhelmed him immediately, but in the airless room, he spent a haunted night. He was constantly pursued but never caught: by Andreas, by Antonis, by his uncle, by Giorgos, and by people from the distant past who still lurked in his subconscious. Wherever he hid, someone found him. He ran and ran, panting and screaming, only just keeping ahead of the chase. He turned into a hunted animal, a creature with matted fur and bloodied paws. He was weighed down by mud and rotting leaves as he tried to find refuge.

When he eventually woke, sweating and crying, his pillow damp with tears, his sheets with sweat, Kyría Agathi was standing by his bedside. The sun was streaming through an open window.

'I thought someone was attacking you, Kýrie Manolis,' she said breathlessly. 'I was sure a murder was happening under my very own roof.'

Manolis sat up, rubbing his eyes. Where was he? Who was this woman holding out a glass? It took him a moment to emerge from the leafy undergrowth of his dream.

'Even the girls were complaining. And it's a mighty strange thing when *they* moan about noise. What a sleep you've had.'

Manolis sat up, took the water from Kyría Agathi and gulped it down. He was aware of her watching him, head tipped to one side.

'It's four in the afternoon,' she said, taking the glass from him. 'You must have needed that rest. I'll be off now.'

Kyría Agathi had not looked at her new lodger closely the previous day, but she did now. In all her years of running this establishment, she had not taken in such a good-looking man.

Manolis was aware of her gaze. He was well used to the stares of women.

'Thank you for the drink, Kyría Agathi,' he said. It was beyond him to smile.

'A pleasure,' she replied. 'And don't worry about the "Kyría".'

As soon as she had left the room, Manolis got up. He tried to forget his nightmares and hoped that the next time he slept, Anna would appear. He needed to see her.

He washed and dressed and then went out into the street. The day had more or less gone and birds were gathering on nearby buildings, some of them preparing to fly south for the winter.

He strolled for a few kilometres along the waterfront. Loading and unloading at the docks had finished for the day, and the shipbuilding and repair yards were silent. Everyone had stopped working, but there were still plenty of people standing about, discussing what they would be doing the following day. The tables outside the *kafeneía* were filling up. The whole of the promenade was lined with places to eat and drink and there were already very few spare tables. Thousands of workers stopped at once and all had the same idea. After a hard day's work, hunger and thirst had to be sated.

Manolis crossed the road and found an empty table. He had not eaten for more than two days, and now he was as hungry as a wolf. The waiter put down bread and water and Manolis ordered. There were three cooked meat dishes ready, pork, lamb and chicken, and he asked for them all, along with a cold beer. His head bent over the plates, he shovelled food into his mouth and mopped the juices with his bread, drained a second bottle of beer, paid and left. He had made no eye contact with anyone, not even with the waiter.

As Manolis was eating his first meal on the mainland, Andreas was being transferred from the police station in Agios Nikolaos to a prison cell in Neapoli. There was no question about his guilt. Only about his motivation.

In the *kafeneía* and tavernas of Lassithi, nobody talked of anything but the Vandoulakis murder. The family's name was known to everyone in the east of Crete, and rumours quickly circulated that the heir to the great family estate had shot his wife in a jealous rage. Everyone who worked for the Vandoulakis family, from domestic servants to estate managers and workers, was instructed by Alexandros neither to speak with family or friends about what had happened, nor to exchange views with each other. It was a pointless edict. Anna's housekeeper, Kyría Vasilakis, swearing a friend to secrecy, mentioned that she had seen Manolis come and go from the house on several occasions. From that moment, gossip and speculation became fact. Manolis had been the cause. And soon his disappearance was as much talked of as the murder itself.

Antonis was one of the few who did not speak ill of Manolis. Even though he now knew that his best friend was probably the catalyst for this terrible tragedy, his feelings were confused. He did not blame Manolis for what had happened, but he did find his loathing of Andreas stronger than ever.

Anna had been lost to him for years now, and love had long ago given way to dislike. Nevertheless, he was obliged to attend her funeral. The whole of Plaka was there, and given his family's proximity to the Petrakis family, he had no choice.

It was a gruelling few hours, standing in the church watching the women of the village weep, the open coffin with Anna's still body at the centre. He did not want to look but found himself unable to prevent himself staring at her waxen face.

This was no ordinary funeral. Such levels of horror and grief were rarely experienced. Some older inhabitants of Plaka remembered a vendetta half a century back where a couple and their child had been murdered, but there had been nothing like that since then.

'How could so much tragedy strike a single family?' they all muttered behind their hands. The return of Maria from Spinalonga one moment, the murder of her sister the next. To most, the two events seemed entirely unrelated. How could such things happen? People were dismayed.

Anna had been mostly absent from Plaka since her marriage a decade earlier, but everyone remembered her as a child and an adolescent. Her father was still a beloved member of the village, all had fond memories of his wife, Eleni, and Maria had always been admired for her kind demeanour.

The absence of the Vandoulakis family at the burial of a woman who bore their name was no surprise, but many felt that they should have sent a representative. 'One of their own murdered her,' they said indignantly. Others understood their absence and could imagine the fathomless depth of that family's shame. 'How could they be here? They would have been shunned even if they had come.'

Instead of being buried in the grand Vandoulakis plot in the Neapoli cemetery, Anna remained in Plaka. The village's *nekrotafeío* was in sight of the sea and of Spinalonga. Giorgos contained his grief with dignity that day, but in the subsequent forty days when he went to Anna's grave, he would look across to Spinalonga and weep bitterly. It could have been some consolation that his wife and daughter were within sight of each other, but it was not.

In the weeks following the funeral, Maria was by her father's side every moment of the day, and often, like him, she looked across at the island. Her thoughts were very different from his, however. She caught herself wishing she was back there. In those latter months on Spinalonga, life had been so much sweeter than it was now.

Chapter Six

F AR AWAY, BEYOND Spinalonga and the Gulf of Mirabello and
hundreds of kilometres north across the Aegean, Manolis was
also thinking of a happier life that had so unexpectedly and brutally
been cut short.

The man who had always faced adversity with good cheer found
himself entirely without resources to deal with the emotions that
swept over him day after day after day. He had lost both parents
as a young child, and then a fiancée to a leper colony, but these
events had scarcely dented him. Life had always been an adventure,
with obstacles and challenges, and each one he overcame had simply
magnified his confidence. Then came Anna. The seismic aftershocks
of her loss followed one after another and never seemed to lessen.

Agathi had no complaints about Manolis. He paid his rent on
time and removed his boots when he came in the front door. He
was clean and well mannered, and when their paths crossed, he
gave her a broad smile that made the back of her neck feel slightly
hot. One morning she decided to change his sheets and give his
room a cursory dust. While she was doing so, she could not resist
a speedy inventory of his possessions as she put away one of his
shirts in the drawer. 'Tidying up', she called it. At first it seemed
that all he owned were a few clothes and a heavy roll of drachmas
stuffed into a sock, but then, at the back of the bottom drawer,
she came across two photographs.

The first, she surmised, was of his parents. The second was more challenging. She scrutinised the image of two men, a woman and a baby. The man on the left could be Manolis, even though his hair was much shorter than her lodger's, but the man on the right looked even more like him. He wore a wedding ring, which she had noticed her lodger did not. She could only conclude that the two men were twins. The baby could have been either boy or girl. The real focus of the picture was the woman. She looked like a Hollywood movie star. She was sensationally beautiful, with pearls around her neck, ornate drop earrings, and a large diamond on her finger. Her hair was glamorously pinned up as if to accentuate not just her long, slender neck, but her jewellery too. It was a photograph that might have appeared on the cover of a magazine.

What a divine trio, Agathi thought to herself. Like royalty . . . and now one of them is living here.

It was all very mysterious, and she held the picture in her hand for a moment before burying it back in the drawer beneath a vest. Perhaps she would coax the information out of him one day.

She continued with her dusting, picking up a saucer on which lay a cut-throat razor and a button that must have fallen off. If she noticed that one of his shirts was gaping, she would happily sew it back on for him. Beneath the razor, something sparkled, so she pushed the blade aside with her finger. It was an earring with pretty blue stones.

Delving into the drawer once again, she pulled out the photograph and held up the earring to confirm that it matched.

Ah, she thought. Something sad happened here. Maybe even something bad.

Agathi was a woman who studied the *flitzáni*, the coffee grounds, to read the past and foretell the future, and she prided herself on her accuracy. She did not need supernatural powers, however, to imagine something from such signs. The image showed a happy moment that had passed. This, after all, was what most photographs portrayed. The presence of a single earring among Manolis's belongings told another story.

The landlady loved the mysteries presented by the scant possessions of her lodgers. A roll of notes in a spare pair of socks was standard. Everyone who found their way to her had a similar amount, otherwise they would be staying somewhere else, either more or less luxurious. Very few came with much more than they stood in, making the things they owned all the more precious and significant. She was sure she could work out if someone was on the run, had stolen or even killed. An earring was a more complex clue, but she sensed that lost love was at the centre of it, and she did not need to wash a tear-stained pillow more than once to detect something tragic.

From that day on, Agathi mothered Manolis more than any other tenant. Every lodger who came was a potential child figure for her, but most of them disappointed her in the end, breaking a bed, never offering even a single smile, or leaving without paying their rent. This man was sad, and Agathi sympathised with a broken heart more than anything else in life. Hearts were like china ornaments. Having collected hundreds of porcelain figures, she was an expert. If they smashed, you stuck them together again, but however well you did it, the fine lines of a repair would always be visible.

Her main interest in the people who rented her rooms was that they were well behaved, did not come home drunk and rowdy at night, and always paid on time, but Manolis had a vulnerability that made her care more. The thin walls of her establishment meant that she was always in tune with his state of mind, hearing when he cried out in his sleep and aware of his sobs when he woke.

A week or so after his arrival in Piraeus, Manolis slept a different sleep. It was the sleep he had hoped for. He had found a local restaurant frequented mostly by stevedores and had filled his belly for a few drachmas before returning to the pension well fed and with enough ouzo in him to induce a state of semi-unconsciousness. Every time his eyes closed, Anna came to him. She was above him, beneath him, next to him, her face close to his. For half the night, his arms were twisted around his pillow, and when he opened his eyes, he expected to see her lying next to him. He thought he could detect her scent, but it was simply the soap Kyría Agathi used to wash the sheets.

He squeezed his face hard against the pillow, his body racked with sobs, with loss, with anguish. The fantasy of his dreams had seemed so real. To wake to this reality, to this absence, to this void, when his sleep had been filled with images of love and beauty and joy. It was like being smashed. Broken.

He found Agathi by his bedside. She had heard his howls from the corridor.

'I thought you'd broken the rule about animals,' she said gently. 'Sounded like you had a bear in here.'

Manolis sat up and took the glass from her hand.

'Dreams, Agathi,' he said, wiping his tears with the sheet. 'Dreams.'

The landlady looked at him with pity. There was nothing that made her sadder than to see a grown man weeping. This one had looked so sure of himself when she found him, and yet she had never seen anyone more defenceless than the man in the bed before her. She suspected some of her lodgers of being the type who broke hearts, whereas this one seemed to have been a victim.

Manolis was aware of Agathi's attention and sensed that it was motivated by simple kindness. Like a cat by a fire, he enjoyed the warmth. It did not matter to him that she saw him at his weakest moment, crying like a baby over his lost love, and he appreciated that she did not bother him with questions.

He happily slipped into playing the role of the son she had never borne.

'You'll feel stronger in time,' she reassured him. 'Believe me, you will.'

He did not believe her, though her words were well meant.

He began to dread as well as desire his nightly dreams of Anna.

Sometimes her appearances had the quality of a vision rather than a dream, making him question whether she really was dead. Not only could he see her as if she stood in front of him, but he could feel her breath on his cheek, her hands on his back. Perhaps if he had gone closer to see her for himself as she lay on that blanket, perhaps if he had touched her cold skin and felt for an absent pulse, he might believe what his subconscious could not accept.

He knew that he must start looking for work soon, but his energy and will were lacking. He spent his days exploring the streets of the town, walking for several kilometres in both directions along the seafront. One day he stopped at the little port, Tourkolímano, where he sat down to eat. The waiter promised him their freshest fish, but it tasted of nothing at all. He thought of the *barbounia*, the red mullet he used to eat in Plaka, delivered by Giorgos from his boat directly to the taverna. In Tourkolímano the buildings were on the same small scale as the island's, but that only made him miss the landscape and intimacy of Crete all the more. He felt like a man in exile.

He went to a different *kafeneío* each morning, having no desire to become a regular in any of them. He was still in the mood to keep to himself. Seeing a newspaper lying on the table next to him one day, he started idly flicking through its pages. The front page was dominated by the Cyprus situation and current proposals for independence. It did not interest him, so he started perusing other stories. Several pages in, a headline caught his eye:

CRETE: JOYFUL HOMECOMING MARRED BY MURDER.

It could only be referring to the release of patients from Spinalonga, a happy moment overshadowed by a killing. *A woman shot at point-blank range was identified by witnesses as Anna Vandoulakis.* Seeing his lover's name in black and white gave him a huge jolt, as if an electrical current had passed through him. Vandoulakis was his name too. He felt more strongly connected with her than ever before. Anna had been *his*. His sense of this was as strong as ever. He was both possessor and possessed.

The author of the piece could not have known how the cure for leprosy and such a killing were somehow connected, and sketchily described the sequence of that night's events. The cure of the patients on Spinalonga and the historic moment of their leaving had been overshadowed by a *crime passionnel*. That was all he had understood.

Andreas's name was mentioned several times, along with the details of his arrest and the scheduled date for the trial. The journalist had done little work to dig into the story. There was no connection made between the victim and the patients. From Manolis's point of view, this was no bad thing.

What he hated most was the way in which Anna was described: 'a fisherman's daughter elevated by marriage into a landowning family'. It was true, but demeaning, as the author of the piece would well have known.

Only one member of the Vandoulakis family had come forward to comment. Andreas's sister Olga had spoken at length to the journalist:

'Our name has been sullied by this. My sister-in-law did not fit into the family. Let's say she was not really born to live in such a way and it is not always for the best when someone marries into a different kind of family from their own. All I will say is that Anna was coquettish and rather spoilt. And she was a negligent mother, too. I won't say more than that. We can't speculate on the reason for this event, but all we know is that this woman provoked my brother to commit an act of homicide. Andreas is a kind and gentle man. One day we hope to find out why he did this, but meanwhile we will continue to regard what he did as completely justifiable.'

Manolis read the article twice, his stomach churning with hatred for his cousin. How *dare* she imply that Anna was the guilty party? May she go to hell!

He left the *kafeneío*, shoved the paper into the nearest bin and strode towards the sea.

It was only a paragraph in a newspaper, but reading it had had a decisive effect on Manolis. Any residual delusion he held onto that Anna had not actually died was gone. The words on the page were definitive proof.

He had spent enough time alone and his roll of notes was shrinking rapidly. It had seemed plenty to start with, but with rent and food he was almost through it. He needed to find a job.

Piraeus had gradually recovered from the devastation caused during the Second World War. The bombing of the huge dock area and the destruction of buildings and ships had been extensive, but now that repairs had been completed, Greek shipping was thriving. Sunken ships had rapidly been replaced and the Greek-owned fleet now surpassed even the British and American in size. Many of the shipping companies had offices in Piraeus, and as the world economy boomed, so did the port.

There was work for anyone who wanted it, in repairs, in loading freight, on the ferries, in construction. Finding the manpower was the hardest part.

That evening, Manolis found himself in a *kafeneío* where a group of men sat together at the next table and cheerfully clinked shots of ouzo. One of them raised a glass in his direction. It was a gesture of friendliness towards a stranger; in Piraeus, lifelong residents happily intermingled with newcomers. There was no suspicion towards an outsider in this town. Everyone was welcomed into the melting pot of the ancient port.

Manolis fell into conversation with the men, and one of them introduced himself as Giannis, the foreman of a repair yard. Manolis had been conscious even before they spoke that the man had been scrutinising him. He had sized up Manolis's strong physique and wrinkled complexion and surmised that he was a man not unused to manual labour. He knew nothing about Manolis personally, but he never took on men with pale skin and soft hands. They always proved workshy in the end.

At the end of the evening, Giannis scribbled down an address and told Manolis to come and see him any time he wanted work. He was convinced that this powerful-looking Cretan would be a useful labourer.

The following Monday morning, after his first decent night's sleep since arriving on the mainland, Manolis got up feeling refreshed. The morning was warm but the heatwave of August had given way to the gentler temperatures of September, hot in the day but with bearable nights.

He went out into the early-morning sunshine, stopping at the barber to have his hair trimmed and his moustache clipped, and then took the short walk towards the shipyards. Dipping into his pocket for the scrap of paper on which the address was written, he knew immediately when he had reached his destination.

PENELOPE. With her name painted large on her bow, she was hard to miss. Her giant hull loomed over the yard, casting everything around it into shadow.

Scores of men were already at work, small figures pushing loaded carts of materials, or suspended in harnesses that dangled them from a great height on the ship's massive dark body. Manolis thought of the ants that hurried in and out of the anthills in the Elounda countryside, each of them purposeful, scurrying to achieve a task without being aware of the scale of the whole.

It was not even eight in the morning, but three or four other men were already gathered outside the wooden hut serving as an office. They were all looking for work. From his desk inside, Giannis, who coordinated repairs, looked up, recognised Manolis and called him inside.

The foreman had taken to Manolis. He had uncles from Crete

and knew that he and this newcomer would find common ground. His team had a lot to accomplish before *Penelope* was due to sail again in six months' time, and he could do with such a type.

'It's fifteen hundred drachma a week, seven until four. One hour's rest at midday. Five and a half days a week. We are stripping the hull of an eighty-metre ship and I have another team waiting to paint it. There's a bonus if we finish on time, a bigger one if we get things done earlier than that. It's gruelling work.'

'Probably no tougher than working in the fields,' Manolis assured him.

'Maybe even less so because you'll be working in the shade half the day.'

The two men shook hands. Manolis was keen to get going. It would take his mind off the all-consuming thoughts of Anna and the newspaper article. His rage towards Olga Vandoulakis still burned inside him.

'I need you on the port side,' said Giannis briskly. 'We had some slackers there. I fired them last week, but we're behind.'

Telling the men outside that they would have to wait, Giannis took Manolis across the yard to meet his new colleagues.

'Dimitris,' he said to the head of the team. 'You have a new man. A good man. I'll leave you to it.'

Just before he turned to walk away, he pulled something out of his pocket.

'Here,' he said, handing Manolis a checked kerchief. 'You'll need this.'

'If you don't wear one,' said Dimitris, 'you won't last long!'

Manolis looked upwards at the great hull. High above, he could see that all the men on the scaffold had their faces wrapped to protect them from dust.

'So, these are your tools,' said Dimitris briskly, giving him a heavy scraper, a large soft brush and a blowtorch.

Manolis had never held a blowtorch before and was surprised

by its weight. Dimitris demonstrated how it worked and Manolis stood back to avoid the flame, which shot out with alarming force. Having tried it once himself and been shown the angle at which to hold the scraper, he was considered ready to start.

He tucked the brush and scraper into his belt and climbed the fifteen metres to the platform, one hand grasping the ladder, the other clutching the cumbersome torch. When he got there, he took a space between two other men. They paused briefly and nodded a greeting. Perhaps they were the men from the bar the other night. It was impossible to tell.

Observing his neighbours for a moment as they worked, he saw for how long he needed to use the flame, how to loosen the paint without damaging the fabric of the hull and how much time to spend cleaning away the dust.

He tied the cotton square around his mouth and nose and started work. After a while, he had found his rhythm: flame, scrape, brush. Flame, scrape, brush. Flame, scrape, brush.

At the end where Manolis was working, only around a fifth had been done. He did not like to imagine how many days were left. He thought of a patch of land up on the Lassithi plateau that his uncle had once asked him to clear in a short time. Thirty hectares needed to be weeded and tilled before seeding could happen. The stony ground had been stubborn; after a whole day he had moved forward only a metre or two, and the area left to clear stretched ahead like a curse. This ship was similarly daunting, but what he had learned back in Elounda was that if you started and kept going, the task grew smaller.

The hours passed slowly. The constant noise of scraping and the fact that their mouths were masked precluded any conversation. With the sun beating down on his head and the sweat pouring down his back, he imagined with every scrape of his chisel that he was paying a penance for Anna's death. Without him, Anna could have continued to be a good wife. *If* he had not returned from his travels, *if* he had not looked so like Andreas, *if*, *if*, *if* . . .

Perhaps he was responsible and the one who should be put on trial.

As the temperature rose, his feelings of guilt became heavier. The work kept his hands busy but gave him many hours to think. More than he needed, perhaps. The fields of Elounda had been a test of endurance, but the dark space on which Manolis worked now was even harder and less forgiving than the dry Cretan soil.

'Manolis! Hey! *Manolis!*'

He did not know how long Dimitris had been calling him. When he looked around, he saw that all the other men had descended the ladder, leaving their torches behind, and were on the ground below. He had been lost in his own world, mechanically scraping but hearing nothing.

Storing his tools in his pocket, he quickly climbed down.

'Good work this morning,' Dimitris said to the group. 'See you back here in an hour.'

The others sauntered off together and Manolis stood alone. He had no appetite and did not follow. All he wanted was to quench his thirst. A cart was going by selling cold soda, and he bought a bottle before seeking shade close to some cargo containers and sitting down. A bale of cotton had been abandoned close by, and he leant his back against it. Before long, his head lolled forward and he fell asleep. In his dream, Anna came strolling by, her hair loose, her dark curls cascading down her back, her bottom swaying provocatively as she passed.

At one o'clock precisely, the team came back. Manolis was woken by the touch of Dimitris's boot on his.

'How are you finding it?' Dimitris asked as Manolis sat up, blinking into the sunlight.

'It's . . . it's good,' he said, for want of anything else.

The work continued, and by the end of the afternoon, Manolis had cleared enough of a patch to justify being there. They were on a rolling scaffold, so they all needed to finish their allocated area at the same time in order to move the structure on. This was individual effort but the work of a team, and the task that still faced them was Herculean.

Manolis found the week went by swiftly, each day the same as the first and progressively more exhausting.

On Saturday afternoon, he began the stroll back home, contemplating how much he was looking forward to his day off. The air was still warm, but a cooling breeze was beginning to come off the sea. He spotted Giannis walking a few steps ahead and caught up with him. The two men exchanged information about where they lived, and Manolis discovered that the foreman lodged with his aunt in a street adjacent to Agathi's.

'Do you want to hear some music tonight?' suggested Giannis. A legendary *rebétiko* singer was billed to be playing in a nearby taverna.

'I'll see you later, then,' said Manolis when they reached the end of his street. The two men went their separate ways.

Manolis counted out what he owed Agathi and slid the notes under her door. Only then did he shower. His hair was stiff with dust, and as he had done each day since he began the job, he stood under the flow for more than twenty minutes watching the dirt run down the plughole, then tilted his face up and felt his eyes and nose fill with water. It was the only way to get rid of the grit. Eventually, once he had scrubbed his body several times with soap, he stepped out and dried himself.

Using the small, cracked mirror above the sink, he began to shave. It was almost dark in the bathroom, and it was only when he had finished that he realised he had nicked himself. A track of blood had run down his chin and woven a path towards his heart. The sight took his mind to the place it always returned to. Anna. He tried not to think about her wound, preferring to remember her perfection, but wondered precisely where the bullet had entered.

He slept for a while and then left for his rendezvous. Giannis's *paréa* mostly comprised other rootless men who had come to Piraeus to find work. Manolis had already met Dimitris, Aris,

Mihalis, Petros, Tasos, Stavros and Miltos at the shipyard, but this was the first time he had seen their faces properly. No doubt each had a story to tell, but Manolis did not ask any questions, since he was not planning to answer any himself.

They ate, drank and sang along with the row of tireless, note-perfect *bouzoúki* players, who strummed as one. The place was noisy, so it was no place for intimate conversation, and as the night progressed, the sound level only rose as singer after singer appeared to deliver their repertoire.

A few girls sat on the periphery of the room. Occasionally one of them approached their table, and some of the men in the group engaged her in conversation. Manolis already knew that the women in Piraeus were very different from those in Crete. These girls dressed unselfconsciously and brightly, unafraid to show cleavage, legs and arms. Many had their hair cut in shorter styles; their nails were scarlet and their jewellery garish. They wore stiletto heels.

He had travelled little more than three hundred kilometres, but conservative Cretan society seemed as far away as the moon. The women here reminded him of those he had met in Paris and Madrid, but even more free and liberated. If one of them tried to speak to him, however, a subtle lift of his head simply indicated 'no' and allowed little room for further engagement. Manolis was not drawn to any of them. He had no desire for female company. There was only one woman on his mind. Anna still filled his thoughts.

On that evening in Piraeus, as often happened late in an evening, Manolis suddenly caught the opening notes of a *zeibékiko* song and felt something inside him stir. The lyrics of this particular song seemed to mirror his life, jabbing at his heart. As if possessed by the power of the music, he rose from his seat.

In the night I reach for you,
But in my arms I feel a void.
I dread those deepest, darkest dreams . . .

His friends immediately dragged their glass-laden tables out of his way to give him space to begin the slow solo dance. With several carafes of ouzo inside him and grief weighing on him like a boulder, he stretched his arms out like an eagle and began to turn. The movements were personal but the tradition of the *zeibékiko* was known to everyone. It was a dance that should only be performed by a man, and only by a man with grief to express.

As the musicians played and the insistent beat thumped and repeated and thumped again, Manolis revolved slowly in a trance-like state, his eyes glazed, unfocused. Someone threw a plate at his feet and one of the girls tossed a flower that she had been wearing in her hair. He was aware of neither. Giannis, Dimitris and several others knelt down, as if in worship, and clapped their hands in time with the distinctive 9/8 rhythm.

The image of you next to me.
All dressed in white, a beam of light,
I wake to see the empty sheets and die.

The dance gave him the opportunity to reveal the darkest corners of his soul. The movements were restrained, tense, controlled, and yet they opened a window into his heart for anyone who looked and cared to understand. All eyes were on him, willing him on. Still turning with arms outstretched, he folded forwards and then bent back in a limbo. The sight of this tall and strikingly beautiful man performing something almost acrobatic held the attention of everyone in the room.

With each turn, he expressed the agony he felt: for the woman he loved, for the tragedy of her death, for his wretched cousin languishing in a prison cell, for his uncle and aunt lamenting the fate of their only son, for Sofia, who had lost both mother and father, for Giorgos, who mourned his daughter, and for Maria, who would be weeping over her sister.

Everyone watched, mesmerised. This was not a man putting

on a display of machismo for the crowd; it was a human being exposing every atom of pain that he was feeling.

The dance was a ritual. It was purifying, a catharsis. The relief, however, did not last. Within a few minutes of sitting down again, Manolis was conscious that his pain was still there inside him.

Giannis clapped his friend on the shoulder in a gesture of wordless sympathy. He poured himself and Manolis another glass of ouzo, which they downed in one.

Manolis remembered how he had danced the *zeibékiko* at Sofia's baptism, recalling the whistles of approval as the men gathered in a circle around him and the moment when he caught sight of Anna gazing at him in adulation. Her admiration had been the greatest prize of all. He had been misusing this majestic dance to show off, even then knowing it was wrong to do so. Tonight he had not danced the *zeibékiko*; the *zeibékiko* had seized him and made him dance.

Throughout the previous week, the men at the shipyard had been suspicious of Manolis. This handsome Cretan with his expensive boots had an air of privilege about him and they assumed that the shadows beneath his eyes were from late nights and *gléntia*, the wild village parties that took place in Crete.

'Raki,' one of them whispered the first day they met him. 'They drink it like water in Crete, and it can ruin a man.'

This Saturday evening changed their view, and it became the first of many that Manolis spent with the group. They regarded him without caution now. After the night of the *zeibékiko*, the man who had turned up that first day with clean boots and hair trimmed like a shipowner was treated like one of them.

Personal information between these men was rationed, but little by little, over the following weeks, Manolis learned something about each of them. He did this not only by asking questions but by listening, waiting and observing. Each of them had lived his own drama.

On hot days when they came down from the scaffolding at

midday, the men sometimes peeled off a saturated shirt and put on a fresh one. During the first few weeks with them, Dimitris caught Manolis doing a double-take as he stripped off.

'Ah,' he said jokingly. 'That's my old war wound.'

'The Nazis?' queried Manolis, assuming he must mean some kind of combat with a German during the occupation.

Dimitris smiled, running his hand down the long jagged scar that went from underarm to hip.

'No, *file mou*, the battle of love,' he said cheerfully. 'And I promise you, she wasn't worth it, though I would have died for her at the time.'

'Yes, I can see,' said Manolis, not really knowing whether Dimitris was telling the truth.

'You know how it is. When you're young, you really believe that women are worth fighting over. I don't any more.'

Manolis nodded, even though he was not sure if he agreed.

'She ended up with him, but make no mistake, he had a scar too.'

Aris was the only one with authentic war wounds. Manolis noticed that Stavros always carried his friend's tools up the ladder for him, and soon discovered that Aris had shrapnel in his legs from the street battle with the British in Athens during December 1944. He hauled himself up the scaffolding with his impressively strong arms, but back on the ground, he had a very noticeable limp.

He was not, however, the only one who had suffered as a result of conflict. One night, a passionate debate about the crimes of the communists during the civil war got out of hand, and Mihalis stormed out of the taverna, overturning a table as he went. His strong reaction demanded explanation. Manolis learned that he had spent three years in the island prison camp of Makronisos and had been subjected to vicious brutality by government troops.

'H-h-he s-s-suffered a lot,' explained Tasos. 'H-h-he t-t-takes it . . .'

69

'He takes it as a personal attack if anyone criticises the left for the atrocities they committed,' interjected Tasos's brother, Petros.

Tasos's stutter sometimes made him difficult to understand, but Petros was always there to finish his sentences. In general, Tasos rarely spoke, but he was built like an ox and did the work of two men.

'Perhaps he imagines that people are justifying the torture he suffered,' said Manolis.

A waiter was calmly sweeping broken glass from beneath their table and picking up the various chairs that lay on their sides. It was clearly not an unprecedented event, and the following morning Mihalis was back to his normal cheerful self. It seemed that he bore emotional rather than physical scars from the past.

Even if Miltos had scars, they would have been concealed by the tattoos that covered his entire torso, neck and arms. Such a sight was unusual even in the Piraeus shipyards, and when Manolis sat with him during a cigarette break, there was nothing Miltos liked more than to relate the story behind each one: when it was drawn, where it was done, its meaning and so on. And with dozens of them – so many that there was not an empty square centimetre anywhere but on his face – he was never going to run out of tales.

'Ah Miltos,' said Manolis affectionately, 'I once went to the Louvre in Paris, and they didn't have as many works of art as you.'

Miltos smiled.

'What's that one, then?' asked Manolis, pointing to a row of figures. 'That's less of an oil painting.' He did not count them, but it was a sixteen-digit number.

'That,' answered Miltos, pointing at the first eight, 'is when I killed a man. And the other numbers are the date when I was released.'

It was a revenge murder; he had served his time and had no regrets. Manolis knew that one day Miltos would tell him more, but for now it was time to resume their work. They still had months ahead of them on the hull.

He had noticed a burn mark on Stavros's arm, but he was the least talkative of the group and never elaborated on what had caused it. Manolis concluded it was a childhood accident.

All the time he was piecing together their stories, the group continued to be puzzled by Manolis. All they understood was that some deep unhappiness had brought him to Piraeus. The *zeibékiko* dance had told them this, but they knew no more. Only when he was ready would he open the shutters. Until then, they would respect his privacy as he did theirs.

Chapter Seven

THE WEEKS WENT by. It was on Manolis's mind that the trial might begin soon, so he wrote to Antonis asking for news. He told his friend where he was staying and what he was doing and waited for a reply.

Antonis was pleased when he received the letter. He was glad Manolis was safe and somewhere not too far distant. He showed it to his sister Fotini, making her promise first that she would not tell anyone what it said. The pair of them had always been close and Fotini always kept a secret if he asked her.

It was now generally accepted that Manolis had been conducting a relationship with Anna, but still Antonis did not judge him for it. It merely made him despise Anna all the more.

'There was no man she wouldn't drag into the dirt,' he told Fotini.

Fotini was annoyed to hear him say this.

'Don't be vindictive, Antonis,' she said. 'I think Anna got enough of a punishment, don't you?'

'It's Andreas's turn now,' he said quietly.

'It's been so many years,' Fotini responded, 'and you're still so angry.'

They were drinking coffee together in Plaka, and Antonis tipped his cup to drain the dregs.

'How could Andreas have known that Anna was yours, in any case?'

Antonis shrugged his shoulders.

'I suppose he didn't know. But it doesn't change a thing,' he said. 'I saw Andreas Vandoulakis almost every day for over a decade. And he treated me like dirt on every one of them.'

Fotini looked at her brother with a touch of sympathy. Everyone knew that Andreas Vandoulakis was haughty with his employees, just as his father had been.

'Maybe Anna and Andreas deserved each other,' Antonis said with finality.

'Please stop, Antonis. You sound vengeful. And it's ugly. Don't forget that she was Maria's sister. And Giorgos . . . These people are like family to us.'

On this last point, Antonis was in agreement. He and Fotini were joined to the Petrakis family through generations of friendship. He hugged his sister and left.

That night, he wrote back to Manolis. He did not have much to tell him, but promised that he would let him know when the trial began.

When the letter arrived, Agathi had trouble reading the name, so careless was the handwriting. The 'M' was clear enough, but the surname was illegible. It was only the Iraklion postmark that gave her the confidence to slip it under Manolis's door. None of her other tenants came from Crete.

Her lodger had seemed a little happier in the past few weeks than when he arrived, but even so there was still a hint of melancholy about him. Perhaps this letter would bring him some good news; maybe it was from that beautiful woman in the photograph.

Manolis's work on the ship was punctuated by late nights of drinking, singing and playing cards with his new *paréa*. Nights of sound sleep followed, but he was never without dreams of Anna. The rest was for his body only.

Andreas's trial took place in Neapoli in the spring and lasted just three days. Eleftheria and Alexandros Vandoulakis were there throughout, pale and rigid with shock and humiliation. Maria and Giorgos sat some distance away from them. Maria was sometimes aware of being scrutinised by people in the public gallery. As the sister of the victim, her emotions and reactions were of particular interest to them, but of course the fact that she had been a leprosy patient was the true reason for their curiosity.

They had all seen photographs of the extravagantly beautiful Anna in the newspaper and at first they were puzzled that this plainly dressed and unremarkable-looking woman with a long plait down her back could be her sister. When they heard a rumour that she had once been engaged to the cousin of the accused, whose name also came up in the trial, their appetite to know more became all the greater. Despite their prurience, however, none of them – not even one of the several journalists covering the trial – had the courage to approach her when the court adjourned each day. Maria knew exactly why. She was protected by their fear.

One by one, witnesses were called and gave their evidence.

Dr Kyritsis, who only remained in the court for the first day, testified that the gun must have been pressed to the victim's chest as it was fired. One bullet had passed through her lung and out through her back. Another had gone directly into her heart and ended her life. He verified that he had pronounced her dead at the scene.

As he spoke, Maria's eyes were fixed on the man she loved. It was several weeks since she had seen him, and the pain of their separation was as great as any she had endured these past months. She knew that he would have to return to Iraklion as soon as the court adjourned.

Several estate workers spoke about Andreas's character. One described his boss as a short-tempered, unfriendly individual. Another said that he was prone to outbursts of violent anger when instructions on the estate were not carried out to his liking. The latter witness was Antonis.

In Andreas's defence, others said that the accused was mild, almost introverted, and that it was very surprising that he had perpetrated such a brutal act. Maria wondered if these were men who were keen to keep their positions on the estate.

On the final morning, Andreas's defence lawyer called his most important witness to the box. It was Alexandros Vandoulakis's *koumbáros*, his best man, who was also Andreas's godfather. Now eighty years old, this former judge spoke with a conviction and gravitas that held the whole court spellbound. Until this moment in the trial, the handcuffed Andreas had sat pale and expressionless. Now he raised his head to look at the man who was speaking.

'It must be clear to all those who have listened to the evidence that the fault lies with the woman. This woman behaved in a manner that would provoke any man. Her insolence, her impiety, her immorality could only hasten the death of such a person. I have known the Vandoulakis family for many decades, and this fine man who sits before you for his entire life. This is an upright family. A decent family. A family with values. There is one belief that is integral to such a family: that these values they hold should be protected! And one of these values is the greatest of them all. *Philótimo.*'

He repeated the word that everyone in this courtroom knew so well, intoning it with even greater emphasis this time.

'*Philótimo!* Honour!'

There was silence for a moment. Every Cretan understood its significance, especially in such a family. In the eyes of this witness, it justified the murder of an unfaithful wife.

Maria listened with disgust to the way her sister was described and to the old man's exoneration of her murderer. It was almost impossible for her to remain sitting there. Out of the corner of her eye she could see that her father was totally motionless. She twisted her fingers together and looked down into her lap, biting her lip hard. The heat prickled on the back of her neck, and for a moment she felt certain she was going to faint. There were murmurs of disapproval from the small group from Plaka who were also in the public gallery but a little way from where she sat with Giorgos.

Before the verdict, there was a break during which everyone went outside. Maria found her father a seat just round the corner from the court and went for a walk. She needed to work off her anger. In a quiet street she saw a church with an open door and went inside.

Kissing the icon first, she sat in the back pew and then, in the darkness, she knelt. With such raging emotions, it was impossible to pray. Anger came between herself and God and she could not control it. She wanted to ask for forgiveness for Andreas, but her rational self wrestled with the very idea of it. Tears flowed unstoppably down her cheeks as she asked herself why such a crime should be erased. Was she the only one, apart from her father, Nikos and a handful of people from her village, who thought her sister had not deserved to be murdered? Did everyone else in that courtroom believe that such an act was justified?

She heard someone come into the church and turned around. It was the priest. Maria got up, crossed herself and swiftly left. It was drizzling as she made her way back to the court. She was not very familiar with Neapoli and took a wrong turning, which led her in a circle back to the church. Her father was not on the bench where she had left him and, anxious and frustrated, she only just made it back inside the court, her hair dripping, before the doors were shut. The judge and jury returned to the room.

The place was even more crammed with people than before, and she was obliged to remain behind three rows of standing spectators. She did not mind for herself that she was unnoticed and unobserved, but she worried about Giorgos, who must be sitting alone. She had wanted to be with him when the verdict was delivered.

Suddenly silence descended. The judge's was the only face that Maria could see as he took his seat on the podium. With his hooked nose and close-set eyes, he reminded her of an eagle.

The 'guilty' verdict was a foregone conclusion, hastily and almost inaudibly delivered by a member of the jury. The judge then allowed for a moment of complete hush before clearing his throat.

His gaze was focused on a single person, whom he now addressed.

Maria could picture Andreas even if she could not see him. She had tried to keep the thought from her mind, but this was the person who had snatched away her own happiness along with her sister's life. On that fateful evening, Nikos Kyritsis, the man who had brought the cure to Spinalonga, had asked her to marry him. Anna's death just a short while later had had many ramifications. One was that Maria knew she had no choice but to remain with her grieving father in Plaka. The wedding had been indefinitely postponed. The new life that was within reach for such a brief time would never be possible now, she was certain of it. Andreas Vandoulakis had ruined the life of every member of her family.

'For me, this is a tragic but simple case,' began the judge. 'I have few words to say to you, Andreas Vandoulakis.'

He was a master of the dramatic pause.

'This young woman, in the prime of her life, was murdered by you, her angry husband. We will never know if this was premeditated. You alone know the truth of that and may well go to your grave with it.'

The atmosphere, already hushed, became electric. He was going to hand down the death sentence. Why else would he mention the grave? This was a shock. What most in the room had expected was acquittal or, at most, a perfunctory sentence.

The judge continued.

'The protection of *philótimo* is important, but it is not a justifiable excuse for such a heinous crime.'

He made several references to those who had described Andreas's tendency to lose his temper. These included Antonis, whose comments had been the most persuasive.

'Andreas Vandoulakis, you are guilty of the murder of an innocent woman. This crime merits the death penalty.'

Someone cried out, 'No!' and sounds of dismay reverberated around the courtroom. Even Maria drew in her breath. A life for a life. There was something utterly appalling about it. She knew such a sentence was not unusual in similar cases, but it would not bring Anna back. It would restore neither her own happiness nor her father's.

The judge waited for the crowd to quieten down. 'However, on this occasion I am *not* handing you the death penalty. Instead, I am sentencing you to spend the rest of your days in prison. I think this will set an enduring enough example to all other men who may lose their tempers with their wives.'

There were more gasps from the spectators, especially from the majority who thought Andreas should walk away a free man. Surely it was Anna Vandoulakis who was the guilty party, not Andreas? The landowner's son being sent to prison? For the rest of his life?

Maria did not like the indignation that she sensed in the room. The crowd did not agree with this outcome. Many of the men amongst them felt themselves criticised. Raising a hand to your wife was not unusual in Crete, and they did not like the warning that had been issued to them.

She was out in the street within a few seconds and waited for her father to emerge. They walked in silence towards the bus stop. There was a bus due that would take them home, and both of them wanted to get as far away from this place as they could, and as quickly.

On the way home, the reflection of an exhausted, bedraggled woman looked back at Maria from the rain-spattered window. There had been so many moments in that courtroom when she had felt she was sitting through the trial of her sister rather than that of Andreas. She had aged a decade in the past three days.

When they reached home, both father and daughter wept. Broken as they were by Anna's death, they agreed that the execution of Andreas would not have mended their own lives.

While the trial was going on, a daily court report had filled the pages of the local Neapoli newspaper, but there had been nothing in the national press.

Manolis knew that proceedings were in progress and vainly scoured the national paper, *Kathimerini*, for information. Only when the trial ended was his curiosity satisfied.

LIFE SENTENCE FOR MURDER OF WIFE

It was buried on page five, with a short paragraph that sketched out the bare facts.

Manolis was ambivalent about the verdict, but admitted to himself, just as Maria and Giorgos had done, that an eye for an eye would not have brought him relief.

Several weeks later, he arrived home to find a large brown envelope propped against his door. Agathi had found it too fat to slip underneath. This time, although it was hardly neat, she managed to make out her tenant's family name. Vandoulakis. What a beautiful Cretan name, she said to herself. Van-dou-la-kis. It had a very pleasing rhythm.

Manolis tore open the envelope and into his hands fell several dozen flimsy sheets of newsprint. There was also a letter from Antonis. His friend always had plenty to say face to face, but he had struggled with his writing ever since school, so on paper he kept his words to a minimum:

Dear Manolis,

I hope things are well in Piraeus. I have left the Vandoulakis estate. It seemed time. I am now working in building construction. There are lots of new houses going up in Agios Nikolaos.

I kept these reports on the trial for you.
The reporter has recorded it exactly as it happened. I think it
marks an end to this terrible story for both of us.
Sending you my best regards,
Antonis

Antonis did not need to mention in his letter the many veiled
references to Manolis during the trial. His friend would surmise
that himself from the press cuttings.

Manolis scanned the letter twice and was puzzled by Antonis's
final comment, 'for both of us'. He knew that Antonis's family
was closely connected with Anna's but still it seemed strange.

He sat on his bed and put the cuttings in chronological order
before reading them. Antonis was right about the reporter. He
had brought the proceedings to life. Every cough or gasp was
there; every time Andreas Vandoulakis shifted in his seat it was
noted; every protest from the people crammed into the courtroom
– apparently a sizeable crowd – was described. By the time it
came to the verdict, Manolis felt he had lived every moment of
those days.

Elli, Kyría Agathi's niece, knocked on his door while he was
reading, but he was so absorbed that he did not hear her insistent
tapping. The evidence that she had been there was a little box of
baklava left outside. When Manolis opened his door, he stooped
down, retrieved it and devoured all eight pieces at once. Reading
about the trial had left his energy depleted and the pastries were
comforting.

He went out alone that night. He wanted to drink without
conversation, to obliterate thoughts, memory and emotion and to
halt the working of his imagination.

Such an objective proved impossible. His mind kept returning
to the man who looked so like him that people mistook them
for twins. His cousin now sat in a prison cell and, as sometimes
happened with actual twins, Manolis felt an involuntary connec-

tion. The trial and the sentence had brought matters to a conclusion in the eyes of the law, but for Manolis, as well as for the rest of his family, and Anna's too, that final day in court had not marked anything like an end.

Manolis sat in a bar opposite the busiest part of the harbour that night and slowly dulled his senses with alcohol. He watched boats leaving the port and followed them in his imagination. They were going to the Middle East, to India, to China and every other destination in the world. Perhaps he should simply take a job on one of them and disappear. He sat for a while contemplating the idea, but ultimately rejected it. For the moment there was probably nothing better than the life he was making here. He liked the men he worked with, and his landlady was a good sort.

He was sitting opposite the area of the port for the Iraklion ferries. The evening boat was just arriving, and he watched as people filed off. He was sure that he spotted a couple from Plaka, and pulled his collar up in case they noticed him.

Agathi came and went from Manolis's room while he was working. The morning after she had left the envelope outside his door, she decided it was the day to change his sheets. It was not difficult to find the package. It was hidden under some shirts in the bottom drawer. She drew the curtains wide to let in plenty of light and sat on the bed to read.

She immediately noted the name of the accused, Andreas Vandoulakis, and the victim, Anna Vandoulakis, and double-checked the name on the outside of the envelope. Taking off her shoes, she stretched out and made herself comfortable, propping a pillow up against the wooden bedhead. She read slowly, running her eyes across each line, paragraph by paragraph, page by page. There was no hurry, because she knew Manolis's movements well, and it would be a long while before he got home. It took her more than an hour to reach the final day of the trial.

She rested the pages on her chest for a moment. She could feel the furious beating of her heart. Then she swung her legs off the bed and started rummaging in the drawer. She was looking for a photograph that she was already familiar with.

Only now did she understand which of the men in it was her lodger. She had been wrong before. The one with the wedding ring was not Manolis. It was his cousin.

Everything made sense to her now. The earring. The nightmares. Poor Manolis. Poor, poor Manolis to have lost the woman he loved. How dreadful it must have been. She was shocked to realise that this young man seemed to have had everything torn away from him.

All the landlady had to offer him was kindness, and she resolved to lavish it on him even more than before. She casually mentioned to her niece that Manolis had a broken heart, which made Elli's fondness for him, and her resolve to cheer him with sweet things, grow even greater. Elli knew that pastries were not a nutritional necessity of life, but they were a magic potion for moods.

The moment Manolis returned to his room that day, he knew that his sheets were fresh: it was the waft of the sweet laundry soap, the smell of which reminded him of Anna. The next day as he left his room, he almost tripped on the midday meal Kyría Agathi had left outside his door. A can filled with rice and green beans and a lump of fresh bread wrapped in a napkin were waiting for him. She must have got up very early to prepare it, and the absence of anything outside other doors suggested that no other lodger was being similarly treated.

In the following days, he saw more of Agathi's niece than he did of the landlady herself. Elli began to appear in the hallway when she heard him coming home after work and they talked briefly. She was always pink-cheeked, and Manolis was polite and kind and asked her about her day.

The girl often had a little package of sweets tied up with ribbon ready to present to him. He took it graciously and always handed back his tin container, asking if she would pass his thanks to her aunt for the meal. Elli would blush even more deeply as Manolis said goodbye and made his way upstairs. As usual, from inside the landlady's own apartment, he could hear the sound of popular music blaring out from a gramophone, and the distorted sound of singing coming through his floorboards.

Everything in Piraeus was booming and expanding. The growth of the shipping industry seemed to have no limit; repairs followed and money flowed into the area. One night in April, a new *bouzoúkia* was opening. The team had worked well this week, and it also happened to be Miltos's saint's day, so they decided to meet up.

A new venue was always a great draw, and Manolis had promised to arrive early to get a good table. The place soon filled up, and all his friends joined him. Musicians filed on to the low stage: eight men with *bouzoúkis* and a drummer. Before the music began, the *paréa* toasted each other and wished Miltos a happy saint's day:

'*Stin yeia sou! Xrónia Pollá!*'

A well-known singer came on almost as soon as they arrived, and everyone sang along. There was not a syllable of his songs that was not imprinted on their hearts. Most of them were *rebétiko* style, the music of poverty and exile. The men sang with swelling hearts and tsunamis of feeling, the singer unleashing deep emotion even in the toughest of them. Nostalgia, longing, loss, desire. All of these swirled in a great collective lamentation.

Very late into the evening, the final act came on the stage. It was a woman with a voice of such strength that it filled the room and halted conversation. Manolis's chair had its back to the stage, but he immediately turned to look.

The singer was dressed very colourfully. She was wearing a blouse that Manolis recognised. He blinked in disbelief. It was his landlady, Kyría Agathi. The only difference in how she looked at this moment compared with when he had seen her earlier in the day was the addition of a pair of jangly hoop earrings that swung from her ears.

Agathi had watched Manolis for a while from behind the curtain, so she was not surprised to find him sitting almost under her nose. She gave him a flirtatious wave and he raised a glass to her as she continued to sing.

Manolis was very happy see her and called out with appreciation.

'*Yeia sou, Agathi. Ela! Ela!*'

She blew him a kiss, and his friends all teased him, demanding an explanation for this familiarity.

When a girl came round selling flowers, Manolis purchased several and showered Agathi with scarlet blooms. She tossed a few back to the table to express her own appreciation. Round after round of drinks went down in this night of surprise, gaiety and joy.

Agathi was tireless, and sang on and on, by far the most popular singer of the evening. Many of the songs had been made popular by the famous Sofia Vembo, and the audience loved her as if she was the diva herself.

'*Ela yélase gliká, pes mou lóyia eroticá,*' she sang. 'Come, laugh sweetly, tell me words of love . . .'

Manolis and his friends were on their feet by the end of her performance. When she had finished her last song, she came over to his table, and he welcomed her before introducing her to his *paréa*.

'Eh, *palikári mou*, you never suspected, did you?' Kyría Agathi said, clinking her glass against his as she nestled between him and Stavros.

'Not for a minute, Kyría Agathi. I have heard plenty of music coming up through your ceiling, but I didn't realise it was you. I thought it was your collection of Vembo!'

'Well, it *was* me,' she said coyly.

Manolis had no idea that Agathi had been an up-and-coming star in Piraeus before the occupation, when her career was interrupted by the wholesale destruction of the area. With her voice still impressive, she was making more appearances again these days, even though younger singers and a new style of music had made her less fashionable.

Stavros suddenly grasped her arm.

'You look just like a singer called Roussa!' he exclaimed, as a memory suddenly came to him. 'You were Roussa?'

Kyría Agathi beamed with pleasure. *Roussa* meant red.

'That was my stage name! You remember it?' she said. 'In those days we were told to have one. Mostly because we were young and it wasn't respectable to be on stage. If we had a fake name, it was less likely our parents would find out what we were up to.'

Stavros was dumbfounded. Once or twice, years ago, he and his friends had taken a trip to Athens from their village near Thessaloniki, and had found themselves in the music dens of Piraeus. He remembered the red-headed Roussa well. Along with the rest of his group, they had all lusted after her. He was astonished to find himself sitting side by side with her now. And Agathi glowed with the pleasure of finding someone who recalled who she used to be.

It was light when they finally left. Kyría Agathi linked arms with Manolis and Stavros and they made their way back to the pension.

'You were wonderful,' Manolis enthused.

'A diva!' murmured Stavros in her ear.

'Should have seen the look on your face, Manolis,' smiled Agathi.

'But . . . you had never said anything!' he responded, squeezing her arm.

It was only three or four hours before they all had to be back at the shipyard, and Manolis went straight up to his room to sleep. It did not surprise him when he saw Stavros emerge from Kyría Agathi's apartment the following morning, and on several subsequent days. It made him smile. Two people, at least, had found some kind of happiness.

After that first performance, Kyría Agathi was booked to make a weekly appearance in the *bouzoúkia*. Every time he passed her apartment, Manolis could hear her practising. It was not just music that filled the hallway, but happiness too.

A few days later, he knocked on the door so that he could return the metal container that had been filled with *spanakórizo*, rice and spinach for his lunch. The singing stopped immediately and the door opened.

'Manolis!' Agathi said gaily. 'Come in! Let me make you some coffee.'

Manolis had never been inside his landlady's apartment before, and it was exactly as he had imagined it. It was predominantly pink, with arrangements of feathers, flounced curtains and floral prints, and it reminded him of a starlet's dressing room. There was even a mirror with bright bulbs all around it. An alcove with floor-to-ceiling shelving was filled with rows of china figures, and he wandered across to take a closer look. They were mostly porcelain figures of elegant grandes dames in European dress from previous centuries, mixed in with a few figures from Disney. Manolis recognised Snow White, complete with her seven dwarves, Alice in Wonderland and Tinkerbell. He smiled. This cheerful display of royalty, fantasy and dreams seemed to fit the collector perfectly.

There was also a newish gramophone player with hundreds of records in messy stacks on the floor.

Elli appeared shyly from her bedroom and blushed the colour of one of her aunt's silk roses. She was just leaving for her evening shift at work.

'Bye-bye, *Theía*,' she said to her aunt, giving Manolis a glance as she passed.

Manolis sat down and looked about him.

'Will you come to my performance next week?' Agathi asked, coming back into the room with a glass of water.

'Of course, *Kyría mou*. You just tell me when.'

'Stavros said he would come too,' said Agathi, beaming.

Manolis took a long gulp of his water and then smiled at her.

A moment later she was back with his coffee and a tiny floral saucer piled impossibly high with rose-petal *loukoúmi*, Greek delight.

Once he had drained his coffee, she reached out for the cup.

'May I?'

It came as no surprise to Manolis that Agathi liked to read coffee grounds.

She tipped them from the cup into the saucer and scrutinised the grainy sludge left inside the cup. She paused dramatically, just for a moment.

'I can see something dark,' she said. 'Something very dark. In your past.'

Manolis sat there playing along with her and nodding. He suspected that she would have drawn her own conclusions from the small number of possessions he owned, and was almost certain that she had read the press cuttings of the trial. It had not escaped his notice that the envelope was on a different side of the drawer from where he had left it, but it did not bother him at all. He trusted her.

'But it's the past, Manolis. And I can see brighter things coming. I can see love.'

Like many people newly enamoured, Agathi wished all those around her to be in the same state.

She reached out and touched his hand. Her fingers felt soft and papery compared with his own hard skin.

'You *will* find new love,' she said with certainty. 'I've had my heart broken so many times, but thanks to you, even an old lady like me has found a wonderful man.'

She meant well, but Manolis was no more ready for love than a man with a hangover is ready for his next cognac.

'Stavros is a good man,' he said sincerely. 'I'm happy for you.'

'Your heart will mend,' she said as he was leaving. 'If mine did, then yours will too.'

'I hope so, Agathi,' Manolis replied. 'I do hope so.'

The summer gave way to autumn and the late-October temperatures were easy enough to work in. Giannis already had another contract in place and was putting his team under pressure to finish the job. Luckily no days were lost to rain, and after a break for New Year, the work was nearing completion by the end of April.

On his final walk to *Penelope*, Manolis passed a yard where boats were under construction. The scale of the operation was immense, with giant cranes positioned around like watchful giraffes and half-completed boats like skeletons of huge animals lying on their backs. Their rows of pale ribs were perfect and symmetrical, just as if God had made them.

He admired their beauty and imagined the pleasure of being engaged in such a long and satisfying process. On that particular day a new ship was being launched down the long slipway. He envied those who stood watching the culmination of several years of their work as the ship entered the water. It was like a birth.

'Hey, Kýrie!' one of the workers called out, noticing Manolis's look of admiration. 'Want a job?'

Manolis shook his head, knowing that he was too integral to his own team to contemplate leaving it.

That night the whole group went out and celebrated the completion of the job. Nine of them clinked their glasses together.

'To the sea!' Giannis shouted above the music.

'To the sea!' chorused the rest.

'May she always create work for us!' Petros cried.

'Man makes a ship and then the sea destroys it,' said Giannis, smiling at Manolis. 'And then we remake it. And so it goes on.'

Manolis looked round at the group. Like all of these men, he had profited from the relationship between time and destruction.

Having spent the past months scraping barnacles and repairing the damage wreaked by salt, he knew this cycle intimately. It was under his skin and beneath his fingernails.

The men had many rounds of drinks and the waiter brought them carafe after carafe of fiery *tsikoudiá*.

'Stay with us,' said Giannis, putting his arm around Manolis. 'There will always be more work than we need.'

Manolis looked around at the faces of these trusted friends. Something held this team together like a magnetic force. From the night he had danced the *zeibékiko*, he had been accepted. It seemed that any man who had suffered pain, whatever had caused it, could become one of them. These men were like the brothers he had never had, all of them with their own reasons for ending up in Piraeus. Their camaraderie was precious to all of them, though they would never admit it.

Giannis's new contract was to repair a massive tanker. Five times larger than the ship they had been working on for the past months, it was owned by one of the 'golden five' owners, a group that also included Niarchos and Onassis, better known these days than the gods themselves. The commission was valuable to Giannis and rewards would be great if the team did a good job. Moreover, the work that could follow was potentially unlimited, such was the exponential growth in shipping.

Manolis made a commitment to stay. His life in the pension was comfortable. Agathi was kind, her niece was sweet, his room was clean and the prostitutes on the floor above did not disturb him since, as she had promised, they usually worked there only in the day.

Occasionally he glimpsed one of them but they aroused no interest in him. When he was in the mood, he went with some of the younger men in his *paréa* to a bar. He would dance with girls but no more than that.

Occasionally one of the others would try to provoke him.

'You like boys, Manolis?'

He smiled. The suggestion did not bother him and he teased back.

'Not for me, Petros. You help yourself, though!'

There were plenty of young men hanging about, and he was never critical if one of his group occasionally paid them for sex.

Even if Agathi proved to be right in predicting that one day he would find new love, he still held Anna close. He looked at her picture every night, and even if he no longer shouted out her name, she often visited him in his dreams.

Chapter Eight

F ROM TIME TO time, Manolis had received semi-legible letters
from Antonis. Through these he had heard of the death of
his aunt and was deeply saddened. Eleftheria Vandoulakis had
effectively been his mother for so many years, and it upset him
that he had not been able to attend the funeral. And surely she
was too young to die? He knew that the events of that August
night would have been devastating for her. Perhaps this was the
cause.

Happier news was that Maria had finally married the doctor
who had cured her of leprosy, and they had adopted little Sofia.
As he had read this, his mind flitted back to his *vaftistíra* for the
first time in a long while. Although Anna had implied he might
be her father, Manolis had always dismissed the notion. They had
always tried to be careful, but even so, he supposed a small chance
remained. Whether or not he was, Maria and Dr Kyritsis now
lived in Agios Nikolaos, and Manolis was glad that the little girl
would grow up in a lovely town by the sea rather than in that
forbidding Vandoulakis house in Neapoli. He had never liked the
heavy oak furniture and the rooms kept in perpetual twilight by
dense lace curtains and heavy drapes.

Antonis wrote about his new work and boasted of the great
rewards it gave him. He was making so much money from construction that he had built his own five-storey block and was renting

out the lower floors. He could not help bragging to Manolis that, in addition to his truck, he now owned a Triumph Herald. It was the only one in Agios Nikolaos and the only thing he lacked was a road long and straight enough to reach its top speed. In every letter he told Manolis that there would always be work for him with his old friend.

There was never any reference to a woman in Antonis's letters, though he always mentioned his sister Fotini and her two children.

Fotini was still the only one Antonis had ever confided in over one particular issue. No one else knew of his passion for Anna that had ended in what he regarded as humiliating rejection. There was a strong sibling affection between them that allowed their exchanges to go to the core.

'Antonis, how long is it going to be?'

'Fotini, I am not going to marry just for the sake of marrying.'

'That's not what I mean,' she replied. 'You know what I mean. When are you going to get over her?'

There was no doubting who she meant by 'her'.

'You've even admitted you didn't like her by the end!' insisted Fotini. 'And it's so many years ago now.'

Antonis knew his sister was right. He had lingered over a love that had long turned rancid. He admitted to himself that this bitter hatred of a dead woman and her ruined husband had become a habit. A habit that was slowly destroying him.

'You're wasting your life,' concluded Fotini.

'You sound like our parents,' teased Antonis, trying to make light of what she had said.

'Don't you want children?'

'I have yours to play with.'

It was true that Antonis was very close to his nephews. He had just been outside kicking a ball with Mattheos, the elder of them. Fotini's children loved their uncle, especially when he took them for outings in his new car and gave them exciting gifts for their saint's days.

It was something very simple that brought about a change in Antonis's mentality. When he got up one morning, he noticed a few hairs on his pillow, and the next day a few more. A brief inspection in the mirror told him what he already suspected. His hairline was beginning to recede. It was his first intimation of mortality. In a few weeks' time, it would be his birthday. His thirty-fifth. At the same age, his father already had a son of fifteen. The realisation gave him a jolt.

A month or so later, Antonis turned up at Fotini's taverna with a girl on his arm. Fotini glanced through the hatch from the kitchen and saw him walk in.

'Look, Stephanos!' she said, tugging her husband's sleeve. 'Antonis! With a *girl*!'

Bringing a girlfriend to the family taverna was significant. Antonis introduced Anastasia proudly. She had just passed her nursing exams in Sitia and had come to work in the hospital at Agios Nikolaos. She was beautiful, sincere and a little shy.

As soon as the couple had left, Fotini observed to Stephanos that there was only one characteristic that this girl shared with Anna. Her good looks. That was where the similarity ended. Anastasia was what Fotini described as *aplí*, meaning simple and honest, and from her this was the highest compliment.

'She's not the schemer that Anna was,' she said bluntly to her husband that night. 'You can just tell she's a good sort.'

Stephanos was a man of few words and simply nodded as his wife continued.

'And I have never seen Antonis in love. Not properly, anyway.'

'Well, as long as Ana-stasia doesn't start shortening her name . . .' quipped Stephanos.

Fotini cuffed her husband round the arm and soon they were laughing together.

A few weeks later, Maria was visiting Fotini in Plaka. Sofia and Mattheos were running about squealing and the two women were chatting over their coffee. Both of them had their backs to the road and were looking out to sea. Above the din being made by the children, Fotini failed to hear the distinctive sound of her brother's car. He always drove into the village too fast and then braked hard.

A moment later, he stole up behind Fotini, put his arms around her and planted a kiss on her head.

'Antonis,' she said, spinning around with delight, 'what brings you here on a Wednesday afternoon?'

Antonis greeted Maria warmly before pulling over a chair for himself. Both the women could see he was impatient to tell them something.

He could not keep his news to himself for another moment.

'We're getting married!' he blurted out, grabbing his sister's hand. 'Anastasia and me. We're going to be married.'

Fotini was startled. Even though it was something she had hoped for, it seemed very soon and she could not stop herself expressing her doubts.

'She's lovely,' she said. 'But you haven't known her that long, have you? And isn't she a bit young?'

'That doesn't matter, Fotini! If your brother is in love, he's in love!' interjected Maria, who was, after all, married to a man much older than herself.

'Maria's right! I don't care about any of those things.'

Fotini was only too aware that Antonis had wasted years over someone who didn't love him, but that could not be said in front of Maria.

'Well, if you're sure,' said Fotini, 'then I am happy. When is it going to be?'

'As soon as we can organise things. Three months' time?'

'And can we have the party here?'

Antonis was beaming from ear to ear.

'Anastasia doesn't have a big family, just her father and a younger sister, so they won't mind if it doesn't happen in Sitia. I am sure they would all be happy to come to Plaka.'

'Let's tell Stephanos straight away! He'll want to start planning the menu!' Fotini hurried off to the kitchen.

'Congratulations, Antonis!' said Maria, squeezing his hand. 'I'm really excited to meet her.'

'I know you'll get on,' replied Antonis. 'She's a wonderful girl.'

When the invitation to the wedding arrived in Piraeus, Manolis propped it on the ledge above his fireplace and contemplated going. What would people do? What could they say if he turned up? He was not guilty of anything in the eyes of the law. This exile he lived in he had imposed on himself. He had every right to return and would face up to anyone who suggested otherwise.

The pros and cons, the what–ifs rolled around in his head for several days. He worked mechanically that week; his limbs moved but his mind was focused on his return to Plaka. Yes, he would go.

When he eventually picked the card up to write his reply, he noticed the date for the first time. It was in much smaller type than the names of the bride and groom, the name of the church and so on. In small type at the bottom of the card he now saw it: 25 August.

It was on that day that a lively *gléndi* in Plaka had been cut short. He assumed that Antonis's bride knew nothing of what had taken place in Plaka, but there would certainly be many revellers who had it on their minds. He wondered if Antonis had consciously chosen this date in order to lay those bad memories to rest. Perhaps for him it represented an ending as well as a beginning. Or maybe it had not even crossed his mind. Manolis could not ask him, but his decision to attend was instantly reversed.

It's a very busy period on this new ship, he wrote to Antonis. *So unfortunately they can't spare me for even a day. I wish you both a wonderful day.*

Once the letter was posted, he had no regrets. The village of Plaka might be ready to dance again, but he was not.

On the day of the wedding, Manolis marked the two-year

memorial of Anna's death by going into a church and lighting a candle for her. In Plaka, Maria and her father did the same.

Antonis wrote a few months later to describe the nuptials. It seemed that everything had gone well. In the same letter he told Manolis that he and Anastasia were expecting their first child the following spring.

One Sunday evening, not long after the birth of her niece, Fotini came over from Plaka to see the baby.

Anastasia was looking exhausted and Fotini took the little one from her arms and rocked her expertly. After a bout of crying that had lasted several hours, she miraculously calmed down. It gave Anastasia an opportunity to rest and she left the room to sleep.

Antonis could see that something was troubling his sister. It was unlike her to turn up like this out of the blue.

'There's something on your mind,' he said bluntly.

Fotini confided immediately that she had just called in to see Maria, who lived only three streets away. Nikos had gone to an international leprosy conference and would be there for a few weeks.

'You will never imagine what she is planning to do, Antonis!'

Antonis could not imagine Maria doing anything either shocking or perturbing.

'She asked me if I would have Sofia for the day next week . . .'

This in itself did not seem very surprising. Sofia loved coming to play with Fotini's children.

' . . . and can you imagine *why*?'

Antonis shook his head.

'She is going to see *Andreas*! In *prison*!'

She was speaking in a hoarse whisper to avoid waking the baby, but the child could feel her aunt's agitation nonetheless and was starting to cry again. Fotini stood up and rocked her.

'I just don't believe it, Antonis,' she said. 'He *killed* her sister.'

Fotini herself was almost in tears now, and Antonis took the baby from her.

'I don't think she should go. And I told her so. I don't think she should go and see her sister's murderer.'

'I agree with you,' said Antonis. 'But you can't really stop her, can you?'

'No,' said Fotini. 'It's as if she is forgiving him. And I don't see how *anyone* could forgive him. Do you?'

'Is she telling her father?'

'No, Giorgos definitely doesn't know about it. Otherwise she would have asked him to have Sofia.'

'I wonder what it's like in there,' mused Antonis.

'She'll tell me, I expect,' said Fotini. 'But I think we can imagine what Neapoli prison is like. Look, promise me you won't tell anyone . . .'

Antonis nodded.

'I think it's better for everyone that she does this discreetly,' he said. 'So of course I'll keep it to myself. She has her own reasons for going, I'm sure.'

The baby was peaceful again now.

'Such sweet innocence,' Fotini said affectionately, kissing her little head.

Chapter Nine

THE FOLLOWING THURSDAY, at around ten in the morning, Maria arrived in Plaka with Sofia. It was a warm early summer's day and the little girl was bubbling with excitement to see her friends. She was nearly five, Mattheos was already six and Petros was almost three. The gang were as close as cousins.

Sofia immediately ran off with the boys and Fotini and Maria had time for a brief conversation before the latter left.

Fotini was taking the day off from the taverna and planned to spend most of it on the beach. In the shadow of the pine trees that went right down to the sea, they would make necklaces from shells and collect the smoothest, palest pebbles they could find. They would take these home and paint them in the late afternoon when they woke up from a siesta, and in the early evening, when they sun had gone down, they would go paddling. The day was all planned out.

As the bus started its journey from Plaka towards Agios Nikolaos and onwards to Neapoli, Maria glimpsed the little group already on the beach. She thought of those endless carefree days of her own childhood with Fotini, and an image came to her of them skimming stones, splashing in the shallows and trying to catch fish. Her friend Dimitris Limonias was often there with them, along with Anna and Antonis. Spinalonga sat on the horizon, the sun caught the sparkle of the waves and a few old men sat in the *kafeneío*. It was all so familiar and yet her whole world had changed. It was two years since the trial, but the events of those months seemed like yesterday.

As the bus trundled along, Maria had plenty of time to worry about what she was doing. The prison in Neapoli had a fearsome reputation. The guards were rumoured to be as tough as the prisoners, and she knew that women were vulnerable when they went in there.

What she encountered was worse than she had imagined. The ordeal began before she even got close. The prison was a long way from the town, and it was a three-kilometre walk to the prison gates from where the bus dropped her. It was a daunting sight, even from a distance. The walls were high and forbidding and, as she got closer, Maria could see layers of twisted and rusting barbed wire running along the top. Even if a prisoner scaled the walls from inside, they would be torn to shreds by the wire, so she imagined that no one ever attempted escape.

As she approached she could see that there was a line of people outside. The queue hugged the wall for a long way. There were women of all ages, fifty or so ahead of her, and soon some behind too. They were ragged, mostly with scarves over their heads to conceal their faces. It reminded her vividly of being on Spinalonga. Several of the women were very bent too, and must have struggled to walk the length of the road that led to this place. All of them were thin, and there was little conversation between them. Maria noticed that the woman directly in front of her was feeding a baby beneath her shawl.

Some of the women seemed to have baskets with them. Perhaps it was food. Maria had not thought to bring anything for the man she was visiting.

As she got closer to the front of the queue, she could see why she had already been standing for an hour and a half. There was a heavy door built into the side wall of the prison. It had a metal grate. One by one the women had to stand on tiptoe and speak to the guard on the other side of it. If he was satisfied with the answer they gave, the door was unbolted and the woman admitted. Some were turned away.

When it was her turn, Maria's heart was beating furiously.

'Name of prisoner?'

'Your name?'

'Relationship to prisoner?'

'Proof of relationship to prisoner?'

For the last question, she was meant to produce some kind of paperwork. She had her sister's marriage certificate and her death certificate and passed them through.

She heard the bolts being drawn back and the door was opened just wide enough for her to pass. As soon as she was in, it was slammed behind her. She shuddered. More memories of Spinalonga came back. She recalled the moment when she had entered the tunnel to go into the island and the sound of the gate clanging shut behind her. Just as then, she was full of trepidation.

In front of her was a scene from hell. On the other side of a wire fence three metres tall were hundreds of men in ragged overalls. They were shuffling around the yard, treading on each other's heels as they moved forward. Over their bowed, uniformly shaved heads she could see a man cracking a whip like a circus ringmaster. None of them looked up.

Perhaps Andreas was one of them, but Maria did not dare scrutinise the pathetic crowd.

The stench was overpowering. The contained space and the temperature within the high prison walls must have heated the human excrement to the point of fermentation. Maria clasped her hand to her mouth and nose. Even so, she almost vomited.

'In there,' barked the guard, pointing to a small hut on her side of the fence.

Maria walked through the open door. There was no sign of the women who had gone in before her. A prison officer was lounging back on his chair, feet up on his desk, smoking.

'Take a seat,' he said, with exaggerated politeness.

She was grateful to be away from the stink outside, even if the smell of tobacco in this small space was asphyxiating. She looked into a pair of cold, unsympathetic eyes.

'Why do you want to see this prisoner? You're not related.'

Maria felt stupid. She had not anticipated having to explain herself.

'He's my sister's husband,' she said simply.

'And your sister is dead, I see.'

'Yes.'

'So he *was* your sister's husband,' the man corrected her.

He got up and began rifling through the messy contents of a filing cabinet in the corner. Once he had found what he was looking for, he held it a few centimetres from his face and started reading. He was small and grey-haired, and his jacket was unbuttoned, a roll of fat bulging over his trousers. Beads of sweat dripped down the side of his face and ran into his neck, making his collar darker than the rest.

'He is a murderer, this man. He killed his wife, your sister, yes?'

Maria nodded, feeling it wise to go along with him.

'We have people like you in here all the time. They come in for revenge, pure and simple. If justice hasn't been done, they come in to finish the job. I don't blame them really. I'd do the same.'

He sat down again and looked at her.

'You'd be surprised how often it's women who do this. They seem to keep the anger in them longer than the men. And it reduces the prison population here. It's very overcrowded, you see. Six to a cell meant for three. What can I do?'

This man obviously liked to talk, and she had no choice but to listen.

'But I can let you in. If you like.'

Maria managed to get in her 'Thank you' before he started up again. She wondered if he was expecting a bribe.

'We usually only let in blood relations. But I suppose you are related by blood,' he said. 'In a way.'

He smirked, amused by his own attempt at a joke.

'Looks like he's never had any other visitors . . .'

Maria had sometimes wondered if any of the family had ever visited. Now she knew the answer. He had not seen a soul in three years.

' . . . and just the one letter.'

A flimsy piece of paper had floated out of the file and landed on the floor by Maria's feet. She picked it up and handed it back politely, but not before noticing the signature of Andreas's sister Olga at the bottom.

The officer held it almost to his face.

'His mother. It's not *from* his mother. It's about her. She died.'

Maria nodded. She did not want to get on the wrong side of this man.

'We don't let prisoners hold onto their letters; they have to be re-filed, you see. Anyway, that lot out there, that's only some of the prisoners. Your Vandoulakis will be locked in today. He has his exercise on a Saturday, according to this.' He waved the file in the air. 'So I'll get someone to take you. He's right over the other side.'

They sat in awkward silence. The man lit another cigarette, put his feet back on the desk, picked up a newspaper and started to read. Many minutes later, another guard appeared.

'Vandoulakis,' said the officer languidly. 'Delta 27.'

Maria was escorted to a block that had been built shoddily against the outside wall. Inside, she saw some of the women who had been let in before her. They were sitting in a row at a long bench divided down the middle. On the other side of the bench, behind a dense wire-mesh partition, were the men they had come to see. There was only one empty seat and Maria took it.

Some of those in the room, both men and women, were weeping, while others were shouting, banging a fist on the bench, or talking earnestly, perhaps sharing endearments or passing secrets. Every time the noise level became too high, one of the four guards who were positioned at each corner of the room would stand up and shout for silence.

The guard had gone to collect Andreas. It seemed a laborious business. Maria sat there trying not to look at anyone. Andreas had no idea that she was coming. Perhaps he even had the right to refuse to see visitors. She was full of questions for herself. Why had she even come? It was hard to justify, which was why she had not even been able to explain it to her best friend. What would they talk about? What did she expect of him? These minutes gave her ample time to doubt if she had done the right thing.

She almost got up to make her escape, but it was too late. There was movement behind the wire grille. And now there was a man standing there. She leaned forward, but the lighting in the room made it hard to see much more than an outline. She could just make out that this figure was handcuffed at the front. He sat down and she could see that he was leaning towards her.

She was alarmed. They must have made a mistake and brought in the wrong person. This bald, bird-like figure was not Andreas. She turned round to see if she could attract the attention of the guards. Then, above the cacophony of other voices, she heard one she recognised.

'Maria? Maria Petrakis?'

However much a man changed physically, a voice remained exactly the same. Sorrow, brutality and lack of food had transformed his body beyond recognition, but this was, beyond doubt, her brother-in-law.

Maria leaned forward to study the face pressed against the other side of the grille.

'Yes,' she said. 'It's Maria.'

She was shocked by his appearance. Even though she had seen a sea of other prisoners in the yard, uniformly abject, she had naïvely assumed that Andreas Vandoulakis would still be the man he had been. She had imagined that his pride and status would have allowed him to retain his air of superiority, even here. She realised how stupid she had been. A place such as this reduced everyone to the same level of degradation.

Since the day Fotini had first questioned her plan, Maria had harboured doubts, and many times since she had got off the bus some hours before, she had wondered what on earth she was doing. But now, with Andreas sitting a metre away from her, she suddenly saw a purpose. It was written in the look of sheer gratitude in his expression. Just by sitting there, she had brought him a moment of happiness.

Everything was hazy through the distorting prism of the mesh, but she could see his eyes. They seemed huge in a thin, shrunken face.

For a moment they peered at each other. The volume of noise around them meant that they had to lean right in so that their faces were almost touching the metal, otherwise it was impossible to hear anything the other said.

'Why did you come?'

It was the only thing that interested Andreas but the one thing Maria could not articulate. She could not really define her motivation.

Even before she had tried to think of something appropriate to say, a bell was clanging. It was loud and relentless and any conversation they might have been having would have been impossible now. There was a mass scraping of chairs as every prisoner got up simultaneously. They did not wait to be told. All of them knew there would be an immediate and violent beating if they dawdled. The four guards were now goading them out of the room. Over their shoulders, many were shouting a few final words to their visitors, but none of these were audible.

The visitors got up with less haste and made their way silently to the door.

Maria felt cheated by the lack of time she had spent with

Andreas. It was little more than a glimpse after so many hours of travel and waiting.

'You have to be here by eight in the morning,' said the woman who had been sitting next to her. She had noticed that Maria had only just taken a seat before the visiting period had come to an end. 'That usually gets you fifteen minutes in here. But that's the most you'll ever have anyway.'

Next time, thought Maria, she would catch the first bus out of Agios Nikolaos. Those few moments with Andreas had not been enough. She understood from the woman who had spoken to her that prisoners were only allowed one visitor each month, so as soon as she got home, she noted in her diary when she could next go.

Nikos was back from his conference in Cairo a few days later. Maria needed to tell him that she had visited Andreas. She waited until Sofia was asleep.

Her husband was a man of great compassion, but nevertheless he questioned whether it was really necessary for his wife to go to a place with a reputation for being one of the roughest prisons in Greece.

'So you went alone?' he said, trying to suppress his annoyance.

'They don't let people in in pairs, Nikos,' she said. 'You *have* to be on your own.'

'But why now?' he asked.

'Sofia, I suppose,' said Maria. 'Every time I look at that child, I see Andreas. And it's just so sad that she doesn't know him. That she has no memory.'

'But it's not logical to tell her. *We* are Sofia's parents now. And that's the reality.'

'I just felt . . .'

'Felt what, Maria?'

Nikos rarely uttered a strict word to his wife, or to his daughter for that matter.

'I think your concern should principally be for Sofia,' he said. 'You shouldn't spend too much time thinking of Andreas Vandoulakis.'

'Perhaps it was because her birthday is coming up,' Maria offered, as an excuse.

'I don't really know what difference that makes. As she gets older, it becomes less relevant, doesn't it, rather than more?'

It was late at night and Nikos was tired after his journey back from Egypt. Maria poured him a whisky and came to sit with him on the sofa.

'Well, even if Sofia never knows what happened, I just thought it would be nice to tell him that she is safe and well. How else will he ever know?'

Nikos shrugged his shoulders. He did not have an answer for his wife. His only instinct was to protect this precious child whom he had so quickly grown to love, just as if she were his own. He put his arm around Maria and she nestled into him.

'They told me in the prison that he's never had any visitors. Not a single one!'

'I'm surprised his father hasn't been to see him,' responded Nikos.

'I'm not,' said Maria firmly. She knew the Vandoulakis tribe better than her husband. 'All that family honour . . . Imagine the shame, *agápi mou*.'

They sat silently for a while.

'And it was terrible in there. Horrific. The smell. The dirt. The look on all their faces. I don't think the old man would manage it. And I'm glad his mother never saw it.'

'I wonder if Andreas even knows that she died?' Nikos mused.

'His sister wrote,' Maria answered. 'I saw her letter.'

A few more moments passed before either of them spoke again. There was a burning question as yet unasked.

'So do you plan to go again?'

The visit to Andreas had lasted little more than two minutes, so Maria had not even considered that it would be her last. She was haunted by that brief moment. She had seen into the soul of an abandoned man, and the look of relief that someone had cared enough to come was something she would never forget.

She already had a date in mind, but she hesitated before answering.

'Yes,' she said firmly. 'I would like to.'

Nikos loved his wife without boundaries and unfailingly showed her respect.

'If you think this is the right thing to do,' he said, 'I won't try to change your mind.'

'Nikos, Andreas Vandoulakis will never be released, so it won't change Sofia's understanding of anything.' She knew that this was her husband's greatest fear: that they might one day lose their daughter.

'Very well, Maria. But next time, I will drive you there and wait outside to make sure you are safe.'

'There's no need, *mátia mou*. You have work to do, and I really don't mind going on the bus. But you could take a few hours off and look after Sofia. That will save me taking her over to Fotini's.'

'Whatever is best. We can discuss all that before you go.'

There was nothing more to be said that night. What Maria was doing made Nikos uneasy, but he could not get in the way of her natural kindness and would never try. It was the very quality that had drawn him to her.

Throughout her time on Spinalonga, Maria's faith in God had given her strength. She had lit more candles in the little church of St Pantaleimon than there were wild flowers on the hillside. She had prayed for mercy for those who were healthy as much as for the sick. She had prayed for those on the mainland as well as those on Spinalonga. She had prayed for the needs of the whole world, for people she did not know, for those who lived close to her and even for those she did not like, such as Spinalonga's bitter school teacher, Kyría Kroustalakis, who had made her life so difficult. She had prayed for the souls of the living and the dead. She had never prayed for an end to suffering. It was part of the human condition.

Certain prayers had been answered so spectacularly that all the days of her life would not be numerous enough to give thanks. When a cure for leprosy was found, there was not enough wax to make all the candles nor enough silver in the mines of the world to make the *támata* she wanted to offer. And when she was finally joined in marriage to Nikos Kyritsis, how could she begin to thank God? After the tragedies of previous years, his arrival on the island and his love for her seemed like divine intervention.

Nikos did not have the same religious faith. He was a pragmatist, but he observed the strength it gave Maria and respected her beliefs and her actions, even though they were sometimes hard to comprehend. Her desire to make peace with Andreas was an example.

Maria's strong sense of God's pity directed what she was doing now. If Christ had preached forgiveness, how could she ignore this teaching? Forgiving Andreas Vandoulakis from a distance was one thing; demonstrating it to him was another.

Every night, Maria brushed her hair fifty times, a habit she had kept to since childhood. As she counted, she imagined the gloomy cell that Andreas would be sleeping in. How could anyone sleep six to a cell? Did they have beds? Did they have water? However abject she pictured it, she knew it could be worse.

The only way this pity of hers would attain any real meaning would be if she demonstrated it by visiting. God's mercy towards her had been shown in tangible ways, not only in the form of a drug that had cured an incurable disease, but also in the form of the wonderful man who lay soundly asleep in their bed.

She began to tick off the days until her next visit.

Chapter Ten

IN PIRAEUS, THE weeks passed by quickly for Manolis, with days of demanding physical labour and nights of drinking and friendship. Nowadays he was earning more than he needed, and for only a small additional sum, Agathi moved him into a much larger room. It had a high ceiling and a balcony overlooking the main street. Shafts of sunlight and the rattle of the first tram woke him each day. The sound of goats and early-morning birdsong that used to be his alarm clock in Crete seemed very distant, and he recognised that he had become fully accustomed to urban life. Piraeus felt like home.

He was as happy as any man could be who had lost the love of his life. At least he had not lost her to someone else, and for Manolis this was great compensation. Jealousy was not a characteristic exclusive to his cousin Andreas, nor to Anna for that matter, and he acknowledged to himself that he would have killed any man who had taken Anna from him. The baptism photograph rarely came out of the drawer these days. He had no need to look at it any more. It meant that he had to see Andreas too, and even the image of himself now troubled him. He had changed so much since then. The photo was tucked inside the envelope along with the account of the trial.

While Manolis lived without love, Agathi spent her days on its cloud.

'We might get married,' she told Manolis. 'It would be nice, don't you think? Just a few of us, then a nice dinner? I've even seen a dress . . .'

Manolis could not imagine his landlady in white, but she seemed determined. She had not been married before and was more than ready now. Whoever had broken her heart in the past had not shattered it entirely. Like a few of her own china ornaments, Agathi was being glued back together.

Stavros now spent most nights with her, appearing by Manolis's side as he left the pension in the morning. They would then walk together to work, stopping to drink a strong, sharp coffee en route. From being one of the most withdrawn members of the crew, Stavros had become a little more talkative.

Every weekend, the four of them, Agathi, Stavros, Manolis and Elli, would go to see a new film. Agathi and Stavros would hold hands throughout and sometimes even kiss in the dark.

The film industry was booming, and new cinemas were opening at the rate of one a month. On this particular Saturday, they had gone to see the latest romantic comedy starring the beautiful Jenny Karezi. Agathi loved her as much for her singing voice as for her acting, and had been waiting eagerly for the film to be released.

Manolis had to put up with Elli's adoring looks when they went out for a coffee and something sweet, a *glykó*, afterwards, but he was kind to her, treating her as if she was his daughter. Agathi had confided to him that morning, 'She'll grow out of it, Manolis. Girls always have a first big crush.' He hoped she was right, but meanwhile he gave Elli no encouragement.

While he was happy that his landlady and Stavros were so content, Manolis doubted that he would ever again find himself in that state of love. He was firmly closed to the idea of it, convinced that he would never feel as deeply or intensely again.

'He's the nicest man I have ever known,' Agathi said, tweaking Stavros's cheek as they sat all together in a pavement café. 'He is as sweet as this ice cream.'

Stavros smiled, taking her hand.

Elli blushed. What seemed to her like geriatric love was embarrassing. Her aunt and Stavros seemed too old for such a thing, and it was only made more mortifying by their openness.

'It's more than twenty years,' continued Kyría Agathi, as though Stavros was not sitting there, 'since I knew love. And when that finished, I swore: never again!' She banged the table with her free hand, making the sundae dishes rattle. 'I tell you, I did! *Never again!* I said.'

A couple at the next table looked across with disapproval at this noisy woman in garishly colourful clothes. Even her perfume made her hard to ignore.

'And then I meet this man! This lovely, handsome man! He is my dream come true.'

Stavros looked shy now. He was anything but handsome and he knew it. Taking Agathi's hand, he kissed it gently and she in turn kissed his.

'Oh, you sweet lovebirds,' teased Manolis. 'What a nice couple you make.'

As Elli shifted awkwardly in her chair, Manolis quickly called for the bill. There was something very endearing about their happiness, even if it made Agathi's niece squirm.

'You'll understand one day, my little one,' she said. 'Love is not only for the young.'

In the early hours of the following morning, when even the noisy drunks who often ended their evening in the street had gone away, there was a huge rumpus down below. A woman was hammering on their door, yelling and screaming. It was May, so all the windows were open. The racket not only woke Manolis, it roused the entire household and the ones nearby.

Manolis leant over his balcony. He could see a woman. Her face was disfigured with anger so it was hard to tell her age, but her hair was bright blonde, obviously dyed.

She looked up when she saw him and screamed, 'I'm going to *kill* them! I'm going to kill *both* of them!'

Other people, also disturbed by the shrieking, were opening shutters on both sides of the street and leaning out. It did not matter what time of night such a drama took place, it always drew an audience. If it did not concern them personally, that was all the better, and it became pure theatre. Most people knew that girls could hire out Kyría Agathi's rooms by the hour and assumed that some regretful husband was about to emerge and be dragged by his collar down the street. They had seen it happen before and it was excellent entertainment.

The woman's shrieking did not abate, and nor did the banging. Manolis had a clear view of her and she screamed up to him again.

'Let me in! You bastard, let me in!'

He could tell that the noise of banging was not created by a bare hand. It was something hard. Probably metal. He also knew that it was only a matter of moments before this woman realised that the outer door was kept on the latch. He withdrew into his room, threw on his trousers and ran down the stairs two at a time. Other tenants stood on the landing in their underpants.

The woman was now in the hallway and Manolis could see that she was brandishing a handgun. She was still shrieking. Recognising Manolis as the man from the balcony, she fired her gun into the ceiling.

'You tell me where Kostas and this woman are, you bastard! You just tell me! Or the next bullet will be for you!'

Manolis raised his hands slowly and cautiously, trying to seem as unthreatening as possible.

'I know who she is,' said the woman, more calmly. 'She's an old singer in the *bouzoúkia*. I know exactly who she is. He was never going to go off with a young one, was he? None of those young ones would even look at him.'

Manolis suddenly realised that the woman was in the right place. Whatever was behind all this, he wanted to protect Agathi at all costs. Her door was still firmly closed and Manolis prayed that it would remain so. If his landlady came out, he had no doubt that she would get that bullet.

He knew that the only tactic was to try and calm this harpy. First he must let her finish her rant.

'It's not so easy to disappear in this country, you know. You think there is a big distance between Thessaloniki and Piraeus? Well, anyone who works on the boats in the north, where would they vanish to?'

'Tell me,' said Manolis gently, attempting to engage her in dialogue.

'To work on the boats in the south, wouldn't they? Any fool could guess that. And I expect he would have gone to the islands next. He would try to vanish into some shipyard in Andros or Chios.'

Her hand was shaking so violently that she could hardly hold the gun, let alone pull the trigger, but Manolis was nevertheless uneasy to see that it was still pointed in his direction.

'I suppose he could be there now,' he said valiantly.

'Well I'm not stupid. It's taken me some months, but here I am. And once you are in Piraeus, you just narrow down the places, don't you? And eventually you find the one you are looking for. *You* know where he is, don't you?'

She drew breath for the first time, giving Manolis the opportunity to speak.

'*Kyría*,' he said, gently. 'Madam.' It was not the first time he had defused the passions of an angry woman with his mellifluous voice. He knew precisely the tone to adopt. 'Please calm down. Are you sure you have the right place? I think there has been some mistake'

She lowered her gun. She was slightly calmer now, as though the narration of her route to Kyría Agathi's house had helped her. She was talking now rather than screaming.

'I am looking for Kostas,' she said. 'Kostas Konstantinidis.'

At that moment Manolis saw the landlady's door open a crack.

Surely Kyría Agathi would not be coming out to confront her lover's wife? Even he might not be able to defuse the situation if she was.

But instead of his landlady, it was Elli who appeared, waif-like in her long nightgown. This vision of virginal innocence seemed completely to change the mood.

'What is it, Kýrie Manolis?' she asked.

The intruder was holding the gun limply by her side now.

'Can we help you?' Elli asked the demented woman, as if she was looking to rent a room.

The woman continued with her rant.

'This isn't her!' she screamed. 'He wouldn't be with this scrawny kid. It's that old singer he's with. Lots of people have told me. Even the waiter in the *bouzoúkia* where she sings. This isn't *her!*'

With her attention turned to Elli, Manolis seized the opportunity to grab the woman's arm and wrestle the gun from her grip. It presented little challenge.

'Go back to bed, Elli,' he told her firmly. 'I'll see this lady out.'

Now that he was fully in command of the situation, he took the woman by the arms and firmly tried to bundle her out of the building.

'You've got the wrong place,' he said. 'And if you ever show your face here again, you will regret it. Just get out!'

She struggled to escape, and the violence of her anger almost fuelled her to succeed.

'Whatever anyone has told you, there's no one by the name of Kostas Konstantinidis here.' With those semi-truthful words, Manolis slammed the door and bolted it from the inside.

He turned around to find Kyría Agathi and Stavros in the hallway. They had heard everything.

Other tenants were leaning over the banisters to see what was happening, and without speaking, Agathi, Stavros, Elli and Manolis went back inside Agathi's apartment and shut the door.

Manolis could see that his landlady was, for once, lost for words.

She sat down in her armchair, pale as a sheet, apparently studying the pattern in the rug. Stavros took an upright seat at the table and lit a cigarette.

Elli vanished into her bedroom.

Someone would have to break the silence sooner or later, but meanwhile Manolis fetched some water for them all. He did not want to leave the pair of them alone.

Finally Kyría Agathi spoke.

'That was your *wife*?' she said, almost inaudibly. 'That mad woman was your *wife*?'

Even if they could hear nothing else, her emphasis on the word 'wife' made her meaning very clear.

Stavros looked too terrified to speak.

'And it was your idea to send my niece out as a decoy?'

Again no answer.

Manolis did not wish to manage another scene that evening. It was around five in the morning and the light was coming up, so he made the only viable suggestion.

'I think we should all try and get a little sleep. Stavros can stay in my room tonight, and in the morning, you two need to talk.'

The two men left the room, and once upstairs, Manolis threw a blanket over a small settee where Stavros could sleep. He had no wish to interrogate his friend. He would leave that to Agathi. He for one needed to grab a few hours' rest.

It was well past nine o'clock when Manolis woke. Stavros had gone.

He leapt out of bed. The thought of Agathi's grief disturbed him as if it was his own. He had a desire to protect this sweet woman, this mother figure, whose vision of happiness had been shattered. And he felt responsible. Without him, after all, Stavros would not have met Agathi.

He washed and dressed, then walked slightly gingerly down the stairs. On the floor of the hallway there was a small pile of shattered plaster.

He looked up and saw the hole left by the bullet, and remembered then that he had left the woman's gun in Agathi's apartment. He had put it down as he poured the water. It gave him a distinct feeling of unease. Pressing his ear against the door, he could hear the sound of low voices on the other side. It was not his business to intrude, so he left the building and strolled along the seafront to find a seat at his usual Sunday-morning *kafeneío* overlooking the water. In spite of his earlier desire for anonymity, he had adopted one or two favourite places. Like any man, he enjoyed being addressed by his name.

It was a perfect early summer's day. There was a warmth that touched the skin rather than scalding it and a breeze that gently rippled the surface of the sea rather than whipping it to a fury. May had a sweetness that was gone by August. He thought back to the time exactly three years earlier. Those were the beautiful times with Anna, before she had driven herself into a state of anxiety over her sister's return from Spinalonga. If only she had kept calm, kept her faith in Manolis and not been so reckless. If only . . .

He hoped that Agathi would keep calm too. Perhaps there was an explanation for the events of the previous night.

Manolis passed an hour reading *Kathimerini*. The main news was an army coup in Turkey. Anything that happened in Ankara affected politics in Athens, but these days, unless it impinged on the vitality of the shipping business, Manolis was unbothered by it.

Eventually, after a second coffee and an accompanying cigarette, he got up to leave. It seemed a good time to be back at the pension.

He tapped gently on the door to Kyría Agathi's apartment and Elli opened it.

'They've gone,' she said. 'They've gone out.'

'Do you know where?'

'No,' she answered unhelpfully.

'Did they go together?'

'Yes,' she said. 'They were holding hands.'

That was enough to put Manolis's mind at rest.

'That's nice,' was all he could think of to say. He was intrigued but happy.

He went out for the rest of the day and returned early evening, by which time there were voices coming from the apartment when he passed. He knocked, and a beaming Agathi threw open the door. She had a glass raised in one hand and a bottle in the other.

'Come, come!' she cried with enthusiasm, as though he was late to a party he had been invited to.

Stavros appeared at the door next to her. He held a glass in his hand too.

'Manolis, come and share this with us!'

They were drinking a bottle of cheap champagne and were in high spirits.

'*Stin yeia mas!*' said Agathi. 'Cheers!'

Manolis was cautious, even though the pair of them seemed perfectly contented.

'So what are we celebrating?' he asked, trying to conceal any trepidation he felt.

'Love!' responded Agathi. 'Isn't that enough?'

'Yes, of course it's enough.'

'We found each other, Manolis. And love binds us together.'

'So . . .' began Manolis, about to ask for a little more of an explanation. In the circumstances, it did not seem unreasonable.

'Why don't we sit down?' suggested Agathi. 'Stavros can explain. He has told me everything.'

They all took seats at the table and Stavros, who was unused to being the centre of attention, began to speak.

'That woman last night. She was . . . *is* . . . my wife. And my name *is* Kostas.'

He paused there. Those were the bare facts, and Manolis was surprised that Agathi had wanted to know any more. But there she was, leaning in towards Stavros and even taking his hand. She was listening to all of this for the second time. He continued, clearly eager to unburden himself to Manolis.

'I was forty-five then, and still a single man, living with my parents in a village up in the north. You know how it is, Manolis, I was called a fag, a pervert, every name under the sun. Even my parents were abused. "Something wrong with Kostas?" "Son a homosexual?" "Your boy a weirdo?" And do you know why I had never got married? For one simple reason. I had never met anyone to love. So why would I?'

Manolis nodded. He understood perfectly.

'The stigma of it got so bad that we moved out of the village and went to Thessaloniki. There was less gossip and people minded their own business more in a city. My parents were much happier, even though they had left a place they loved.

'In the apartment below us there was a family. The couple had four grown-up children. Three of them had moved out, but the oldest one, a daughter, was recently widowed and had returned to live with them. She was ten years younger than me, but nobody seemed to mind about that. My parents became friendly with hers and they were keen on the idea . . .'

Stavros paused to gulp down a glass of water. The evening was warm and the apartment stuffy. Agathi got up to throw open a window.

'The moment I married her, I knew I had made a mistake. You see, I didn't really know her. We moved into an apartment on the other side of the city, closer to the docks. And then it all began. When we were alone, not with her parents or mine, she was a different person. She beat me, she scalded me and one day she went at me with a knife. But how could I ever prove it? I had scars, but even my own mother didn't believe me when I told her it was my wife. She thought I was getting into fights. I suffered like that for two years, but it felt like twenty. And I never lifted a finger against her.'

Manolis was shocked by the story, but, having met the woman the previous night, he could well imagine her behaving like that. She had been crazed, deranged. Stavros did not give her a name and Manolis did not want to know it.

'I planned it for a while, and one day, when she was visiting her sister, I left. I couldn't go to my parents in case *her* parents saw me. So I got a train and then another train, and fled to Athens, the only place where I thought I could disappear. And then I came down here to Piraeus because I knew there was plenty of work to be had. At that moment, I had nothing. No possessions, no money, nothing.'

Kyría Agathi put her arm around Stavros. Her love for him seemed to pour out of her.

'Poor Stavros,' she murmured. 'My poor Stavros.'

'And then Giannis gave you work?' enquired Manolis.

'Yes, and that was the beginning of my new life.'

'Were there any . . .'

Stavros anticipated the question. He would have asked the same.

'No, no children, and I thank God that he never blessed her with any.'

'And "Stavros"?'

'That's my father's name. I always preferred it to Kostas.' He laughed. 'It reminds me of him every day. You see, I can't go back. I have written to my parents, but they understand why I don't even want to tell them where I am. My in-laws would come after me too.'

'I wish you had turned that gun on her, Manolis,' said Kyría Agathi.

'I'm not sure that would have helped anyone,' said Manolis with a touch of irony. 'Least of all me!'

Stavros had a little more to say.

'I was free. That was all I wanted. I wasn't looking for anything else. I wasn't looking for any*one* else. And then that night in the *bouzoúkia*, I heard this voice. And it belonged to this beautiful woman . . .' He was gazing at Agathi as he talked. 'I never expected to find such happiness. This woman, this goddess. She is the dream I never allowed myself to have . . .'

'Oh Stavros,' said Agathi, stroking his arm.

'I know I should have told you all this before,' he said. 'But I couldn't risk losing you.'

She shook her head.

'I'm not blaming you for anything,' she affirmed. 'And if she comes back here, she'll have me to deal with.'

Manolis had worked with Stavros for nearly three years now and felt he knew him. He did not doubt either the veracity of his story or the sincerity of his love for Agathi. No man could have performed such lines, even if he was a star actor in one of those films they all loved so much. His own confrontation with the violent wife only added to his certainty that this story was the truth. He even felt suspicious about the death of Stavros's predecessor.

'So can we have a toast now?' said Agathi, filling the glasses almost to overflowing.

Manolis picked up a glass, as did Stavros and Agathi and they all clinked them together.

The gun was still sitting where he had left it on the shelf. It was incongruous next to a small figure of Marie Antoinette. Stealthily he slid the weapon into his pocket.

That night, Stavros collected his clothes from his lodgings and moved into the apartment.

Agathi bought a new dress that same week – not the white one that Manolis had envisaged, but a pale green one – and the following Saturday, as soon as he got his wages, Stavros bought a ring.

The four of them went out for dinner in one of the finest restaurants in Piraeus, to be paid for by Manolis. With the best bottle in the house, they raised their glasses.

'To love,' said Agathi.

'To us,' said Stavros, taking Agathi's hand and putting the ring on her finger.

'To your happiness,' said Manolis.

When he had taken a sip, he put his glass down, took one each of their hands and placed them together, with his on top. The moment seemed no less binding than a marriage ceremony.

From then on, Agathi and Stavros lived as man and wife, with as much trust and love between them as anyone could have. They existed in a state of happy gratitude for having found each other, and Agathi's boundless affection and bonhomie spilled over onto her tenant even more than before.

For Manolis, this couple were more than friends. They were his family. He had never known such stability. He had never lived a life where someone cared as Agathi cared. When he returned to his room at night, there might be a jug of roses on his dresser, an ironed shirt lying on his bed, or his boots brightly polished beneath the window. Sometimes there was a sprig of lavender on his pillow to help him sleep. Always there was lunch waiting outside his door when he left for the boatyard in the morning, and when he came in after work there was a cheery greeting as he passed her door.

Several times a week, Manolis ate with Agathi and her 'husband', but it was never an obligation. He passed most of each day with Stavros, but the two of them were always happy to spend another hour or so together. Changed out of their grimy overalls, they were different men, and enjoyed sitting at the same table to eat the irresistible dishes that Agathi set in front of them. She was putting on noticeable weight, something that Stavros and Manolis avoided thanks to the hard physical labour they engaged in each day.

The three of them were always out on a Saturday night, when Agathi sang at the small *bouzoúkia*. The same audience came each week to hear her unchanging repertoire. But her love songs now had a specific focus, directed without embarrassment to the man in the front row.

'*Olo ton kósmo orízo kai ílio plimyrízo ótan sta mátia me koitás . . .*' she sang, gazing directly at Stavros. 'When you look into my eyes, I hold all the world . . .'

The 'wedding' sparked a change in Elli. It had motivated her to seek love for herself. Within the month, she had stopped going to the cinema with her aunt, and started going instead with the son of her employer at the *zacharoplasteío*. Philippos Papadopoulos would one day inherit the shop, so Agathi gave her plenty of encouragement. Manolis was relieved that the girl no longer blushed every time she saw him.

Manolis wrote occasionally to Antonis and related any news in his life. Naturally, he told Antonis about the couple he lived with, and his recent role as their *koumbáros*, but he knew that his friend enjoyed technical detail more than personal, so he wrote mostly about the ship he was now working on.

It was a luxury yacht, and Giannis had put half his team on the deck and half on the body. Manolis had shown real aptitude with wood. It required more skill than the hull, and great precision was needed even for the apparently simple job of mixing varnish with turpentine. That was not all. His tools included pumice stone and chamois skin, linseed and rottenstone, oil paint and shellac. All of them had to be used correctly, and he became a master of his craft. He found it more satisfying to work on the area of a boat that an owner would appreciate than the part that would largely be submerged beneath the waves and never seen. Nevertheless, he did sometimes reflect that it was strange to spend his days on the deck of a boat on which he would never sail.

He always looked forward to Antonis's replies, which still came irregularly. Antonis wrote that he occasionally saw Maria in town with little Sofia, and described to Manolis what she was like.

She is very pretty, seems quite shy and if we meet in the street she hides in Maria's skirts. But my sister tells me that she and Mattheos are very close friends and that she is quite talkative and noisy when they play together. She's just started school. Maria has started training to work at the hospital and Dr Kyritsis is still travelling a lot.

He assumed that Manolis would be interested to know about his goddaughter.

What Antonis was really keen to write about was cars. The last vehicle Manolis had owned was the truck that probably still sat abandoned in Iraklion. Now that he was making plenty of money, he had more than enough to buy something new, and Antonis fuelled his appetite for a fast modern car. One day, on his friend's advice, Manolis ordered an Alfa Romeo. In bright green.

It lived in the street outside the pension, and he would often come home from work to find a gang of boys crowded around it. They all thought that someone with such a car had to be a film star. Manolis was sorry to disappoint them, but was happy with the attention this gleaming possession attracted.

Life had become easy enough for him, and only occasionally did he wish that there was a woman in the passenger seat.

Aside from the occasional letter from Antonis giving small glimpses of life in Agios Nikolaos, Crete seemed very remote to Manolis. His old life and the new were linked nowadays by only the finest of threads. Without the press cuttings of the trial and the baptism photograph, which were now together in his bottom drawer, he might have wondered if the past they recalled was really his.

The photograph of his parents was in a frame and sat on his dresser, but the image of the baptism still caused him too much pain. Even without looking at it, there was no possibility that he would ever forget Anna. Sometimes he rested the single earring in his palm or held it up to the light. It must still bear a tiny trace of her.

Chapter Eleven

SOMETHING THAT ANTONIS's letters never even alluded to were Maria's visits to Andreas. Whenever he was writing to Manolis, the temptation was great, but a promise to his sister was unbreakable.

Maria now went to the prison in Neapoli once a month. After that first time she took the earliest bus, which left Agios Nikolaos at six, so that she was nearer to the front of the line when she arrived. This allowed her a little longer with Andreas.

Visits had not become less of an ordeal. The heat of the summer brought even more pungent smells of excrement, sweat and drains, and like most other visitors, she now held a handkerchief to her nose when she went in. She always folded some herbs into it, believing it might reduce the smell as well as alleviate the chances of picking up any infection.

Each visit began with an encounter with the same officer, who always put on an act of false joviality, and she soon came to realise that a bribe of some kind was expected. Ostensibly, the two hundred drachma she handed over was to purchase a privilege of some kind for Andreas – additional bread, a clean shirt twice a week rather than once, and so on – but she suspected that this money went straight into the officer's pocket. Andreas's abject state was evidence of this. He had the same stains on his shirt from month to month and looked more emaciated each visit.

Several visits in, the prison officer greeted her with his usual false bonhomie and she smiled back blandly, knowing this was the expected response. Nothing seemed to be different and she was expecting to be taken through to the visitors room as soon as he had made a note in Andreas's file.

'Kyría Kyritsis,' said the officer, clearing his throat. 'When a visitor comes as regularly as you, I am obliged to make spot checks. You understand that sometimes we discover goods are smuggled into this prison, and the only possible conduit is through the visitors.'

Maria knew that she had nothing to hide, but nevertheless she felt a strong sense of unease. What did he mean, 'spot checks'? She held out her handbag to him. He was more than welcome to take a look.

He ignored the gesture.

'Get up, please, and take off your coat.'

Perhaps he was going to check her pockets too. She followed his instruction, standing up and placing her coat over the back of a chair.

'Arms out . . .'

She stood there, dumbfounded. It was obvious that she was carrying nothing in her clothes. Her skirt did not even have pockets.

To her astonishment and disgust, the officer began to run his hands over her body, first of all patting her down, then moving them over her breasts and belly and towards her thighs. He squeezed her buttocks gently at first, then more aggressively, all the while breathing his foul breath into her face.

Then he lifted her skirt and slid a hand between her legs. Maria froze. Her eyes appealed to the young guard who stood in the corner, but she was sickened to see that he met her look with a leer. He was enjoying the spectacle.

She held her breath and shut her eyes. It would be over soon. It had to be. After a few minutes and when there was no part of

125

her body that the officer had not touched, he stopped. She was aware that he had stepped back because she could no longer smell the repellent mix of garlic and stale cigarette.

She opened her eyes.

'Delta 27,' he barked at the guard.

Despite the immensity of her disgust, anger and humiliation, Maria managed to suppress her need to vomit and calmly put her coat on. She did not look the officer in the face. With her legs shaking so violently she was not certain she could make it to the door, she picked up her bag and left.

Afterwards, she could remember little of her time with Andreas. His expression of gratitude was as immense as ever, but all she could think of was getting away from this place.

That night she said nothing to Nikos, but he sensed that she was in a strange mood.

'Was everything all right today?' he asked, puzzled.

'It was fine,' she said. 'Tell me about your day.'

She had managed to deflect his question, but she faced a great dilemma. Could she tolerate such an assault a second time? Would she risk it to see Andreas again?

For the next couple of months, she made her excuses both to herself and to Andreas, in bland letters that simply apologised for her absence without providing any reason. Even Fotini asked her why she had not visited lately, but Maria skilfully covered up.

One night, lying sleepless in bed and trying not to wake Nikos with her tossing and turning, she suddenly had an idea. It was so obvious that she could not imagine why she had only just thought of it.

Two days later, she was on the bus towards Neapoli.

She was not far from the front of the visitor queue that day, and in no time she was next in line to be admitted. Her heart was beating at twice its healthy pace and she clenched her fists to try and stop every part of her visibly shaking.

'So,' said the officer with insouciance, 'tell me who you have come to visit.'

'Andreas Vandoulakis,' answered Maria, trying to quell the tremble in her voice.

'Andreas Vandoulakis . . . Mmm. Ah . . . yes.'

How she loathed this man. She could tell from the smirk on his face that he remembered exactly who she was and who she came to visit. He was enjoying this charade, that much was obvious.

'I have a question . . .' she said innocently.

'A question?'

She looked him straight in the eye, with uncharacteristic boldness.

'Well?'

'Did you ever work on Spinalonga? As a guard, I mean?'

She had rehearsed the words so many times in her head and even in front of a mirror.

'What do you mean by that, *Kyría*?' demanded the officer.

'It's just that you remind me of one of the guards we had,' Maria answered. 'You're the spitting image. I was there, you see, for a few years, and—'

'You're a leper?' he asked, with obvious disgust.

'Well, not any more,' Maria replied with a hint of a smile. 'Not since the cure was found.'

She tilted her head to one side to measure his reaction. It was exactly as she had hoped. She knew that he would never again lay a finger on her. For the first time ever, she had used stigma as a weapon. Nikos would be proud of her.

That visit seemed to flash by. Andreas's pleasure at seeing her made the effort she had gone to more than worthwhile. Their conversation followed a similar pattern as the preceding visits. Andreas asked about Sofia, and then about his father. Maria answered as best she could, with any details she could think of that would vary the response.

She told him that Sofia had started school now, that she liked painting and enjoyed listening to stories, but there was a blankness in his eyes. It was such a vacant look that she contained her own enthusiasm. Of course he could not even imagine what his daughter looked like now. More than three years had passed since he had seen her, and she had probably changed beyond recognition in that time.

Concerning Alexandros Vandoulakis, she tried to give full answers. She told Andreas what she knew about his relatively good health, how Olga and Eirini and their children went to see him most weekends, and even small changes that his housekeeper, Kyría Hortakis, had made in the arrangement of the furniture, plus any other trivia she could recall from her most recent visit there with Sofia.

Andreas always enquired politely after Giorgos. All Maria could tell him was that he fished every day except when the winds blew too strongly, and even she did not have the skill to make this sound less repetitive than it was. She knew that Andreas had no interest in the life of Agios Nikolaos, and she found the details of the Vandoulakis estate hard to report on, especially now that Fotini's brother Antonis was no longer connected with it.

She rarely asked Andreas any questions. How could she enquire about his life in prison? She could see what the conditions were like, and the officer had confirmed the first time she visited that he shared a small cell with five others.

Conversation was made harder because everything they said had to be shouted above the din and often needed repetition. As the bell sounded for everyone to leave, Andreas always leaned forward to say thank you, and even if she could not hear it clearly, she could read his lips. Each visit, she saw the same look of profound relief that she had noticed the very first time she came. To witness this gratitude in his eyes for being forgiven made her own sting with tears.

That October evening, when Nikos returned from the hospital, Maria told him about her visit. His main concern was that she would pick up a disease when she went there.

'That prison is full of sickness, Maria,' he said. 'And if the sanitation is as bad as you describe, it's just not safe for you to go.'

Maria smiled.

'*Agápi mou*, I survived leprosy. I think I can protect myself from prison germs.'

'As long as you are careful,' he said gently. 'And wash your hands as soon as you get home.'

'You know I do, Nikos,' she assured him. 'I scrub them.'

'And your clothes?'

'The same. Until they are threadbare,' she teased.

It was a balmy night, and they were having dinner in their small garden. Nikos was due to leave for another medical conference the following day and would be away for a few weeks. She never complained about his dedication. How could she when he had saved her life and was now saving the lives of so many others? Nevertheless, she would miss him hugely, not only because she loved him, but also because Sofia was always harder to deal with when he was absent.

'I worry so much about you going to that place,' he said tenderly. 'Even though I understand why you do it.'

There was a pause as they looked up at the dazzling display of stars above them.

'And have you thought more about telling Alexandros Vandoulakis that you visit? Will you?'

This was Nikos's other concern, and it was almost as great as the worry over his wife catching a disease from prison bacteria.

'Can you imagine if he finds out that you visit his son and you have never mentioned it?'

'But he never will find out. None of the family has ever been inside that place and Andreas isn't permitted to write letters. So there is no communication.'

'Just suppose that one day Alexandros decides to go. Then he will discover that you have been visiting. Imagine how he might react!'

'I just don't think it will ever happen, Nikos. I don't think he would even manage to stand in that queue outside the prison for long enough. He's quite frail now.'

'Well I think it's wrong that you go and see Andreas and then when you sit there chatting in Alexandros's drawing room you never say anything. Doesn't it weigh on your mind? Please tell him, *agápi mou*.'

Nikos's entreaty was strong and pricked Maria's conscience.

'You are right. I know you are,' she admitted. 'The next time I go, I'll do it. I will find the right moment.'

'Promise me?'

'I promise.'

Nikos went to pack for his trip and Maria cleared away their plates. While she was washing up, she contemplated when she would tell Alexandros about her visits.

The following weekend she took Sofia to see *Megálos Pappoús* – Big Grandpa, as Sofia had named Alexandros. The child was too young to question why this grandfather was not the father of either of her parents. One day they would have to explain, but that day was a long way off. To differentiate the two grandfathers, Giorgos was known as *Mousátos Pappoús*, Bearded Grandpa.

Sofia looked forward to these visits because the housekeeper, Kyría Hortakis, always prepared her favourite biscuits, and she never tired of running around the spacious house. *Megálos Pappoús* had also bought her a rocking horse, which lived in his drawing room, and she was happy to sit on it for hours at a time. Back and forth. Back and forth. She had named it after Alexander the Great's horse, even though she could hardly pronounce the name, and in her mind she galloped far away across the mountains, wild and free, goading the beast to go faster and faster. With her wild curly hair flowing down her back, crying out 'Bucefali, Bucefali!' she never looked more like Anna than in those moments.

Over the past few years, Alexandros Vandoulakis had grown fond of Maria Kyritsis. The reality was that he preferred her to her late sister, and there was no doubt in his mind that Maria was a more suitable mother. Anna's name was never spoken out loud.

As they sipped their coffee and Sofia, totally absorbed, rocked on her horse, Maria knew that the moment had come. Since her first visit to Andreas, every trip to see Alexandros had been burdened by the unsaid, and Nikos was right. She had used many excuses to herself – that Alexandros might be displeased or angry, that it was the wrong thing to do, that it was not her place to go, and many more – but the time had come to tell him.

There was no way that the subject could glide smoothly into conversation. She simply had to be bold.

'I need to tell you something, Kýrie Alexandros,' she said.

The seriousness of her tone made him lean forward with concern.

'What is it, my dear?'

'I have been to visit your son. I have seen Andreas.'

Alexandros looked astonished, and for a moment did not speak.

Maria was so nervous that she had to put her coffee down on the table. The chattering of cup on saucer revealed her anxiety.

'I w-went to see him in prison,' she continued.

'My . . . son?'

The face of this dignified elderly man, a person who so rarely showed any emotion, crumpled.

The housekeeper, Kyría Hortakis, sensing that something had happened, lured Sofia off her horse and into the kitchen for biscuits.

The last time Alexandros Vandoulakis had spoken to his son was on that August evening three years ago when Andreas and Anna had agreed that they would go to the celebration in Plaka. Two days later came the terrible news. He and Eleftheria had eaten and were about to go to bed when the telephone rang. They both commented that it was unusually late for a call, and Eleftheria left the drawing room to pick it up. A moment later, Alexandros heard his wife scream, and hurried into the hallway, where he found her sitting on the chair next to the phone, sobbing. He took the receiver from her hand. Antonis, one of the estate workers, was on the other end of the line. Anna was dead and Andreas had been arrested.

In one moment, a bullet had changed their lives.

'You have seen Andreas?' he asked quietly.

It was the first time he had spoken his son's name since that terrible night, and Maria could barely hear him say it now.

'Yes.'

Alexandros Vandoulakis, the proud and dignified owner of this great estate, a man who had kept control of his emotions since that August night, was weeping into his hands.

It seemed overfamiliar given their formal relationship, but Maria got up and put her arm round him. It was instinctive. The man needed comforting.

After a few moments, he pulled a handkerchief out of his pocket and gradually composed himself. Maria could see that he needed time to recover and took her place opposite him again.

Eventually he was ready to talk, and he was full of questions.

'How is he? What does he look like? How does he manage? What is it like in there?'

His relief at being able to speak about his son was palpable, and the gentle interrogation flowed on and on. Maria answered every question she knew the answer to, and told the truth unflinchingly.

Eventually she could see the old man's energy beginning to fail, and he sat back in his chair, emotionally spent. One question he did not ask was *why* she had gone to visit. It seemed to Maria that he understood. Perhaps there was a river of compassion flowing through him that she had not imagined. Only someone capable of forgiveness themselves would not find it necessary to ask.

As the questions ended, Sofia came running in and raced towards her grandfather. The old man adored this little girl and gave her a hearty embrace.

'It's time to go now, Sofia,' said Maria.

'*Mamá!* I don't *want* to go,' protested Sofia. 'I want to stay here with Bucefali!'

'I'll feed him and look after him for you, *moró mou,*' said her grandfather kindly. 'I promise.'

Sofia gave him a hug and then took her mother's hand.

Maria felt a lightness that she had never experienced in this house before.

Alexandros Vandoulakis got out of his chair and held her arm very gently.

'Thank you for coming, Maria,' he said. 'It was lovely to see you. Please come again soon and bring me news.'

She understood what he meant. She was certain that from now on, Alexandros Vandoulakis would be hungry for word of Andreas. Since the death of his wife, he had become much frailer, and when she touched his hand, she felt how bony it was. It made her reflect once again on the dangers of visiting that prison. She might be strong enough to resist illness and disease herself, but she was not so certain about this elderly man. She would have to be his ears and eyes in that hellish place.

With Nikos away for a few weeks, Maria did not plan to visit Andreas until he returned. It was Sofia's first full month at school and she had to take her each morning.

It perturbed her to miss a month. She fretted that Andreas would feel abandoned by her again, and planned to go as soon as Nikos was back and could take their daughter to school.

The still, calm days of late October gave way to a new season. November brought rains that were rarely seen in Crete, thunderstorms that blackened the skies mid morning and bright flashes of lightning that lit up the mountains behind Agios Nikolaos in the middle of the night. Several days running, Maria postponed her trip to the prison, but finally she woke one morning and was aware that the shutters were not rattling as they had been for so many days.

She got out of bed, dressed quickly and whispered to Nikos:

'I'm leaving to get the bus, *agápi mou*. Sofia's clothes are all ready.'

Nikos stirred.

'Take care, Maria,' he said sleepily.

She bent to kiss him lightly on the ear and tiptoed from the room.

As she left their house on the hill, she could see the sun slowly appearing over the horizon. It was a spectacular dawn. She walked quickly to the bus station, her breath making clouds on the chilly morning air, and regretted that she had not put on a thicker coat. She was the last to get on before the bus left promptly at six. She recognised a woman who had once worked at the hospital and politely acknowledged her with a nod. To her slight chagrin, the woman got up from her seat and came to sit closer to her. Maria noticed that she did not actually take the seat beside her, but preferred to shout above the grunts and groans of the bus from a few rows further forward.

The woman now had a job at the orphanage in Neapoli and wanted to tell Maria all about it. Naturally she wanted information in exchange, in particular gossip from the hospital, what was Maria doing these days, how was Sofia, and so on.

Apart from the fact that it felt a little early in the morning for conversation, Maria was unwilling to divulge too much about what she was doing and was determined not to say where she was going. She was aware that a hint of stigma continued to hang over her from her time on Spinalonga and concluded that this was why the woman kept her distance. If she revealed that she was visiting her sister's murderer, it would be more than enough to make the woman get off the bus in the middle of nowhere. Maria had no time for such a person and the thirty-minute journey was awkward. She was happy to get off before her.

She was close to the front of the queue that day. The weather must have deterred some of the other usual visitors. As she waited, she was full of anxiety. It was a while since she had seen Andreas, and she worried that he might think she had stopped coming. She paid the usual 'pocket money' for the prisoner and was shown in to the visitors room. Gradually the room filled up as other visitors and prisoners shambled in. The seat opposite Maria continued to be empty. She looked at the clock on the wall and saw that fifteen minutes had already passed. At any moment the bell would ring, and she felt a rising sense of disappointment. Against the regulations, she stood up and went to speak to the guard seated closest to her.

The man did not give her time to ask a question.

'If he comes, he comes. Even prisoners have some choices. Whether or not to come in here is one of them. The other is whether to eat.'

The guard did not look at Maria as he spoke, but straight past her towards the clock on the wall. Those who came to see prisoners merited no more respect than those they visited, and it was not the first time that she had felt the contempt of a guard. Everyone, whatever their relationship with a prisoner, was treated as if they too had been convicted of a crime.

'Looks like he didn't want to see you.'

The guard's words were blunt. It might have been the truth, but it was a truth that hurt.

She returned to her seat for the remaining moments of the session. There was a small possibility that something had detained him. She could not imagine what that might be in this place, but she felt obliged to stay in any case.

As the minute hand moved inexorably towards the hour, Maria struggled to hold back her tears. She made it out of the room, across the courtyard and into the road before she lost control of her emotions. Nobody took a second glance at a woman who cried in the street. It was a common sight outside these prison walls.

It would be a whole month now until she could visit again, and there was no means of getting any information about him. Her imagination gave her no rest.

Nikos was pragmatic.

'Maria, if something bad has happened, I am sure they would communicate with his next of kin. And Alexandros would have contacted you. There is no question of that.'

'But—' protested Maria.

'Please try not to worry,' said Nikos gently. 'There is nothing you can do. And next month will come soon enough.'

When Maria took Sofia to see *Megálos Pappoús* at the end of that month, she did not tell him that Andreas had failed to turn up when she went to see him. She just answered his eager questions blandly and said that she had been allowed very little time with Andreas on the last visit. She hoped it would help justify why she had so little to say about him. Next month, she reassured Alexandros, she was sure to have a little longer with him.

She was eager for the December visit to come. Andreas was always in the back of her mind.

He soon appeared in front of her and she was relieved to see him, even though he looked thinner than ever. He explained that he had been very sick with suspected cholera and they had put him in isolation for so many days he had lost count.

Time was galloping, as it always did in this place, and Maria was eager to tell him that his father now knew about her visits.

'I have told your father I come to see you,' she said, perhaps too quietly.

He did not hear her the first time, and she found herself repeating the words. They were met with an unexpected blankness of response, so she decided to rephrase.

'I went to see Kýrios Alexandros and—'

It was the sound of the name that stirred Andreas, and he leaned forward, needing to check he had heard correctly.

'Alexandros. My father?'

'Yes. I told him that I come to visit you. It seemed only right.'

Rejection by his father and the total withdrawal of parental love had been a blow to Andreas greater than incarceration itself.

Both Eleftheria and Alexandros had idolised their only son, and he had basked in their love from the moment of his birth. At the moment he brought the family name into disgrace, this boundless supply of affection was cut off. Then, when the letter had come from his sister informing him that Eleftheria had died, her words left him in no doubt that he was responsible not only for the death of his wife, but for that of his mother too: *You broke your mother's heart, Andreas, and now your father is twice destroyed.* Olga's words had been like a knife in his side, and two years on he still bled from the wound.

'What did he say? Tell me what he said, Maria.' He was always eager for any news of his father, and this time even more so.

'He asked how you were, what it's like in here, all the things you might expect.'

'So he wasn't angry that you come . . .'

'Of course not, Andreas. Perhaps the opposite.'

Andreas's relief at hearing this showed in his eyes. For a moment they glittered. Perhaps these were tears, even if they did not fall.

The bell was ringing now and Maria was one of the last to leave. It was the first time she had left the prison feeling lighter than when she had arrived.

The next time she visited Alexandros Vandoulakis, it was with both Nikos and Sofia. She knew that the old man loved to see her husband, and it was a delightful afternoon, with Sofia enraptured by Bucefali, as usual.

'When you are a little older,' her grandfather told the little girl, 'you will ride a real horse.'

'Silly *Pappoús*, he *is* a real horse,' replied Sofia, who was busy combing its mane.

Her parents sat and talked for a while, and Nikos told Alexandros about new developments at the hospital and the latest conference he had attended.

Out of earshot of his granddaughter, Maria then told him about her recent visit to Andreas.

'He seemed pleased that you know,' she said.

Alexandros looked thoughtful for a moment.

'Next time you go,' he said, 'please will you give him my love.'

Maria was relieved to hear these words and hoped that Nikos might hear them too. She wanted him to share her sense of why these visits mattered more than ever.

Chapter Twelve

WINDS FROM THE north and the east blew in over the next few weeks, bringing snow that coated the mountains of Crete. It would be several months until there was enough warmth to melt it.

The night before her visit to Andreas in February, Maria had been up with Sofia, who was suffering night terrors. Her broken sleep meant that she overslept by just fifteen minutes, but it was enough to make her miss the first bus, and by the time she eventually reached the prison, the queue in front of her was long. It was raining heavily, and the downpour turned to sleet as she waited. In her haste she had forgotten to pick up her umbrella when she left the house, so by the time she went through the main door, she was soaked. The process of registration seemed to take longer than usual, and when she reached the visitors room, her hands and lips were numb with cold.

It was a short visit that day, and this time it was she who tried to put on a brave face for Andreas.

He looked pleased to see her, but there was not much to talk about this time. He asked how Sofia was enjoying school, and Maria gave the briefest answers. She was so distracted by her discomfort that she almost forgot to pass on the message that she had been given by Alexandros. It was only as she was leaving that she remembered it.

'Your father,' she said, 'sends you his love.'

The bell was ringing but she barely heard it. All she was aware of was Andreas's smile.

Between the bus station and home, Maria endured another soaking. As she trudged up the hill, rainwater was cascading down the steep streets, and by the time she arrived at her front door, her shoes were squelching. She was shivering so violently now that it felt as if her bones were rattling inside her body.

Nikos came in with Sofia soon after and found his wife in bed, delirious, her teeth chattering. Her saturated clothes lay scattered across the bed.

Memories of seeing her like this once before came flooding back. It was when she had first taken the drugs for leprosy. Like many other patients, she had gone through several days of extreme fever before turning a corner to recovery. Some had not survived at all, their bodies lacking the strength to fight back.

When Nikos Kyritsis looked after strangers in the hospital, it was easy for him to be dispassionate, and he had a reputation for a calmness of manner that many doctors envied. With his own beloved wife, it was very different, and he struggled to contain his anxiety. His memories of those days on Spinalonga were vivid.

For several days Maria's temperature remained dangerously high and she drifted from fitful sleep to delirium and back. Nikos diagnosed pneumonia, and during several long nights he held his wife's limp hand, agonised by the possibility that she might not survive.

Little Sofia was sent to stay with Fotini. In Plaka she could also spend a few nights with her *Mousátos Pappoús*. Even as a highly trained doctor, Nikos could not say how long it would take for Maria to recover.

He took time off from work to care for her, sitting all day at her bedside to mop her brow and monitor her temperature. Twice a day he changed her sheets. Neighbours brought in food for him and a thin egg and lemon soup for Maria, a traditional recipe for recovery. She could not even lift her head to taste it, and could only sip the occasional mouthful of water.

All those weeks as she lay in bed, she was aware of very little except the presence of the man who watched over her. When he was in the room, she felt safe. He sometimes sat and read to her, and the sound of his voice soothed her. It was usually poetry, and the way he read, whether it was Cavafy or Elytis, the lines sounded more like music than the spoken word.

The worst phase of her sickness lasted for three weeks, but in late March she was strong enough to sit up, her head propped against several pillows. She was missing Sofia now, but knew that it was better for her daughter to be in Plaka.

In early April, the little girl came home. She bounced into her parents' bedroom and threw herself into Maria's arms, scattering the small posy of flowers she held all over the bed.

'*Mamá*! I have missed you so much!'

She sat and chattered for hours, telling her mother everything she had been doing with her friend Mattheos. Sofia seemed to have grown up a lot in those weeks. She had learned to write her name and had produced enough drawings to fill an art gallery. One by one she displayed them to her mother, with great pride.

Soon Maria was out of bed for a few hours a day. Nikos returned to work in the hospital and gradually life resumed some kind of normality.

Easter fell on the second weekend of April that year, and the most important festival in the Orthodox calendar was celebrated all over Greece, as lavishly in Piraeus as in Agios Nikolaos.

Agathi had a strong religious streak that manifested itself on important festival dates, and she insisted that both Stavros and Manolis accompany her to the great church in the main square of Piraeus on three consecutive days. On *Megáli Paraskeví*, Good Friday, Manolis followed the *Epitáfios*, the float festooned with flowers that represented Christ's funeral bier, and the following day he waited in the street with an unlit candle ready to receive and share the flame disseminated from Jerusalem. '*Christós anésti*,' he chorused with all the rest. 'Christ is risen.' He spoke the words, but he did not share this belief that the human body could be resurrected. If only it were so.

On Sunday, he went again to church with Agathi and Stavros. On the way in, he lit two large candles and stood there watching them burn for a while before taking a seat. One was for Anna. Unlike the flame, his love for her would never die. The second was for Sofia. Although he gave her less and less thought, she was still his goddaughter, and if life had been different, he would be in church with her now in Crete, she proudly wearing the brand-new shoes he had bought her, the traditional Easter gift from *nonós* to *vaftistíra*.

He contemplated this as they sat there for some hours listening to the chanting of the priests, before emerging into the spring sunshine more than ready for the feast of lamb waiting for them in their favourite taverna.

For the first time in almost three months, Maria left the house that Easter Sunday. She checked her hair in the mirror as she was about to set out for church and was shocked to see the thin, pale face that looked back at her. She pinched her cheeks, then took her husband's arm and they walked the short distance to the main square, with Sofia skipping along happily next to them. Dozens of people flowed along the pavements in the same direction to celebrate the Resurrection.

Nikos was not a devout believer, but he could not stop himself reflecting that his wife had been reborn. There had been times in those early days of her illness when he had watched a dying woman, and now here she was next to him, alive, almost well and greeting her friends with a smile.

Sofia was just as Manolis might have pictured her. She was wearing a new blue dress that her father had bought for her and some matching shoes from her mother. She was six now, and with her long corkscrew curls tied back in a ribbon, she looked very beautiful. Nikos could not help wishing that she looked less like Anna.

For many months afterwards, Maria wrestled with the idea of how to broach the subject of resuming her visits to Andreas. She knew Nikos would be resistant.

Finally, around the end of September, she brought the subject up.

Nikos answered with a rare display of anger.

'Absolutely *not*, Maria,' he said. 'How can you even think of going there?'

'It's more than six months since I went. He must wonder—'

'Well write to him then,' snapped Nikos. 'That last visit practically *killed* you! And you talk of going *again*?'

'But—' she protested.

'You are not strong enough yet. Even if you go at some future time, it's far too soon even to contemplate it now.' The words were said out of love, but their delivery was harsh. 'It's obvious that you picked up the infection in that filthy place.'

'It was the cold . . .'

'The cold may have made it worse, but . . . Well, you know what I think.'

Maria got up and left the room. She did not enjoy conflict with Nikos, and it was worse when she knew he was right. Even on that very first visit, a woman she had talked to outside the prison had warned her it was easy to catch pneumonia inside those walls.

She went into the living room and pulled a piece of writing paper out of the desk drawer. She should have written to Andreas before, and now she hastily scribbled a note to explain why she had not visited in all these months. She posted it that afternoon but knew that she could not expect a reply. Letter-writing was one of the privileges that convicted murderers were denied.

A few weeks later, when she felt well enough to visit Plaka, she poured her heart out to Fotini.

'I feel such terrible guilt,' she said. 'Imagine that poor man alone. It's so awful. And if they don't give him my letter, he will never understand why I suddenly stopped visiting.'

'I still can't understand why you feel so sorry for him,' said Fotini, with the honesty of an old friend. 'He killed your sister.'

'Fotini!'

'Maria, it's the truth.'

'Yes, but the truth isn't all that matters. You haven't been there and watched how his face changes when he sees me in front of him. It's more than gratitude, Fotini. He looks at me as if I have saved his *life!*'

'Couldn't his father visit him?'

'I really don't think that's a good idea. He is old and quite frail now.'

'Well I'm certainly not going in your place, Maria.'

Fotini was tough with her friend. Maria sighed.

'I've promised Nikos that I won't go again just yet. But one day I will. And meanwhile I'll just hope that he gets my letters.'

Chapter Thirteen

Maria waited until the following spring to raise the subject of going to see Andreas Vandoulakis again. She was well enough to visit now and put the date in Nikos's diary to make sure that he would be able to take Sofia to school.

Two days before the appointed day, Nikos came in from the hospital and put the newspaper down in front of her.

'Look,' he said, pointing at the headline.

PRISONERS PROTEST. FIFTY ON HUNGER STRIKE.
FOUR DIE.

Maria read the entire story, with Nikos looking over her shoulder. It was dramatic. Several prisoners had died as a result of violence, dozens more were on hunger strike and others were occupying the prison roof. Fires had been started. With something close to terror, Maria looked for a name she recognised and was relieved not to find it.

Over the ensuing days, there were more confrontations between prisoners and guards. An officer had been stabbed to death with a dagger that must have been smuggled in by a visitor, and the prison authorities were cracking down hard. Fifty members of the police force had been brought in from Iraklion to help control the uprising, and residents of Neapoli reported that they had heard gunshots.

'I don't think you'll be going to see Andreas at the moment,' said Nikos.

Each day Maria read the developing story with horror. She hoped that Andreas was not involved, but it sounded as if all the prisoners had been united against the prison governors and were demanding a number of improvements.

'The conditions are terrible in there,' she said. 'Inhumane. And what do they have to lose by complaining about them?'

'So you sympathise with this?' said Nikos, with a note of indignation.

'That place is hell,' Maria said. 'You haven't been there.' She wished that Nikos could sometimes see things from her point of view.

'I doubt it's worse than any other prison in Greece,' he said.

'That might be true, but it doesn't make it acceptable to put six men in a cell, does it?'

Nikos did not have an answer.

The disturbances in the Neapoli prison continued for another few months, and when they died down, the authorities announced that there would be a ban on all visitors for the foreseeable future. This was both a punishment and a way of guaranteeing that nothing else could be smuggled in.

It was not until the following year, when order had been thoroughly re-established in the prison, that Maria was finally able to return.

She was filled with huge apprehension when she got off the bus that day to take the long walk to the prison entrance. She found herself almost sick with anxiety, just as she had been after the officer had molested her.

When she arrived, everything looked the same: the same guard at the entrance and the same officer to make a note of her visit.

'Haven't seen you in a while,' he said with sarcasm.

She did not know what the correct response should be, and said nothing as he turned his back and began rummaging in his filing cabinet, humming all the while. He was even more rotund than she remembered.

'Vag . . . Val . . . Van . . . Vandoulakis . . . Where are you, Vandoulakis?' he muttered. 'Mmm, Vandoulakis. Vandoulakis . . . Vandoulakis . . . Vandoulakis . . .'

The more jovial he was and the more he repeated the name, the more irritated Maria became. How could they have lost a prisoner? She could see from where she was sitting that the filing system was chaotic, and had to restrain herself from getting up and taking a look herself.

She started to become worried. Perhaps Andreas's file had been thrown out. Or had he died? In all the chaos of the rioting, could that have happened? Yes, she told herself, that must be it. He had after all been one of the prisoners who had died in the riots. The authorities just hadn't reported it.

Just as she was about to ask a direct question, the officer suddenly stopped his search and slammed the drawer shut.

'I know!' he said, as though he had been touched by inspiration. 'I know!'

He turned round and leered, his face coming within a centimetre of hers. Maria flinched.

'I've just remembered!'

She could smell the nicotine on his breath.

'He was moved!'

He sauntered over to another cabinet in the corner. Maria was so relieved that she did not speak. She simply willed him to get a move on. Every moment that he procrastinated was a moment of her time with Andreas lost. She thought of all the women outside, and how some of them would probably not even get in today because of this officer's dithering.

He quickly found the Vandoulakis file.

'Here you are,' he said, reaching inside the cabinet and pulling it out. 'He's gone to the other wing.'

Maria did not even know there *was* another wing, but was

relieved when she understood that he had not been moved to a different prison.

'Gamma 10,' he said, to the young guard hovering by the door. 'Take the leper to Gamma 10.'

The words were like a hornet sting. It took all her will not to react and for the sake of her dignity she succeeded. This man disgusted her on every level.

She hurried out. It was an effort to keep up with the guard, and wherever it was that Andreas had been put, it was a lot further away than his old cell. She tried not to look at all the miserable buildings she passed, but she could not help noticing a few faces peering out from behind bars. Expressions of anger, sadness and curiosity were visible from the shadows.

Finally they reached a building that was more modern than the rest. There was a scent of fresh paint in the air as they passed through one door and then another. Maria wondered how on earth anyone knew which key opened what in this place. They all appeared to be unmarked.

She followed the guard down the corridor almost to the end. There were thirty doors on each side. They must all be cells, she thought, but how many men occupied each one she was yet to discover. It was a relief that the normally ubiquitous smell of human waste was masked by the whiff of emulsion.

The guard stopped at the penultimate door and slid open the hatch so that he could see inside.

'There's your man,' he said. 'You have five minutes and I'll be back. They say he's not dangerous.'

He slammed the hatch closed again and once more produced the correct key without hesitation.

The door was thrown open and with great trepidation Maria went inside. She heard the sound of the key being turned in the lock behind her.

There was a man sitting on the end of the bed. It was Andreas, his head shaved, in a shirt as white as the freshly painted walls.

The shock for Maria was not his appearance but to find herself alone with him in a room four metres by three. Was this solitary confinement? Was Andreas being punished for something?

'Maria!'

It was that same look of sheer amazement that she remembered from her very first visit.

'I'm so sorry,' she found herself apologising. 'I'm so sorry I wasn't able to come.'

As soon as she said this, she realised how strange it was to be apologising to Anna's murderer, but her words were sincere. She hugely regretted this absence.

'I got your letter,' he said. 'How terrible that you were so ill. How terrible. And I do hope it wasn't because you had been here. There is so much sickness in this place.'

'I am sure it was nothing to do with coming to see you,' Maria fibbed. 'But I am glad you got my letter. And then the ban on visitors for so long . . .'

'Yes. I thought they might stop outsiders coming in for ever,' said Andreas, offering her a chair. It was neatly tucked under a small table, the only other pieces of furniture in the room aside from the bed.

The floor tiles were spotless, the blanket on the bed was clean, and she caught a reassuring smell of disinfectant. Even Nikos would have approved.

'So . . .' she began.

This was the first time there had been the possibility of a proper conversation. In all her previous visits they had only managed a series of short questions and brief answers shouted above the noise of more than fifty other prisoners and their visitors. Now they were face to face in the silence.

'Thank you for coming, Maria.'

'It's . . . it's my . . .'

'Pleasure' was not the word. Neither was 'duty'. Maria's voice trailed off, but Andreas had plenty to say, and his words came tumbling out. This was not the pompous and aloof man who had married her sister. This was not the man who had carried about an air of superiority, and spoken down to everyone but his father.

'It is because of you that my life has changed,' he said, very seriously.

Maria was momentarily bemused.

'My father is writing to me now! Since I last saw you, he has been writing every month. I don't have the letters. They take them away from me. But they have changed everything.'

Maria was eager to understand what he meant.

'At the beginning, he told me of his anger, his grief, his humiliation. I understood all of it. I really did. He told me that he and my mother scarcely spoke of me after that night. It was their way. He made it very clear to me that I had broken my mother's heart. That it was my fault she had died. Olga had already told me that, but to hear it from my father was a thousand times worse.

'Those first letters gave me the darkest days I have had since being here. I began dreading them. Sometimes I didn't even want to open them. I cursed you, Maria, because I felt that it was because of you that he had started to write. And everything he wrote was true and drove deeper the dagger of shame.'

Maria shifted in her seat, on the point of apologising for causing this pain, but Andreas was in full flow.

'I was torn apart at the beginning, but even though I have my father's words of sadness and regret going round and round in my head, at least the letters acknowledge my existence. He is saying to me: "Andreas, you are my son." You can't imagine what that feels like.

'I wait for each letter. We are only permitted one a month, but something is better than nothing. Sometimes he just writes one or two sentences, but the letters have kept coming, Maria, and that's all that matters to me.'

He paused for a moment.

'I was sad when I thought you had given up on me, and then there were the riots . . .'

Maria interjected with a few muttered words. 'I know, I know. It's been so long . . .'

Suddenly there was the scraping of bolts and the sound of a key in the lock.

Andreas could not speak for a moment, but quickly wiped his face on his sleeve.

'Maria, please come again soon. There's so much more I want to tell you. And if you see my father, please thank him from me.'

'Come on,' barked the guard. 'Time's up. Out now.'

A moment later, Maria was out in the corridor, being ushered towards the exit.

It was a very different visit from the previous one, and that evening, Nikos could tell that she was glad to have seen Andreas again.

'He's been moved,' she told him. 'And it's very clean there. It almost smells like the hospital.' She said this almost teasingly. She knew how much hygiene mattered to her husband.

'Why has he been moved?' enquired Nikos.

'He didn't say. He had too much else to tell.'

Nikos did not ask for any more detail. The resumption of his wife's visits to the prison did not please him. She had nearly lost her life as a result of going.

There was, of course, an even deeper angst. This connection with Andreas instilled a profound fear within him. What would happen if Sofia discovered who her real father was? Along with his love for Maria, his bond with Sofia was the most treasured thing in his life. For some time they had known that Maria could not have children of her own. She was one of the unfortunate leprosy patients whose fertility had been affected by the disease, so they were both very conscious that Sofia would be their one and only child.

Sofia was eight now, growing tall, learning to read, asking

questions about the sun and everything under it. Everything was 'Why?' Being a scientist, Nikos could answer most of her questions, and satisfied her with clear and simple explanations for everything she wanted to know. He adored her and she idolised him. He seemed different from the fathers of most of her friends at school. He wore smarter clothes and had silvery hair and he even spoke with a different accent. Sofia knew he was very important at the hospital and that gifts sometimes arrived from people he had helped. One boy at school told her that he had saved his father's life.

For Nikos, even the smallest risk that he could ever lose this child who called him *Babá* was insupportable. The prison visits were the one source of conflict between him and his wife, and the day or so after they took place there was always a frostiness in the air. Maria was taking a part-time job at the hospital soon, so perhaps she would no longer have the time to go. This was his hope.

Maria was eager to see Alexandros Vandoulakis. She wanted him to know how pleased his son was that he had finally begun to write to him. The following weekend, she and Sofia went to Neapoli to visit *Megálos Pappoús*.

'He told me straight away,' she said. 'It means so much to him.'

Alexandros Vandoulakis leaned forward a little.

'I should have done it before, perhaps. But you're the person who made me realise—'

Sofia interrupted by running in.

'*Mamá!* Kyría Hortakis has shown me how to make the biscuits. They're in the oven now!'

'That's so exciting, *agápi mou!* Will you bring your grandfather one when they're cooled?'

'And one for you too!' Sofia sang, skipping out again.

Maria was eager to carry on her conversation.

'And he's been moved! He's no longer in that dreadful crowded wing with six to a cell. He has one all to himself. And it's *clean!*'

Alexandros Vandoulakis gave a contented smile.

'I didn't have time to ask him why or when it happened. It's right at the far end of the prison, so by the time I got there, it was almost time to leave again.'

Sofia had come back in.

'They're nearly ready, *Mamá*,' she said. 'They won't be long.'

Off she went again, and for a few minutes, the elderly man and Maria talked about the ill health she had suffered. She was very careful to avoid any suggestion that it was a prison visit that had given her pneumonia.

Before it was time to leave, the biscuits were ready to eat.

'They're delicious, *moró mou*,' said Alexandros Vandoulakis to his granddaughter. 'They're the best biscuits I have ever tasted!'

'Can we take one home for *Babá*?' asked Sofia.

'I'm sure we can,' said Maria. 'I expect Kyría Hortakis can even spare two. Will you ask her to wrap some up for us?'

While Sofia went off to do this, Alexandros asked Maria when she would be going to see his son again.

'Soon, I hope. It has to fit with Nikos's shifts at the hospital. He has to take Sofia to school and collect her again when I go,' she answered. 'And I am starting a part-time job at the hospital next week, so my time will be a little more limited.'

'Well whenever you go, please will you give him this?' With a visibly trembling hand, Alexandros Vandoulakis handed Maria an envelope. They were both aware that prisoners were not allowed to keep letters. They had to read them and then hand them back. Unless, of course, they did not come via the prison authorities and the officers did not know that they had received them.

She took it from him and silently slid it into her bag. It felt illicit even to possess it, but she could not refuse the old man.

It was time to go now. Alexandros got up and bent down to kiss his granddaughter on the top of her head. He had several other grandchildren, all a little older, but none of them competed with Sofia in his affections.

That evening, when Nikos and Maria had eaten and dinner was cleared away, Maria remembered the carefully wrapped package of biscuits that had now slipped to the bottom of her bag. As she put her hand in to retrieve it, her fingers felt the smooth surface of an envelope.

She calculated that it would be a few weeks before she could visit the prison again. It was frustrating, but she knew that the days would pass quickly enough. For Andreas, though, every hour must be slow torture, with the future stretching ahead into nothingness.

'What's on your mind, *agápi mou*?' asked Nikos, noticing that his wife was gazing absently at the ground.

'Oh! Nothing, Nikos. I suddenly remembered that Sofia made these biscuits for you. She was so proud of them. Here!'

He opened the little package and ate them enthusiastically.

'They're perfect,' he said. 'And did you have a nice time with Alexandros today?'

'Yes,' she said. 'He loves seeing Sofia so much, and we always have such a nice chat. He likes company and I don't think his daughters go very often.'

She did not mention the letter, and was very conscious that it was an omission on her part. She knew exactly what Nikos would say. It was strictly against regulations to take anything into the prison for one of the inmates and they both knew it. No doubt it would result in some kind of punishment for Andreas if it was discovered, and was probably a personal risk to herself.

The envelope remained in her handbag. It was the safest place, but over the following weeks she was very aware of its presence. Every time she reached in to find her purse or her keys, she felt it. She would be glad when it was no longer in her possession.

Chapter Fourteen

ANTONIS SOMETIMES NAGGED Fotini for information about Maria's visits to Andreas, but his sister was reticent. She still found her brother's *Schadenfreude* over his old love rival's fate very distasteful.

Maria shared everything with her friend – how Andreas looked, what he said and what the conditions in the prison were like – but Fotini passed nothing on. She felt uncomfortable that Antonis gloated at the notion of this great man brought low by his crime. It was wrong in her view to give any fuel to her brother's decades-old resentment. Antonis had so much in his own life. Several building sites, plans to build a hotel, two cars, a big house, a beautiful wife and a second child on the way. Andreas Vandoulakis had nothing. Not a drachma.

Fotini was particularly cautious because she knew that Antonis was still in touch with Andreas's cousin Manolis. No, she told herself, whatever Maria said about the poor man remained with her alone. She loved her brother, but on this subject she did not entirely trust him.

Antonis had concluded that Manolis would never come to see him in Crete, so one weekend that year, he left his wife and child in Agios Nikolaos and went to Piraeus for a few days.

Manolis arrived at the harbour well before the ferry appeared on the horizon, excited to be seeing his friend after all this time.

The two men had missed each other these past years and embraced each other heartily with affection and friendly abuse.

'Hey, *maláka*! You bastard!'

'*Gamóto!* Fuck! How good you look!' exclaimed Manolis, as he stood back to admire his groomed and handsome friend.

Antonis looked like a man who had done well for himself. There was no dirt under his fingernails these days. His hands were well scrubbed and he wore a thick gold band on his right hand and a heavy gold watch on his left. He sported well-cut trousers and a jacket made to measure by a tailor in Iraklion; his hair and moustache were perfectly clipped. Despite his concerns of a few years back, he still had a reasonable head of hair, though nothing like his friend's copious thick locks.

Manolis still looked like a man who worked outside and used his hands for a living. His skin was very lined now, but he had not lost the looks that often turned heads. The clothes he wore were casual compared with Antonis's, and his boots were dusty, but anyone who looked at them as they strolled along in the sunshine saw two tall and unusually handsome men, happily lost in each other's company.

They walked back to the pension and Antonis left his bag in Manolis's room. Agathi appeared in the hallway as they were leaving again. She knew Manolis was expecting a friend and was curious to meet someone from his Cretan past. To this day, her lodger had never formally shared anything about his former life. All she knew of it was what she had deduced from her snooping.

The pair of them spent the first night of Antonis's visit drinking and talking. Manolis wanted to hear about married life and fatherhood. He also asked about Sofia, whether she was happy and what she looked like now. He was glad to discover that she was still best friends with Antonis's nephew Mattheos.

Antonis had plenty of questions about his old friend's new life and wanted to know all about the boat he was working on.

The following day they drove a long way down the coast in

Manolis's Alfa Romeo, and then inland to Athens. Antonis had never visited his country's capital city and wanted to see everything. They climbed up to the Acropolis and strolled the shopping streets of Kolonaki. He was enthusiastic about everything he saw, bought new shirts for himself and dresses for his wife and little daughter, and footed the bill for the enormous dinner they ate in Monastiraki.

They had forgotten how much they enjoyed each other's company and found their friendship untarnished by time.

They ended up in Au Revoir, a popular bar in Patission that stayed open until the very last drinker left. There was only one moment in the evening when the conversation hovered over the night that had changed both their lives. It was around two in the morning and there was a whisky bottle almost empty on the table in front of them. It was that stage of the night when alcohol made them maudlin.

'So,' said Antonis, leaning forward a little lopsidedly, 'you haven't met a nice woman in all this time?'

'Me?'

'All these girls around,' said Antonis, waving his arm randomly around him. 'All the girls in the whole of Athens. And you, Manolis Vandoulakis, you're . . . you're alone.'

Manolis picked up the bottle and topped up their glasses with what was left in it. The waiter was there almost instantaneously putting another one down on the table.

'No,' said Manolis firmly, shaking his head. 'There's no one. There hasn't been . . .'

'Not since . . .?'

The unfinished sentences were wholly understood by them both. The conversation quickly moved on.

They arrived back in Piraeus around five in the morning. It was already getting light. A good part of the day was spent dozing in an attempt to recover from the excesses of the previous night, and at eight in the evening, they went to meet some of Manolis's *paréa*.

'Antonis! This is Giannis, Dimitris, Tasos, Mihalis, Miltos.'

He introduced them with ease and affection and the evening was noisy and boisterous, with Antonis forming an ever clearer picture of Manolis's new life. These men were as bonded as brothers, that much was clear.

Stavros came by for an hour, only to be mercilessly teased by the others.

'He's not allowed out much these days!' taunted one of them.

'Not that he wants to come now he's a happily married man!'

It was true that amongst the rest of them none had a stable relationship; most just had occasional love affairs. These were men enjoying bachelorhood. In due course they might seek greater permanence, but for now, independence was the source of their contentment.

It was late when they all went their separate ways. After a few hours' sleep, Manolis drew the curtains back. Antonis groaned. It was already eleven in the morning and time for Antonis to leave for the lunchtime ferry. It would get in to Iraklion in the early hours of the following day, in time for him to be on his latest site that morning. En route, Manolis took him past the luxury yacht he was working on.

'Beautiful,' said Antonis admiringly. 'But don't you dream of sailing somewhere on it?'

Manolis shrugged. There was no time for such a conversation.

'Will you come again?' he asked as Antonis was about to board.

'Keep me away, Manolis! What a time! What a place!'

'It's livelier than Agios Nikolaos,' Manolis agreed.

'I don't think you're ever going to come back, are you?'

'Unlikely,' said Manolis.

'Ah,' said Antonis. 'That means I'll be coming to visit you more often, then?'

'Any time, my old friend, any time.'

A few weeks later, Fotini told Maria that Antonis had been over to Piraeus.

'They had a good time together,' she said. 'And it sounds as if Manolis is quite happy there.'

Maria gazed out of the window of Fotini's taverna towards Spinalonga. It was bathed in golden sunlight and, despite its proximity, felt a thousand kilometres away.

She watched a boat chugging across the water. It was her father, and in his boat was another man. It must be the priest, the only person who regularly visited the island these days. The bones of several hundred people still lay in the cemetery on Spinalonga, among them, of course, Maria's mother. The priest was required to observe the rites of remembrance.

Maria had once asked her father if he remembered the day when he had taken her mother there. As soon as she had said it, she realised it was a ridiculous question.

'I relive every moment of that journey each time I go with the priest,' he said, his eyes filling with tears. 'And the same for the time when I took you, too.'

Maria had apologised for upsetting him.

'But on the way back, I always remember bringing you home,' he said with his sad old smile.

Maria was lost in a reverie.

'Don't you want to know any more about Antonis's visit?' asked Fotini, who had expected a barrage of questions.

Maria shook her head. She had no interest in Manolis Vandoulakis. She saw him as the catalyst for her family's terrible loss. Whatever people had said at Andreas's trial, she was now certain that he was not born to be a murderer. She was glad that Manolis had disappeared from their lives. She prayed to God to lighten the burden of this anger she still felt towards him. The most she managed was to keep thoughts of him to a minimum, and she was momentarily irritated by Fotini for mentioning his name.

Giorgos's boat was almost at the jetty now; he would arrive in five minutes or so. They would all eat together, including Sofia, who had been with Fotini for the afternoon. It was Monday, and the taverna was closed to customers today.

While they were still alone, Fotini asked Maria if she had been to the prison recently.

'I'm planning to go as soon as I can,' she answered. 'But it's been busy at the hospital.'

Fotini's husband, Stephanos, appeared.

'Ah, you sticky friends! You never run out of secrets to share, do you?' he teased. 'You've had your heads together for long enough. It's time to eat now. I've called the children.'

He was right in some ways. The two women, friends since birth, always had plenty to talk about, but for the first time Maria could remember, there were secrets she did not want to divulge. She knew how much her friend would disapprove if she confided about the letter secreted in the handbag at her feet.

When the day arrived for the prison visit, Maria was visibly uneasy. Nikos noticed it.

'If it worries you to go, then don't go,' he said, always hopeful that she could be dissuaded.

'I'm fine, Nikos.'

'Well, you know my views . . .'

When she left that morning, there was a distinct chill in the air. It was late October, and she was glad to have brought a woollen scarf of Nikos's, which she wrapped several times around her neck. Alexandros Vandoulakis's letter had been in her bag for some months now.

As always, her heart was thumping when she arrived at the prison. The trauma of feeling that man's hands on her would always be there. Several women in the queue talked of similar experiences to hers, though almost without exception they had had items removed from their bags that they were trying to sneak in for a prisoner, after which they had been banned from visiting for six months. The prisoner they had come to see had then been deprived of all privileges. The officer relished his power, and Maria knew how much he enjoyed inflicting a little cruelty on the innocent as well as on the guilty.

It was probably her imagination, but today the process of finding Andreas's file, making a note of her visit, taking the dues and so on all seemed to take even longer than usual.

'What's that you have there?' asked the guard, pointing at her side.

Maria looked down. She had stuffed the scarf in her inner pocket and it was bulging. She pulled it out to show him.

It seemed to be an invitation to further scrutinise her.

'Take your coat off,' he said. 'I want to check if you're hiding anything else. Put it on the chair, please.'

Maria obediently did as she was told, putting her bag down on top of it. She had no option. Please, God, she prayed. Don't let him touch me again.

'Turn around slowly,' he instructed. 'Very slowly.'

She followed the instruction. She completed two revolutions before he told her to stop.

'You can put your coat on again now,' he said, smiling.

She managed to suppress her fury at this intimidation. She did not want to give him the satisfaction of the slightest reaction.

The same young guard as usual was leaning against the wall. She wondered how many times he had looked on as his boss behaved in this way. No doubt he was waiting for the time when his own turn came.

'Gamma 10,' came the instruction.

Clutching her bag to her chest, Maria left the room. She was holding back tears and her legs shook so much that she had trouble keeping up with the guard. The walk across the compound seemed longer than the previous time.

Eventually they reached the building where Andreas was now kept, and Maria was admitted to his cell. He looked at her with concern.

'Maria, something has happened . . .?'

She brushed his question aside, but it was obvious from the look on her face that she was upset.

'I'm fine, I'm fine, I was just worried about not getting in on time,' she said.

'Well I am very happy to see you.'

'How are you?' Maria was determined to put what had just happened to the back of her mind.

Andreas looked as he had the previous time, similarly haggard, but clean, right down to his fingernails. His hair was shaved, as was compulsory here.

One thing she had been wanting to know since the previous visit was why he had been moved here. She had imagined he was being punished.

'It might look like solitary confinement,' he told her, 'but it's not. Before I was moved here, I was with five others in a cell this size. It was terrible. I wanted to die in there. It was subhuman. Just the stench . . .'

Maria tried to picture six men living in a space this size. It seemed a physical impossibility.

'We heard that a new block was going to be built, and then the noise and dust of construction started and went on for a few months. There were rumours that all the prisoners from Iraklion were being moved to Neapoli too. We could see that we were losing one of the exercise yards and calculated that with all those extra prisoners and half the open space, we would not even be allowed out once a week to exercise. Plenty of people were losing their minds already. It was one of the reasons for the riots. I went on hunger strike.'

That explained why his bones looked as if they might pierce through his skin.

'They suppressed the riots violently. Even by the standards of this awful place it was shocking. Several prisoners died.'

'We read about some of this,' said Maria. 'But I am sure most of it went unreported.'

'Of course it did,' responded Andreas, pausing for a while before continuing. 'After a few weeks things went back to normal. Or worse than normal really. All of us were punished in one way or another for what had happened. As well as no visitors, we couldn't receive letters, and food portions were halved.'

Maria sat there horrified. However harsh people on the outside might imagine it, the real cruelty in this prison was ten times worse.

'Then one day – it was only just light, so it must have been around five in the morning – two guards came into the cell and pulled me off my bunk. They handcuffed me and led me out. It was a moment of terror because I had no idea what was happening. I thought I was being taken somewhere to be punished, but suddenly I found myself here! It was the opposite. As if I was being rewarded. And everything has changed. I still don't have my freedom, but I can breathe in here. I can think. I am alone!'

'You even have a book!' exclaimed Maria, noticing a copy of the Holy Bible lying on the table.

'It's all we're allowed,' smiled Andreas. 'But it's better than nothing.'

'But why did this happen?'

'I have an idea, though I can't be certain. I think it's to do with money. I think someone is paying a large sum of money.'

'Your father?'

'It can't be anyone else, can it?'

'He didn't say anything to me,' said Maria.

'I don't think he would.'

Maria looked around her. It was a very small space, but the sense of tranquillity within it was palpable. She had visited a few monasteries in Crete and had seen the kind of cells where monks slept. It was not so different.

'We never see the other area now. We're kept separate. Exercise, eating, everything. We don't have any contact with the other inmates. But when someone new comes in here, we learn what they think over there. There's huge resentment.'

'There must be,' said Maria. 'But do you really think the prison authorities would take such a bribe?'

'Of course they would.'

Maria was getting anxious. She glanced at her watch. Time was running away and she must give him the letter before the guard returned.

The envelope was a little grubby and creased after all these months inside her bag, but Andreas's name was still legible on the outside. She deftly took it out and slid it underneath the Bible.

'What's that?'

'It's a letter from your father,' Maria said nervously. 'I know you aren't allowed to receive letters this way and they'll be able to work out who got it in here, so . . .'

They heard the sound of the bolt being drawn back.

' . . . so read it when I've gone.'

'And you'll explain to my father why I don't write back?'

'He understands,' said Maria, picking up her bag.

Chapter Fifteen

IT WOULD BE a while before Maria was in the right frame of mind to go to Neapoli again. Hard as she tried, she had never managed to banish that sexual assault from her mind and the prison officer's renewed intimidation of her had revived her fear and made her even more reluctant to visit than ever. It was something she could not share even with her best friend.

Eventually she felt ready to go but, a few days before, she went to see Alexandros Vandoulakis, taking Sofia as usual.

It had become a habit now that the little girl would make biscuits for them all with Kyría Hortakis. Maria was a good cook but not a very proficient baker, and she was glad that Sofia had someone else to teach her this skill.

It was spring now, and they were practising making *koulourákia*, the delicious Easter biscuits flavoured with orange zest and vanilla. Sofia was impatient with stirring the ingredients, but Kyría Hortakis insisted that the dough of flour, sugar and olive oil should be perfect before they began to shape them. This was when the little girl became excited. They took a section and twisted each one into the form of a snake.

'And you know why we do this?' asked the housekeeper.

Sofia shrugged, too busy concentrating on her task to answer.

'Because thousands and thousands of years ago, the people who lived here, who were called the Minoans, worshipped snakes!'

Sofia laid her uncooked biscuit carefully on the baking tray and looked up at Kyría Hortakis with her big brown eyes.

'So why would they want to eat them?'

'That's a good question, *mátia mou*,' the housekeeper answered, smiling.

They both continued silently fashioning the dough until the whole tray was filled and ready to put into the oven.

Maria and Alexandros Vandoulakis knew they had some time ahead of them to talk privately.

'I gave him your letter,' said Maria. 'And he seemed very happy to get it.'

'Ah, good. And he is still in that room of his own?'

'Yes,' answered Maria, understanding now why the old man had smiled in that knowing way all those months before. It had puzzled her at the time, but now it confirmed that he had paid the cost of Andreas's move to a more civilised place.

They chatted for a little while longer, and then Maria went to the kitchen. The old man had asked her if she would fetch him a glass of water.

The biscuits were just out of the oven, and Sofia was arranging them carefully on a cooling rack.

'She did them all by herself!' Kyría Hortakis reported with delight.

'I'll bring them in in a moment,' said Sofia. 'But only when they're ready.'

She would be nine in a few months and was very capable and determined. She wanted to do everything properly, and planned to sprinkle the biscuits with sugar and put them on a particular plate.

'Don't worry, *agápi mou*,' Maria assured her. 'I won't interfere.'

She and the housekeeper exchanged a smile.

Maria returned to the drawing room.

Alexandros Vandoulakis appeared to have fallen asleep. Maria knew that he often had an afternoon nap, but not usually until they had left.

She tiptoed across to his chair and put the glass on the table adjacent to him. She noticed that his head had tipped forward slightly awkwardly, and then that there was no rise and fall in his chest. He was completely still. With a shaking hand, she took his wrist and felt for a pulse. There was nothing.

Moving his head into a slightly more natural position, she ran from the room and called Nikos from the telephone in the hallway. He would come immediately from the hospital.

In the kitchen, she took Kyría Hortakis to one side and managed to convey what had happened without telling Sofia. The devoted housekeeper, who had been with the family for more than half a century, dashed out of the room. Maria could hear her sobbing in the drawing room, and put on the radio to muffle the noise.

Time went by slowly. Maria kept Sofia playing in the kitchen, telling her that her grandfather had fallen asleep and they must not wake him.

Eventually Nikos arrived. He often came by to collect them from a visit, so it was not such a surprise for Sofia to see him there, but she had never seen him with such a worried look on his face.

'What's wrong with *Babá*?' she asked her mother as Nikos hurried from the room.

'I think he's tired, *moró mou* . . . He's probably had a very busy day.'

Ten minutes later, Nikos reappeared looking even more grey-faced than before. He sat down at the big kitchen table with his wife and daughter and took the girl's hands.

'Sofia,' he said. 'A long time ago, when you were very little, your *yiayiá* passed away. *Megálos Pappoús* was very sad for a long time, but he knew that one day they would be together again.'

'And is that where he is now? With *Yiayiá*?' Sofia replied very matter-of-factly. One of her friends at school had lost her grand-father the previous week, so she was familiar with where grandparents went.

Maria looked at Nikos, knowing that her husband did not really believe in what he was saying, so she helped him out.

'Yes, Sofia. He is with *Yiayiá* now.'

Sofia began to cry, but once her parents had both hugged her, she stopped. She wanted to see her grandfather and was allowed to look at him one last time from the doorway.

Kyría Hortakis was inconsolable, and Maria stayed with her while Nikos took Sofia home.

As soon as Alexandros's daughters and their husbands arrived, Maria left. They were always very frosty with the sister of the late Anna Vandoulakis, and she could sense their resentment that she had been the last person to see their father alive.

It was the duty of immediate family to go through the formal processes of mourning, and Olga's driver was instructed to give Maria a lift home.

Alexandros Vandoulakis was buried thirty-six hours later. The funeral was held in the large church in the centre of Neapoli and attended by several hundred people. There were too many of them – estate workers, local dignitaries, family and friends – to fit in at once, but everyone had the opportunity to pay their respects to this well-loved man.

It was a warm, still afternoon, and as she stood on the steps of the church after the service and listened to the tolling of the bells, Maria wondered if Andreas might be able to hear them. The prison was less than five kilometres away.

Suspecting that Olga and Eirini would not make it a priority to write to their brother, she resolved to go and see him within the next day or so. She knew that Alexandros Vandoulakis would have wanted her to do that.

She put aside her fear of the prison officer to make her visit. He was there, perspiring and leering as usual, but perhaps even he had a modicum of respect for someone in mourning. He found the Vandoulakis file, made his notes without the usual quips and summoned the guard to escort her across the yard.

Her black attire was the first thing Andreas noticed.

'Your father?' he said, as soon as the door was bolted behind her. 'I'm so sorry . . .'

He had assumed she was in mourning for Giorgos, who was several years older than his own father.

'Can we sit down?' Maria asked quietly, taking the wooden chair as Andreas sat on his bed. 'I'm afraid it's *your* father, Andreas. He died two days ago. I am so sorry.'

Andreas put his head in his hands for a few moments. It was as if he was praying. There were tears in his eyes when he looked up, but they did not fall. Andreas found it hard to cry.

'I was at the house when he died,' explained Maria. 'It was very peaceful. I had just told him that you now had his letter.'

Andreas was quiet for a moment.

'Let me show you something, Maria,' he said at last, with great composure, reaching for the Bible on his desk. Inside, almost as if it was being used as a bookmark, was a sheet of paper. He drew it out carefully, as if it was as precious as a sheet of gold leaf. The envelope had been dispensed with. 'Look! Do you see what he says?'

He showed it to Maria but without letting it go, and before she had a chance to cast her eye over it, his eagerness got the better of him.

'Let me! Listen.'

As Andreas read his father's words, Maria sat and marvelled at how alike father and son sounded.

Dear Andreas,

I am sorry it has taken me so long to realise this. I have been slow.

I merely want to tell you one thing.

If Maria can forgive you, then I can forgive you too.

Your loving father

Maria looked down at the floor as he repeated the words. He spoke them as if they were from the Holy Scriptures.

"'If Maria can forgive you, then I can forgive you too.'"

She saw that tears now flowed down his cheeks, and felt a great lump in her throat.

'My father forgave me, Maria. I never imagined . . . Before he died, he forgave me . . .'

She wanted to touch him on the arm, just as a sign of comfort, but restrained herself.

Andreas looked directly at her.

'Maria, there is no doubt in my mind that you are an angel.'

She felt very uncomfortable with the word. She tried to do her best for people, but there was nothing angelic about her. If there was, she might not get so upset with Nikos, with whom there was always a level of friction when she came to see Andreas. And she might be more patient with Sofia when she refused to tidy her room. No, she was no angel.

'I don't think so, Andreas,' she said firmly.

'But you are definitely an angel in the purest sense. *Angelos* – from the ancient Greek for "messenger". That's you. Like Gabriel. He was God's messenger.'

Maria looked slightly bemused. Andreas's theological knowledge surprised her.

'You brought this letter, Maria, and it conveyed the most important news I have ever received. Just as the Angel Gabriel's message was for Mary.'

There was the now familiar scraping of a bolt being drawn back, the same ugly noise that heralded the end of every visit. Andreas hastily hid the letter back inside the Bible.

That night, Maria had a vivid dream. Alexandros, Eleftheria, Anna and Andreas were all together at a long table under some trees, eating, laughing and talking happily.

It was a beautiful, peaceful scene. It was only later on that she began to analyse it. Why had Andreas been there, eating with the dead?

Chapter Sixteen

OLGA IN PARTICULAR was eager for the reading of the will. How had her father divided the estate? Had he given Andreas's daughter a share? Perhaps he had even left a portion to his absent nephew Manolis? There were various possibilities and all of them made her anxious.

She had married a man who was less wealthy than his family had made out, and not only that, she had discovered he had a penchant for gambling. With four children and a husband who regularly lost hundreds of thousands of drachma playing cards, Olga was praying for salvation.

Eirini had made a much better match. She hoped for something from the will, but fully expected that her father would have left Olga the lion's share, given that she was clearly the favourite daughter.

The lawyer's offices were even gloomier than the Vandoulakis house, with dark wooden panelling and low-wattage lights. It was with great effort and much stumbling over his words that the old lawyer read out every last sentence of the will.

Olga sat next to her husband trying unsuccessfully to appear relaxed. Eirini was there alone. Her husband was in Athens finalising the purchase of a new building in the city centre.

Although it took the lawyer more than an hour to finish reading it, the essence of Alexandros Vandoulakis's last will and testament was very simple. The great estate, with its vast swathes of olive groves and vineyards, had been left equally to his two daughters.

Although the old man had very precisely and fairly divided the land to the last half-hectare, the two sons-in-law immediately squabbled over the boundaries, and the sisters each felt that the other had been given the more fertile vineyards, the more productive olive groves, the larger share of land that might be ripe for development in what was now considered to be the new gold rush: tourism. Of late, areas closer to the sea, which were unusable for agriculture, were seen as potential sites for hotels.

The sisters quarrelled viciously over the monetary value of what they had inherited. Neither of them gave a moment's thought to the circumstances that had brought them such riches. Olga had been left the Vandoulakis house and Eirini was to have Andreas and Anna's house, which had stood empty since that terrible August night. During and after the reading of the will, none of them even mentioned Andreas, who if circumstances had been different would now be the owner of all this land.

One morning, Maria bumped into Kyría Hortakis in the market in Agios Nikolaos. She was very happy to see the housekeeper and asked how everything was in the Neapoli home. She assumed that Kyría Hortakis had remained there to work for the new incumbents.

'I stayed a week,' answered the elderly woman. 'That was all I could manage. I couldn't work for those people. Not for another moment. They bickered about everything. She bickered with him. The children bickered with each other. Bickering, bickering, bickering. I couldn't stand it, Kyría Kyritsis. Not at my age. Not after working for that lovely Kýrios Vandoulakis. He didn't smile very much, but he was always kind to me. And you know what he did? He left me some money. I never expected that. Enough to rent a nice house and to live on for a few years. I'm seventy-three now, Maria. I don't need those . . . people.'

Maria was not surprised to hear any of this. She had no illusions about Andreas Vandoulakis's sisters and was glad that she had no need to come into contact with them now. She was relieved – and Nikos even more so – that they showed no interest in their niece.

Some weeks after she had seen Kyría Hortakis, a letter arrived for Maria and Nikos addressed to 'The Legal Guardians of Sofia, formerly Vandoulakis'. The letter was from the lawyer in Iraklion and informed them that Alexandros Vandoulakis had placed in trust for Sofia Petrakis the sum of five hundred thousand drachmas, to be released on her twenty-first birthday.

Maria blinked and thought she had misread the noughts. Nikos had to read it out to her twice before she believed it. It was a huge sum.

Manolis was the one person in the family unaware of Alexandros's death, but given that he had been left out of the will, there was no legal obligation to track him down.

Maria asked Fotini if her brother had any plans to go and see him in the future.

'I think he's hoping to visit in the next couple of weeks,' answered Fotini brightly. 'Anastasia isn't too keen on him going, but it does him good to see the bright lights.'

Antonis had already booked a ferry ticket and arrived one fine Friday afternoon full of his usual excitement and anticipation at seeing his friend. He found Manolis in the same frame of mind as ever, living for the day and never looking beyond the horizon.

Manolis still lived with Kyría Agathi. A big change at the pension was that Elli had moved out to get married to Philippos, her boss's son. They had a small but joyful wedding and everyone said how sweet the bride looked in her candyfloss gown.

Antonis had promised to mention the news of his uncle's death to Manolis.

'Ah, the old man,' said Manolis with fondness. 'He was always kind to me. Shame those daughters were such witches.'

'I don't think they've improved,' smiled Antonis. 'As far as I've heard, anyway. I still see some of the workers for a drink and their new boss isn't making himself popular. You remember Olga's husband?'

'He always was a *maláka*,' Manolis confirmed.

'Much better to work for yourself,' said Antonis. 'That's what I think, anyhow.'

'To the old man!' said Manolis, raising his glass.

'Yes,' agreed Antonis. 'To your uncle, my old boss! To Alexandros Vandoulakis.'

The two men spent the evening getting drunk in Piraeus, and not for a moment did they run out of conversation.

Antonis told his old friend about every aspect of his latest building project, a hotel not far from the sea.

'It's the future, Manolis! Foreigners coming to Crete to spend their money in Agios Nikolaos. The sun never shines in northern Europe! They come to Greece and they go mad on it! They can't even believe the colour of the sky. I tell you, there aren't many yet, but in ten years, there'll be thousands of tourists in Crete.'

Manolis listened. He enjoyed his friend's enthusiasm.

'And the wine. It's so cheap for them! They drink until they fall over. And they love the food. Did you know they don't have feta cheese in Scandinavia? And the Austrians – none of them have ever seen watermelon! Can you believe it?'

Manolis had travelled to those places, so he well knew how different the eating habits were, but he did not interrupt his friend's flow.

'There's money to be made, Manolis! Why don't you come back and we can do something together? We can make a partnership. I just bought a piece of land for the next hotel. Now, I know you're not meant to build on sand, but this place will have its own beach so guests can walk straight from their rooms into the sea. It's going to be unique.'

Manolis gazed out towards the shipyard opposite the bar where they were sitting.

'I am happy enough here,' he said. 'For the moment, it's all I want.'

Antonis shook his head. He was going up in the world. He had bought a second car, moved to a bigger house and was exploiting his healthy financial position to take out large loans for future projects. He failed to understand his friend, believing that Manolis could be doing just as well as him.

'Well, you should think about it. You're wasting your time here, Manolis. We would make a good team.'

Manolis did not like to be too blunt with his friend, but even if it was the last place on earth, he could never return to Crete. Such a tragedy as Anna's death cast a long and deep shadow, and he did not want to live in such darkness. It would be decades more before tongues stopped wagging. Everything about Crete, its scents, its sounds, its flavours, would always remind him of Anna. How could he create a new life in a place where she would be a constant presence?

He made light of his reasoning.

'Perhaps one day,' he said to his friend. 'But the work is good here. I'm earning plenty. Saving a bit. Who knows what the future holds?'

The weekend passed with great merriment. Both men had plenty of cash in their pockets. Antonis loved to spend, and on Saturday he splashed out on a new watch for himself at a jeweller in Ermou, a central Athens street lined with glamorous and expensive shops.

'You don't get all these brands in Agios Nikolaos,' he laughed as he handed over a wad of notes to the shop assistant.

When they came out of the shop into the late-afternoon sunshine, they strolled up towards Syntagma, Constitution Square, and soon found themselves outside the Grande Bretagne. Everyone, even on the remotest island in the Aegean, knew the name of this iconic hotel. It was the smartest, most expensive and most beautiful establishment in Greece and a place that Antonis had always wanted to go.

'Time for a drink?' said Manolis.

Without a second thought, he led the way. A doorman smiled and with a gloved hand pulled the door open. These two were well dressed, and he recognised them as the type who would tip well when they left.

They were immediately shown to a table and Manolis ordered a martini.

'The same, please,' said Antonis.

He leaned forward.

'How did you know what to order?' he asked his friend.

'It's the best cocktail there is. The simplest, the best, the purest. And they make the finest ones in Europe right here.'

'You mean you've been here before?' Antonis asked, looking around at the lavish decor. His eyes were wide as he surveyed the mirrored walls and ceiling, the gleaming chandeliers and the jungle of mighty potted palms. The gentle sound of a grand piano rolled towards them from the far corner of the room.

Antonis had never thought much about Manolis's previous life, but it was obvious now that this was not his first visit.

It seemed light years away from Plaka and the bar where they had spent so much time together, a place where the choice had been either beer or raki. There were moments when Antonis realised that he hardly knew this man. Manolis was the sort who fitted in wherever he went, whoever he was with, like the lizards that could change the colour of their skin. Antonis noticed for the first time that his friend had shed his Cretan accent. Yes, this man was a chameleon.

He turned to look at the barman, who was vigorously rattling the cocktail shaker, chilled glasses neatly aligned on the bar. A waiter brought them iced water in cut glasses and small silver dishes of nuts and cheese biscuits the size of grapes. White linen coasters were positioned beneath each item.

He returned a moment later with the martinis.

'Anything else for you, sir?' he asked.

'Not for now, thank you,' replied Manolis.

Antonis watched as his friend carefully lifted his glass.

'Don't knock it back in one,' Manolis instructed with a smile. 'It's not raki. Savour it.'

Picking up his own glass, Antonis looked through the clear liquid and removed the olive that had been threaded onto a stick and carefully balanced on the rim. It was his first cocktail.

'Try it!' urged Manolis.

Antonis had soon drained the glass and put it back on the table. '*Panagía mou*,' he said. 'That was good. Not enough of it, though.'

The pair of them had several more of the same.

'So are you a regular here?' asked Antonis.

'Not a regular, but I call in whenever I come through Athens,' Manolis replied. 'I've lived all over Europe, Antonis, you know that. I've ordered martinis in Rome, Paris and Salzburg, but none of them ever compared with this.'

'So why did you go back to Crete then?' slurred Antonis. 'I never understood it.'

'Money, really. I ran out. If you spend and spend and don't earn any, then money disappears sooner or later.'

He was stating the obvious, but Antonis nodded politely.

'I never thought I was coming back for ever,' admitted Manolis. 'I just thought it would be good to be in one place for a while. To be with family.'

'And then—'

'Let's get the bill!' Manolis cut his friend off. Antonis was about to stray into forbidden territory.

With a slight nod of his head, he summoned the waiter. He gave the bill a cursory glance and left a large note on the tray. A small gesture with his hand indicated that he did not want the change.

Even in his state of mild inebriation, Antonis knew that he had touched on something that Manolis wanted to keep to himself. The subject of Anna was still a raw nerve and Manolis's defences were in place, as ever.

As the doorman had hoped, Manolis discreetly slipped a few drachmas into his hand as they left. Antonis took in every nuance of his friend's behaviour. This was the kind of place he wanted to frequent more often in the future, and he could see that the smallest details of etiquette were key to blending in.

The two of them wandered up the street in the direction of Kolonaki. They needed to pick up Manolis's car before driving back to Piraeus. Agathi was singing in a *bouzoúkia* in an hour's time and Manolis had promised her that they would go.

The landlady was in good voice that night. Manolis and Antonis sat with Stavros at a table close to the stage, and some other members of their *paréa* joined them.

Perhaps it was alcohol that had induced this melancholy. Or perhaps being with Antonis had brought back too many images of Crete. It certainly felt to Manolis that Anna had been present with him more than usual today, but nevertheless he resisted the urge to dance the *zeibékiko*.

Eventually the two friends made their way home. The sun was already rising.

Chapter Seventeen

MARIA WAS WRITING to Andreas, but it was a long while since her last visit. She hated to admit it, even to herself, but her loathing of that prison officer still deterred her from going. Even Nikos asked why she had not been to see Andreas for such a long period, and she had to make up an excuse.

Accompanied by Giorgos, Nikos and Maria had both attended the one-year memorial for Alexandros Vandoulakis. A week or so on, Maria felt a pang of guilt. She put aside her fears, took a day off work from the hospital, caught the bus and joined the queue outside the prison.

The officer pretended not to recognise her. It was disconcerting but also a relief, and the process of admission was swift.

The building in which Andreas was held was still clean and sanitary, just as it had been when he moved in. Maria had worried that after his father's death the payments for this special accommodation might have ceased. To her great relief, it appeared that Alexandros Vandoulakis had allowed for them to continue. She was happy that he had protected both his son and his grandchild from the avaricious daughters and their husbands.

Andreas was little changed, still thin, still shaven-headed. He was happy to see her and asked all about Giorgos and Sofia. It had been the child's ninth birthday since the last visit, and Maria had brought some recent photographs to show him.

'That's at school . . . on a trip to Knossos . . . when we went to Sitia . . . on the beach in Plaka . . .'

He looked at them almost absent-mindedly as Maria gave a running commentary, and then handed them back to her. She would have expected more interest, given that he was Sofia's father, and it surprised her that he did not ask to keep even one. She supposed that this was because he knew the risk as well as she did. Inmates were not allowed any possessions, except for the book that still sat on his table.

Now that the photographs were back in her bag, she worried that conversation might run out. What, after all, was there to talk about? News of the outside world was not particularly relevant to someone who was never going to see it again, and there was nothing to say about his father now.

When visits had been held in the large room, time had always flown. The level of ambient noise had meant that everything needed to be repeated, sometimes more than once, and there were no awkward silences.

This time, Andreas seemed quieter than usual. Maria could have filled the space with tactless gossip about the behaviour of his sisters and their husbands. There was a feud brewing between the two couples, and the local paper was already referring to it. There was talk of a law suit. Olga was now contesting the will, believing that she had not received a fair share.

It was contemptible in Maria's view, and she did not want to bother Andreas with it.

Just as she was about to tell him of some new breakthrough in medical science that Nikos was involved in, Andreas leaned forward and picked up his Bible.

'I've been reading it, Maria,' he said. 'Cover to cover.'

She could see from where his father's letter was placed that he had reached the Gospels.

'It's beautiful,' he said. 'Full of wisdom.'

Maria smiled. She was familiar with much of the New Testament but had never methodically read the Old Testament as he had done.

'It's full of stories. Full of people. Full of poetry.'

'I wonder how many people have actually read it all the way through,' she commented.

'I suppose not many people are stuck with just one book,' Andreas replied, almost smiling. 'But I have been glad of it, Maria. And it's only now that I am getting to what seems the best part.'

'I wish I could bring you some other books to read too,' she said.

'No! Don't worry. This is all I need for now. It's probably more than any man needs.'

Maria looked into Andreas's eyes, uncertain whether his words contained a hint of sarcasm, but she could see that he was serious.

'And in any case, it's the only book permitted in this place,' he added with a smile.

Maria was glad to see him so at peace.

'I have to tell you about the priest,' he said. 'About six months ago, I asked to see one. We're allowed to ask for a priest any time of day or night. They don't ration God in here.'

Maria was intrigued. Talk of religion was the last thing she had expected from Andreas.

'This wasn't an ordinary priest,' he continued. 'Or not like any I have met before.'

He began to speak very rapidly. The clock was always ticking on these visits, and he had to finish telling Maria his story before the guard came. She could see it was a matter of urgency to him and resolved not to interrupt.

'There was something in his eyes. Nobody is born with such eyes. They are eyes that look *beyond*. He can look into the soul, Maria. Anyway, he wasn't always a priest.

'He is Cretan – born somewhere near Anogia – and there was a vendetta between his family and another. He tried to kill a man in revenge for the death of his brother, but his victim survived and he was arrested the following day. He was given a ten-year sentence and got sent to the prison in Iraklion, a barbaric place compared with here and the conditions even worse. An epidemic of tuberculosis swept through the place and about one third of the inmates died. He was one of them. There was no treatment and he was pronounced dead.'

'He died?' interrupted Maria incredulously.

'Yes. He remembers a cold sheet on his skin as they laid it over his face. He remembers a smell as sweet as a lily. He felt with his own hands the inside of the coffin in which they had placed him. Suddenly there was a very bright light as he came out of the darkness, a sense of the divine. Before they had time to nail down the lid, he managed to sit up.'

Maria sat spellbound. She had never heard of anything like it.

'There is only one reason for such a thing to happen, Maria. God. God wanted to save him. And there was only one way he could thank God. As soon as he was released, he went to a monastery and gave his life to the service of the Lord. Eventually he was permitted to enter the priesthood.'

'So it's as if he was resurrected,' said Maria, not really knowing what to think.

'He came back from the dead,' replied Andreas without hesitation. 'And if you met him, you would have no doubts. He is like Christ. He is not like you and me.'

Maria knitted her brows. Andreas had more to say.

'It is impossible not to believe in . . . *this*,' he said, holding the Bible aloft. 'And if I had one day of my life to be a free man, I would go and find that priest again.'

'You mean you haven't seen him since that visit?' Maria was slightly aghast.

'He just came on that one day, Maria. But it changed my life. I am no longer afraid. I used to watch the sun fall on that patch of wall and weep. I could not bear that one more day of this miserable life had gone. Now I look on it and rejoice, for I am one day closer to the Lord.'

The bolt was being drawn back. Maria stood up. She was bemused. Andreas was talking like an octogenarian, not like a man in his forties. It was disturbing and strange.

She assured him she would not leave such a gap before the next visit, and was escorted quickly to the prison gates.

On the way home, she had plenty of time to reflect. She went regularly to church herself, listened to the chanting of the priests and knew the sense of peace it gave her, heard passages of the gospel being read and believed them. She followed the *Epitáfios* and wished everyone '*Christós anésti*' two days later. When she said '*Alithós anésti*' – 'Indeed he is risen' – it was with sincerity. She believed that a man had once conquered death, on one occasion all those years ago in Jerusalem, but not again in a prison in Iraklion.

Was the priest who had visited Andreas really a priest? Or was he a fraud? Perhaps even a figment of his imagination? Though if Andreas had found solace, did it matter?

She mentioned Andreas's new-found faith to Nikos, but his response, as she expected, was a little sceptical.

'If he thinks God himself will shorten his sentence, he might be disappointed,' he said.

Maria managed to see Andreas again a few months later. The prison officer was ready and waiting to intimidate her. This time he demanded that she empty her bag out onto his desk. He picked over every item: keys, purse, a shopping list, her lipstick, a hairbrush. It was of no possible use to any prisoner here, but he took the brush in any case. He came close enough for her to smell what he had eaten the previous night, but did not touch her.

Full of disgust, she followed the guard to Andreas's cell. When she walked in, he was on his knees, praying. For a few minutes he continued as if unaware that she was there.

Finally he opened his eyes and stood up. It was obvious just from looking at him that he was even more consumed by religious conviction now than the last time she had been there. There was a strange expression in his eyes, as if he was looking at something that she could not see. She was reminded of an image of the shepherds enraptured by the sight of the Christ Child.

Like the priest he had described, Andreas himself now had eyes that seemed to penetrate, to look *beyond*. They were luminous.

He told her he had come to the end of the Bible now and wanted to talk about certain passages. She pretended to listen intently, mostly because she did not want to hurt his feelings, but for the first time she was glad to hear the sound of the guard in the corridor and the scraping of the bolt.

Chapter Eighteen

M ANOLIS WAS NOW supervising a team of his own in the shipyard. He and Giannis worked side by side in the office during the morning and then joined up with their respective teams on practical work in the afternoon. Manolis's gift was to create a sense of loyalty among those he recruited. He found that this halved the time in which a job could be completed, and the guarantee of a bonus further increased the speed of work. They had bookings for repairs that would keep them busy until the end of the following year.

'We'll be able to buy our own ship one day,' joked Giannis.

'I think I'll stick to working on other people's,' said Manolis.

Manolis loved the process of making an old ship new again. What could be more satisfying than bringing a shabby boat back to its former glory? Occasionally he wished he could do it with his own life.

Stavros was only working part-time now. In the afternoons he did all the maintenance that was needed in the pension, repairing bathrooms and one by one giving the bedrooms a fresh coat of paint. The guest house was always full and all the tenants paid on time, so he and Agathi had more than enough income for a comfortable life.

Their happiness had been untarnished since the day of their 'wedding', and Manolis had never known two people more contented in each other's company.

One day, as he and Stavros were walking together to start their morning's work, Stavros grabbed his arm.

'Look, Manolis! Look!' Stavros had frozen, his lips pale.

They were passing the ferry terminal and people were being disgorged onto the pavement in front of them.

'It's her!' he said in a whisper. '*Theé mou!* Oh my God! I am sure that's her.'

Manolis looked for a woman he recognised. It was many years since his encounter with Stavros's wife, and from the back it would not have been easy to identify her in any case. Stavros, however, was insistent.

'In a green coat! Look!'

He shrank back. Manolis saw who he meant. If the woman turned now she would see them. She had bright blonde hair just as he remembered it, but more than that he could not really see.

Stavros pulled Manolis back and across the road into a *kafeneío*. Manolis ordered two coffees and they sat for ten minutes to drink them while Stavros calmed down.

'I know it was her,' he said, trembling. 'I *know*.'

Manolis could not persuade him otherwise.

'Even if it *is* her, which I admit it could be, she doesn't know where you live, Stavros. When she left last time, I left her in no doubt that she was in the wrong place. She doesn't even know what name you use. So the chances of her finding you again are—'

'They aren't slim, Manolis. She found me once. She'll find me again.'

'Well I've still got her gun in my drawer,' said Manolis, trying to cheer his friend.

Nothing would convince Stavros that he and Agathi were not in danger, and for the next few weeks he was racked with insomnia. He contacted his parents to ask if his wife was still in Thessaloniki, and to his horror they confirmed that she had left her parents' apartment some weeks before. They would not say where she was.

Agathi tried constantly to put his mind at rest, and Manolis was present on many occasions when she tried in vain to comfort him.

'I'll look after you, *agápi mou*,' she reassured him. 'Nothing is going to come between us.'

'But you don't know her!' Stavros said. 'You didn't even see her that night when she came.'

It was true that Agathi had no idea what the woman was capable of. Only Manolis had any notion of it.

Fear changed Stavros. He was no longer the relaxed and contented man that Agathi had helped him to be. Instead he was constantly nervous and frequently glanced over his shoulder. He would not go out after dark and his eyes were hollow with lack of sleep.

One evening a year or so later, Manolis came in from work and picked up a pile of letters that lay on the hall floor. He leafed through them. He always hoped for a letter from Antonis, and it had been a while. He enjoyed his friend's correspondence and Antonis was supposed to be confirming the date of his next visit.

But there was nothing for him. There were some letters for other long-term tenants and one for Agathi. Hers was an airmail envelope with multiple brightly coloured stamps showing exotic flowers. It was from Australia.

He slid it under her door and left the others on the table in the hall.

That night, Elli and her husband Philippos joined Agathi, Stavros and Manolis for dinner. The young couple had some important news. Elli was expecting a baby.

The mood of the evening was jovial and they toasted the blushing young woman and her unborn child. Stavros, as he had been since the sighting of the woman at the ferry terminal, was a little subdued.

The pale blue envelope with its bright stamps was propped up against a vase in the centre of the table. Manolis was intrigued to know why it merited pride of place at the meal, but his curiosity was soon satisfied.

'I've had a nice letter!' Agathi said cheerily, holding it aloft. 'My second cousin in Melbourne has written to me.'

'Uncle Pavlos?' asked Elli.

'Yes, *agápi mou*,' Agathi replied. 'You remember him? But you were so young when he left!'

'It's only ten years ago, *Theía*,' said Elli.

Agathi was full of excitement and wanted everyone's attention back.

'So,' she said, explaining to the men in the room, 'I have lots of cousins. A few of them went to the US, but Pavlos went on one of those assisted passages to Australia. To be honest, I thought we would never hear from him again. Things weren't so good here then, but even so, it seemed a bit rash to go to the other side of the world.'

'So how has he found it over there?' asked Manolis.

'Paradise!' Agathi said, beaming. 'Paradise.'

She looked around at the faces of her audience.

'All these years go by without hearing anything, and then—'

'*Theía!* Tell us!'

'Listen. I'll read some of it.'

Kyría Agathi drew in a breath and her breasts swelled over a daringly décolleté blouse. Everything, even the reading of a letter, was a performance. Manolis loved this about her.

'"I now have three tavernas in Melbourne and two *kafeneía*, and I am planning to open two more next year. They're all completely traditional and full seven days a week. All my customers are Greek. We have musicians and singers every Friday and Saturday night in every taverna." But now comes the really important part.'

There was an inaudible drum-roll. Manolis leaned forward, the most enthusiastic member of her audience.

'"And now I am opening a *bouzoúkia*. It will be the biggest in Melbourne. It's my most ambitious venture yet, but I know it is going to be a success."'

'That all sounds very exciting,' said Manolis.

'I haven't finished, Manolis,' said Agathi, waving her hand in mock irritation at his interruption. '"I want you, Agathi, to come here and sing! And I want you to be here for the opening night. If you say yes, I will send money for your passage. You will see how sweet life is. Australia is like Greece but without any of the bad things. It's warm and sunny and you don't even need to speak English! There is a whole community of us here, and most of us don't have a word."'

She finished reading and looked up at the faces around her to take in their reactions. Elli surprised her by being the first to speak.

'Well I think you should go, *Theía,*' she said decisively. 'Especially if he's going to pay for the journey.'

Manolis glanced across at Stavros and for the first time in several days saw him smile. It was clear that he was already familiar with the contents of the letter.

'What do you think, Stavros?' Elli asked.

Manolis was watching his friend's face.

'I think we should go,' he said.

'You could probably get one of those assisted passages too, couldn't you?' offered Philippos.

Manolis knew Stavros well enough to know what he was thinking. Not only would a new life in Australia be an exciting opportunity, but being on the other side of the world would also remove the fear of being found by his wife.

Elli was looking tired, so she and Philippos got ready to leave.

'Thank you for dinner, *Theía,*' she said.

'And thank you for the wonderful news about the baby, *agápi mou.*'

'I mean it, I think you should go,' she said quietly to her aunt. 'You know you don't have to worry about me.'

189

'Yes . . . but the baby! Will you manage?'

'Of course I will,' she said sweetly, glancing up at her husband. 'I have Philippos now.'

'And who knows?' chipped in Philippos. 'Maybe one day we'll join you. I am sure there's a market for a *zacharoplasteío* over there.'

'Well it's only an invitation to go and sing . . .' protested Agathi.

'You know it's more than that, *Theía,*' said Elli, touching her aunt's hand.

They all knew she was right. There was every chance that they would not return.

Once Elli and Philippos had gone, Stavros poured them all another drink.

'Stay for a bit, Manolis,' he said.

They sat around the debris of dishes on the kitchen table. Stavros was unusually eager to speak.

'I really think we should go,' he said. 'Imagine it, Agathi. We wouldn't need to rent out rooms any more. There's no gold rush now, but there are other kinds of treasure out there. And a new life . . .'

Agathi looked at him with fondness. She too liked the idea of escaping from the threat of another appearance by his wife.

'What do you think, Manolis?' she asked.

'It sounds a wonderful opportunity. I think you should take it.'

A life-changing decision was often more easily made than a trivial one. Agathi had spent longer selecting pastries for their supper that evening than it took her to mull over her cousin's invitation. Her mind was made up before they all went to bed.

Manolis did not sleep well that night. He felt an almost immeasurable sadness. He could not imagine life without the two people who had become as precious as family.

As the day began to break, he got out of bed and drew back the curtains. He wanted to watch the sun rise. It was only then that he realised something: the melancholy that he had felt the previous night was not because he was bidding farewell to his friends. It was to Greece that he would be saying goodbye. Almost without realising it, he had made the decision to leave with them.

Australia would be a new start for him too. Everyone said it was the land of opportunity, and who had ever met a Greek who had returned? Apart from anything, he would not be sorry to leave a place living under a military dictatorship. It was a couple of years since a group of army colonels had seized power and, though Manolis's day-to-day life had not been affected, everyone knew that political detainees were being locked up and tortured. His friend Mihalis, like many on the left, had already gone to live in France to escape such persecution.

There was another more personal reason to go. Finally he might be free. After all, Stavros was not the only person with someone to escape. Manolis too was still followed by a shadow from his past.

Within a few days, Agathi was making progress with all the necessary arrangements. She sent a telegram to her cousin, and money was wired into her bank account. Pavlos was obviously a rich man. He sent enough for Stavros's ticket too, and his secretary had looked into the schedules of any boat leaving for Australia. There was one sailing in three weeks' time.

Agathi began carefully packing her ornaments and folding her clothes in a trunk. Elli and Philippos had asked for her dining table and chairs, and the rest of the furniture was being left.

The lease on the pension was easily dealt with. The regime was actively encouraging tourism and a hotel owner on the main street, looking to expand, eagerly grabbed the opportunity for a new property. A growing number of tourists and travelling salesmen needed somewhere to stay the night before taking an early-morning ferry to the islands, and the location was ideal.

Every day, Agathi became a little more tearful at the thought of leaving. She was particularly sentimental about Manolis, who had not said a word to anyone about his plan. He wanted to surprise her and Stavros on the day.

'Where will you live?' she asked him, her lashes damp.

'I've found somewhere, Agathi,' he said, hugging her. 'Don't you worry.'

'And will you keep an eye on Elli for me? If she needs anything, will you be able to help her?'

'Of course I will,' said Manolis reassuringly. 'But I think Philippos is a safe pair of hands.'

Stavros had already had his last day in the shipyard a while back, and a few days before departure, Manolis told his *paréa* that he was leaving too. Giannis took the news very badly. He was devastated to be losing the best person he had ever worked with and one of his most loyal friends.

'You can always come back if it doesn't work out,' he said, turning away to hide unmanly tears.

That night they all went out and drank and drank until they could scarcely stand. It was the only way for such men to say goodbye. The *paréa* made promises to come and visit, and Manolis swore that he would be back to see them before they knew it. All these things were said with enough sincerity to make the parting bearable. Only time would tell if they would be as good as their word.

Manolis had a few loose ends to tie up, some bills to pay at the tailor and one or two *kafetzídes* to bid farewell. Then there was the complex matter of a passport. Time went quickly. He had planned to let Antonis know that he was leaving but never found the moment to write a letter. He would surprise him with a postcard from Melbourne.

In a moment of melancholy, he thought of Sofia. They would not even recognise each other if they met in the street. Presumably she was growing up without knowing that he existed. Even the smallest possibility that he was her father made this thought unbearable, and it was one that he had to dismiss. Perhaps he would write to Maria and her husband from Melbourne, even send some money next Easter. He imagined that most twelve-year-old girls loved a new pair of shoes.

The day before the boat was due to sail, Agathi came up to see Manolis in his room. The tenants all had another week before they had to vacate.

'Can I come in?' she asked.

She had something in her hand and was holding it out to him.

'I thought you might like this,' she said. 'Do you remember? We had a photographer at our wedding.'

It was a picture taken on the day of their celebration, with the two men on either side of Agathi. Almost a decade had passed, but they had all aged well.

'That's so nice,' he said. 'Thank you. I'll put it next to my parents for now.'

'Who will cook for you, Manolis? Who will wash your shirts?'

Agathi was getting sentimental again. Her tears were never far away.

'I wish you had met a nice woman,' she tutted. 'Then I wouldn't be worrying about you so much. I can't understand it myself, when you're the most handsome man in Piraeus. The girls here must be blind.'

In the past two or three years, Manolis had enjoyed plenty of mild flirtations, evenings of dancing, the occasional night in a different bed. But that had been all.

'Ah, Agathi. If only there were two of you,' he said, knowing how much she loved her ego to be stroked.

She blushed.

'Manolis,' she said. 'You don't know how much I'll miss you.'

He hugged her and she left. Today she was packing her precious record collection. Some were on vinyl but the majority were made of shellac and were rather brittle, so all four hundred must be individually wrapped.

That night, the five of them had a farewell dinner in a nearby taverna. Agathi's apartment was virtually cleared out now.

They tried to be merry and made toasts for the future, but their smiles were forced and the underlying mood was one of deep melancholy and loss.

Elli was in on Manolis's plan and almost spoiled the surprise he was planning to spring on Agathi by embracing him too hard at the end of the evening and wishing him farewell. Agathi did not notice, but Stavros was puzzled.

The following day, at five in the morning, the couple emerged from their apartment, having spent their last night there. The shipping company had already collected their belongings and taken away eight large trunks. Agathi was assured that they would see them in six weeks' time, when the boxes were offloaded from the same ship on which she and Stavros would be travelling. She needed a lot of persuasion from Stavros that this would actually happen.

'Even if it doesn't, *mátia mou*, we can buy you some more blouses in Australia,' he said in his most reassuring voice.

'But what about my ladies?' she asked, very agitated. 'They're so fragile, some of them!'

'I saw you wrapping them, *agápi mou*,' he said affectionately. 'They're in so many layers of tissue that they'll probably have a more comfortable journey than we will.'

Some of the tenants had got up early to wish the couple farewell. Manolis was among them. He was waiting in the hallway and had his car parked outside. He had told them that he would take them to the ship. He had already stowed his bag in the car. His own possessions fitted into the same holdall that he had brought with him from Crete all those years before.

It was a ten-minute journey to the port, and when they got there, he opened the door for Kyría Agathi and then took their two suitcases and set them down on the ground. Finally, he took out his own bag.

'Where are you going now?' queried Agathi, seeing the holdall at his feet. 'You have another week in the pension before you have to move out.'

'Just getting myself organised,' said Manolis, hugging her.

It was then that she saw the twinkle in his eye and understood. This was a man she knew and loved so well.

She threw her arms around him with a scream.

'Manolis!'

She wept profusely. There were others nearby saying goodbye to their loved ones for the very last time, and they imagined that she too was leaving someone she cherished.

'Manolis! Manolis! I can't believe it. I just can't believe it,' she cried in joy and disbelief.

Stavros shook his head, smiling.

The foghorn was blasting out. It was a sign that they only had fifteen minutes left on Greek soil before the ship sailed.

Manolis saw his friend Tasos approaching and extricated himself from Agathi's embrace.

'M-m-Manolis!' Tasos said breathlessly. 'S-s-sorry I kept you waiting! The b-b-bus was late.'

'Don't worry,' said Manolis. 'You won't be needing to use the bus any more.' As he said this, he handed his friend his car key.

Tasos took it, bemused.

'B-b-but . . .'

'It's yours, *file mou*. Enjoy it.'

Tasos was literally speechless. Manolis had not told him why he had to come, and he had never in his life received such a gift. A bright green Alfa Romeo. Gleaming and polished. Every man's dream.

'Look, we have to go,' Manolis said. 'I'll drop you a line when we arrive. Take care . . . She goes at quite a speed!'

He turned away. Agathi and Stavros were waiting for him, still on shore. The three of them were the last passengers to board, and there were formalities to be gone through with tickets and visas. Above them they could see the passenger decks, full of people waving handkerchiefs and calling out to family and friends below.

Manolis looked up at the boat. He had been working on ships for so long, but it had been years since he had actually travelled anywhere on one. It felt very strange, and his palms were sweating as he picked up his bag and began to walk up the gangplank. It was a bridge that would lead him from one life to another.

The great hawsers that held the ship in place were being loosened, the anchor was being hoisted up, and the slow process of moving out of the port began.

The trio soon found their cabins, stored the luggage they had with them for the journey and then went up on deck. They found a space big enough for the three of them by the rails.

Agathi had insisted that Elli and Philippos did not come, so there was nobody for them to wave to. Once the ship had swung round, they had a good view of the city of Piraeus from their position on the aft deck. They all gazed at it, knowing they were seeing it for the last time.

Agathi was dabbing at her eyes. She saw very little through the mist of her tears. Stavros had a comforting arm around her.

As the ship moved slowly and steadily south, Manolis could not take his eyes away from the view. The city became smaller and smaller, a speck in the landmass. And then everything solid – mainland, islands, homeland – gradually vanished from view. There was nothing to interrupt the flat line of the horizon.

For a while he experienced the full force of nostalgia, a sensation so deep and powerful it almost made him swoon. Most people, including Agathi and Stavros, had gone inside now as the wind began to strengthen. Manolis stood there alone for a full hour, his hands gripping the rails. The middle of the ocean was a lonely place.

He recalled the last time he had stared down into the waves. It was the day after Anna's death, when his grief was still fresh and his memories of her touch were still warm. Her earring had been in his trouser pocket that day. He still had it all these years later, and felt for it inside his jacket now.

It glinted in the palm of his hand and he looked at it one last time, imagined it hanging from the lobe of her ear, imagined her smile. And then he let it drop. It was a long way down, and the stones were the colour of the sea. He did not even see it touch the water. Finally he was leaving Anna behind.

Chapter Nineteen

IN AGIOS NIKOLAOS, Sofia was soon to experience true grief for the first time. *Mousátos Pappoús* had been living with them for over a year, after failing to recover properly from a chest infection, and in the autumn of 1969, he died peacefully in his bed.

When Alexandros Vandoulakis had passed away, Sofia had been too young to understand the full force of such a loss, but this time she was inconsolable, and Maria found her daughter's sadness almost harder to deal with than her own. It was weeks before Sofia stopped crying herself to sleep. The event seemed to mark the moment when she lost the sparkle and innocence of childhood and her adolescence began.

During the entire time that she was nursing her father at home, Maria had not visited the prison. She did not want to bring home any infections.

Once the funeral and the forty-day period of mourning had passed, she made it a priority to go and see Andreas. She had often thought of him during the intervening time, but had not even had time to write him a letter. She felt she had been neglectful.

'It's not enough just to think of someone,' she said to Nikos, who was hoping that she might not resume these visits. 'You have to *show* them that you think of them.'

Andreas was lying on his bed when she walked into the room, and did not stir. Was he asleep? Was he ill?

'Andreas? It's Maria . . .'

She could see that his eyes were open.

'Maria? Ah, Maria,' came a faint voice from the emaciated figure on the bed. He struggled to sit up, just about managing to lean his back against the wall behind him.

Maria found him greatly changed. The image that she had in her mind of him, religiously transformed, smiling, was not the reality now. Inside his prison uniform, he was just bones, and he had aged by a decade.

He seemed very preoccupied and did not ask her a single question, even about Sofia. The only thing that interested him was his own spiritual state.

Maria had to lean in to hear him, his voice was so weak.

'I have been fasting,' he said. 'It brings me closer to the Lord.'

'I sometimes do that for a few days too,' Maria answered. In Holy Week she had often tried to be observant when she could, though she found she could not sustain it for five whole days, particularly when she was working in the hospital. It was impractical to feel weak with hunger when she had patients to take care of.

'Not just for a few days, Maria. I do this for months at a time. It began last year. You know our Lord was in the wilderness for forty days and forty nights without food.'

'Yes, Andreas. That's why we have Lent, isn't it?'

'Well, nothing passed my lips for forty days. I came so close to him, Maria. He was with me, next to me, within me.'

Maria was torn between the notion of faith and her knowledge of the human body. She did not want to be cynical, but she found herself imagining the state of delirium that such deprivation would induce.

'Do you know the Lord, Maria? Has he visited you? Has he sat beside you? Have you felt that warmth? That light?' As he spoke, he gesticulated wildly. His hands looked unnaturally large at the end of his emaciated arms.

His direct questioning left Maria feeling slightly uncomfortable. He challenged her own very private ideas of faith and spirituality.

Yes, she had known God's peace. Yes, she had understood the strength that faith brought. For all those years on Spinalonga, she had seen the fortitude and the hope expressed by so many patients, and the desire for healing that had been dashed for them. She had nursed dozens through the moment of death and seen them sustained by the belief that this was not an end, but a beginning. The presence of God next to them was unquestioned, even as they left this life, some of them in terrible pain.

She nodded to avoid giving Andreas an answer, and he continued.

'After those forty days, I had no wish to eat. I wanted to remain with the Lord. I saw him surrounded by light, surrounded by angels. I was given a glimpse of heaven, Maria.'

Maria listened. There was nothing else demanded of her. This fanaticism seemed to need no response.

'I am getting closer to him all the time now. I eat a small amount of bread and take a little water each day. But that's all.'

Maria looked at him. It was obvious that he was ill — even dying. Any words she wanted to say simply dried in her mouth. There in front of her was a man slowly killing himself.

His tone changed suddenly, as if he had some new source of energy.

'I am moving towards him, Maria. What I mean is that I am moving towards being with him for eternity. He is calling me, Maria. I know he is calling me!'

There was a maniacal excitement in Andreas's voice that suddenly made Maria feel afraid. She was locked in with him and there was no way out until the guard came.

'But there is something *between* us! There is something in the way! There is something between me and God, Maria! I feel his crown of thorns as though it is on my own head! I feel the nails in my hands! And in my feet! But there is something between us . . .'

Maria watched him warily. Hallucinations were a frequent result of food deprivation. He was getting more and more agitated by the moment. It was a small comfort to her that she would easily be able to defend herself if he attacked her. He must be half her weight now and looked as if he could be snapped in half.

'I know what it is that keeps me from him!' he cried out. 'There is a truth that has to be told, Maria. There is a truth that I must tell!'

'A truth?' she asked calmly. 'Can you tell it to me?'

'No!' he said, with a hint of anger. 'There is only one person who must have this truth. There is someone it *belongs* to. It is *his* truth, Maria. He must have it. *He . . . must . . . have . . . it!*'

He was almost raving now. Maria glanced nervously at the door, willing it to open.

'I need to write to him, Maria. I need paper. Give me paper. Do you have paper, Maria? Quickly, I must have paper.'

Maria's pulse was racing. She grabbed her bag from the floor and rummaged in it frantically. She knew she did not have a sheet of paper. It was not something she carried with her. As she pulled out a pencil from the depths of its darkness, she could see Andreas getting frustrated.

'Not just a pencil! Paper! I need paper! Paper, Maria! Paper!'

Maria was almost in tears. She was panicking. In a side pocket she felt something and heard a crinkling sound. She almost cried with relief as she pulled it out. It was a shopping list scribbled on a sheet of exercise paper, and the back of it was blank.

Andreas almost snatched it out of her hand. He grabbed the Bible, which lay on the bed next to him, and used it to rest the paper on.

Maria handed him the pencil and he began to scribble furiously. It was as if he was possessed. She could not see what he was writing, but he filled the entire side of the sheet, signed his name and folded it twice before holding it out to her.

'Please,' he said, as if addressing his secretary. 'Please can you see that this is delivered to Manolis Vandoulakis.'

'But I . . .' She wanted to tell him that she did not know exactly where Manolis was, but Andreas was not listening.

'It is confidential. Totally confidential. *Only* Manolis should read this. *No one* else!'

He was brusque to the point of rudeness, but nothing surprised Maria on this visit. All she wanted was to get out of there.

'Do you promise me?'

Suddenly the guard's footsteps could be heard outside.

'Maria? Do you *promise*? No one else!'

'Yes,' she said, and deftly took the letter from Andreas's hand.

As the door swung open, she was zipping up her bag.

She had never been so relieved to leave the prison. She wanted to get away as fast as she could, and almost fell as she ran along the road away from its heavy door and forbidding walls.

Andreas's state of religious mania had shocked her. She had never encountered anything like it before. She had read of monks who lived alone and meditated all day, of those who crawled for many kilometres on hands and knees to reach a holy place, of those who sought solitude on mountaintops. But they were still connected to the earth, to life. Andreas seemed distant from both.

When she got home, Nikos was sitting at the kitchen table with Sofia. They were tackling her maths together.

The prison visits were never mentioned in front of Sofia. Nikos took one look at Maria's face and could see that something was wrong. He followed her to the bedroom, where she was hanging up her coat.

'What happened?' he asked with concern.

'He's gone mad,' she answered simply. 'And he's dying.'

She slumped down on the end of their bed. The visit had exhausted her.

'I don't really know what else to tell you,' she added. 'He was crazed.'

'I'm so sorry, Maria,' said Nikos, kissing the top of his wife's head. 'You look really upset.'

'I'll be fine in a minute,' Maria reassured him. 'You'd better get back to the maths!'

She closed her eyes and sat for a while.

What was she going to do? It was the greatest dilemma she had ever faced and one she had to confront alone. She glanced at the brown shoulder bag sitting next to her on the bed. Nikos had given it to her for a birthday half a decade ago and she had used it every day since. Over the years, the leather had softened in a pleasing way and its worn straps had been repaired many times over. It had been a constant companion wherever she went. But now it seemed like an unexploded bomb.

Manolis Vandoulakis. It had shocked her to hear Andreas saying that name.

Inside her bag was a letter. There was no barrier to her reading it, no envelope securely sealed down that she would have to steam open or tear apart. Just two folds. One, two and she would know what it said.

It was not addressed to her. But she knew that the contents were of concern to her. Did that give her a right to read it? She wrestled with the question.

Downstairs she could hear Nikos with Sofia.

'Bravo, *agápi mou*! Bravo!' he said.

Sofia struggled with her maths, and Nikos spent hours each day patiently helping her to understand it. The cheerful sound of her daughter's hands clapping together with pleasure came up through the floor. There had been a breakthrough.

Maria felt inside the bag. The letter was still there.

She took it out. Before she had a chance to yield to the temptation, she should find an envelope, put the letter inside and seal it up. This was her obligation. Not because she owed anything to Andreas Vandoulakis, but because it was her moral duty. She had been entrusted to act as postman. And by a dying man.

She ran downstairs with the letter in her hand. In the living room, she rummaged through her small desk, which sat in the corner of the room. She felt a sense of panic. There was plenty of writing paper, but she had run out of envelopes.

'Nikos,' she said, hurrying into the kitchen, 'I need an envelope!'

'*Mamá*, please,' complained Sofia. 'Can *Babá* just finish this for me first?'

'I'm sure I have one, *agápi mou*, but just give me a second.'

Neither of them felt that an envelope could be a greater matter of urgency than the algebraic equation they were in the middle of solving.

Maria retreated into the living room. She was sweating so much that the folded paper was almost sticking to her hand. It felt like it was burning through her palm.

A moment or so passed. She felt nauseous as a war continued to rage within her. Just to peel up a corner of the sheet – would that be wrong? Was she not entitled to learn some kind of truth from the man who had killed her sister? Did he have a right to keep anything from her? What exactly had he written to Manolis?

From the other room, she could hear that father and daughter were still immersed. If only Nikos would come in at that instant to hand her an envelope, this moment would pass. She felt the panic rising within her.

With a shaking hand, she opened out the sheet and ran her eyes over the list: *flour, eggs, sugar, coffee, cheese, soap* . . . It would be so easy to turn it over. She even held it up to the light so that she could see the faint scrawl coming through from the other side. It looked even untidier than her husband's.

The rumours about Manolis and her sister had preoccupied Maria when she was on Spinalonga, but she had always told herself that Andreas must be Sofia's father, because she had never wanted to believe otherwise. She was convinced that on the reverse side of her banal list of household goods was an important truth, and a battle raged within her.

What held her back, but only just, was a promise. She had promised that the letter would be given to a particular person and that nobody else would read it. There was no possibility of breaking such a vow, and she found her resolve hardening.

She folded the letter up again and concealed it in her desk drawer.

It must leave her possession as soon as possible. It must find its way to Manolis.

She had a further rummage for an envelope and eventually found a heavy brown one at the back of a drawer. She stuffed Andreas's letter inside, sealed it up and put an additional strip of tape over the flap. The outside was left blank. She said nothing to Nikos and put the envelope in her bag, knowing that he never looked inside.

The only person she knew who had any kind of contact with Manolis was Antonis. So a week later, when they went to Plaka for lunch in the taverna, she took Fotini to one side.

'Can I ask you a huge favour?' she said. 'Do you think your brother would post something to Manolis for me?'

Fotini looked very surprised.

'To Manolis? What on earth do you want to send to that rogue?' she asked.

'Just a letter . . .'

'You're writing to him? What on earth for, Maria?'

'Nothing important. But I do want him to get this.'

Fotini could see that her friend was being cagey.

'Well, I could get his address from Antonis, I suppose. Then you could send it yourself.'

'I don't really want that,' admitted Maria. 'Do you think he would actually send it for me?'

'All right, *fili mou.* You're being very mysterious, but go on, give it to me. I'm going over to see them next week, so I'll ask him then.'

Antonis was more than happy to do his sister's friend a favour.

It seemed a while since he had contacted Manolis, and he wrote a letter of his own. It was the usual brief and semi-legible précis of news about his business, names of some new cars that had come on the market, and two suggested dates for his next visit to Piraeus. He enclosed Maria's letter with his and put it on the table ready to post.

Chapter Twenty

E VEN BEFORE ANTONIS had got round to going to the post office, Maria and Nikos received a letter. It was from the governor of the prison.

Andreas Vandoulakis had died. The letter informed them when the burial was to take place but arrived after the event.

Nikos read the letter first and then passed it to Maria.

Maria felt neither surprise nor great grief. She had seen close up the strength of religious faith that had made Andreas yearn for death. Now he was where he wanted to be.

She noticed a look of relief on her husband's face. As far as Nikos was concerned, Andreas's death meant an end to his irrational fear that the Vandoulakis family might take Sofia away from them. One careless comment from Maria and the calm expression she saw on her beloved husband's face would be wiped away. In a few years' time they would have to consider what Sofia was told, and only then would she tell him about the possibility of Manolis being the girl's father. For now, it was enough that the man who had killed her sister had died in peace. She was happy to have enabled that.

Without discussing it with Nikos, she decided to visit Andreas's grave.

She went on a day in early February when the sun could not break through the low clouds. At the entrance was a flower stall, and having purchased the least desultory posy on display, she went through the gates. Unless they had families who demanded other arrangements – and very few did – all the life-sentence prisoners who died in the Neapoli prison were buried in one corner of the sprawling cemetery situated on a hillside above the town. In this dark, neglected area where weeds grew waist high, there were no well-tended graves with sentimental expressions of love inscribed on the headstones. There were no photographs of the deceased or oil lamps with flames kept alight by grieving relatives. It was a bleak environment, and particularly so on this colourless day.

Maria soon found the place she was looking for. The name was marked on a wooden cross and the grave was long and narrow. She remembered how painfully skeletal Andreas had been on that last visit. There were rarely any visitors in this area of the *nekro-tafeío*, and two attendants who were hacking away at some frost-hardened ground not far away regarded her with curiosity.

She crossed herself several times, then stood over the grave for a few minutes before laying her flowers.

'*Anapávsu en iríni*, Andreas,' she said, under her breath. 'May you rest in peace.'

After a moment or two of contemplation, she crossed herself and turned away, knowing that she would never return.

She was home in time for Sofia's return from school. They chatted about what had happened in classes that day, and Maria began to make the supper.

'My friend Despina has a boyfriend!' revealed Sofia.

'A boyfriend? But she's only thirteen!' exclaimed Maria, who had been dreading the moment when Sofia started to take an interest in boys. She was already taller than most of the other girls and looked older than her fourteen years.

'And he has a friend . . .' admitted Sofia.

'Well, you're both too young to start going around with boys, Sofia. So the answer to whatever your question is is *no!*'

Sofia flounced from the room and Maria heard a door upstairs slam.

She tried to stop herself thinking it, but Sofia was reminding her more and more of Anna when she was that age. It was not only as an adult that her sister had been disobedient and wild.

When Nikos came home, Maria had a quiet word with him about Sofia's friend and her boyfriend.

'Will you say something to her when we're having dinner?' she asked. 'She listens to you more than me.'

With great subtlety, Nikos steered the conversation round to Despina that evening, and by the end of it, he had agreed that Sofia could go with her after school that Friday for an ice cream along with two boys in their year at school.

'I'll be home by five, *Babá*,' she promised, giving her father a peck on the cheek before going up to bed.

'She's got you wrapped round her little finger,' Maria said indulgently.

'A visit to the *zacharoplasteío* is not worth fighting about, is it?' responded Nikos.

Maria nodded in agreement. She suspected that there were bigger battles to come.

During these weeks, a new hotel was being fashioned on the site of Pension Agathi. As soon as the previous tenants had left, scores of workmen had moved in. They had stripped out all the old furniture. One of them had pocketed the small gun he found in an old chest of drawers, and another had taken Agathi's mirror with the lights round it for his wife.

Their first task was to fit the place out with more modern lighting, and a shower cubicle was installed in the corner of every bedroom. To advertise 'en suite' put it in a category above every other establishment in the immediate area.

Within a short time of the previous tenants vacating, the Sunrise Hotel was ready, and after only a week of opening, it was overwhelmed with business. When a guest left, the efficient and fastidious manager immediately sent in a cleaner to get the room ready for the next client. The place quickly gained a reputation for cleanliness and value, and he often had someone waiting in the foyer with a suitcase for the first available vacancy.

One morning, the manager was at the front desk taking a payment for a departing guest. Three new guests were queuing to check in, and he realised there had been an overbooking. There were only two rooms available. The phones were both ringing and one of the cleaners came down to say that all the lights had fused on the top floor.

At that moment, in walked the postman with a stack of letters in his hands.

'Just put them down there, please,' the manager instructed irritably, indicating a small table already supporting an overfilled rack of printed ferry timetables.

The postman did as he was instructed, but the timetables scattered across the floor.

Generally the manager was a patient man, but this concatenation of annoyances tipped him over into a state of annoyance. He hated mess. He grabbed the mail to stop the whole table falling and marched into his office.

First he called an electrician, and then a neighbouring hotel. The overbooked guest would have to stay there. Then he quickly sifted through the post. At the end of each week he dutifully returned anything addressed to Pension Agathi to the postman, who in turn handed it back to the manager of the local post office, one of the laziest civil servants around. His task was to trace people who had left no forwarding address, but he rarely bothered. 'Half of them will be in Australia by now!' he joked.

The bulk of the mail comprised bills, which the manager put to one side, and a few booking requests, which he opened. There was one letter without the name of the hotel, but the address was theirs, and although the name on the envelope was scrawled, it bore some resemblance to his own: Markos Andreakis. Perhaps it was a booking. Using his silver opener, he slit open the envelope and withdrew the contents.

The first thing he saw was a list of food items – flour, eggs, sugar . . . – which seemed strange. Puzzled, he turned it over. Although he immediately realised the words roughly pencilled on the other side were not meant for him, the first line grabbed his attention.

Dear Manolis,

You will know that I am in prison serving a life sentence for killing my wife, Anna.

The receptionist came into the office to seek help with a customer complaint, but the manager waved him away with his hand.

'Give me a moment,' he said curtly, compelled to read on.

My days are hastening to an end and soon I will be with my maker. He will not take me until I have shared with you, Manolis, the reason that I committed the worst sin known to man: to take a life.

Anna and I were married for some years and we did not produce a child. Then, as if by a miracle, she conceived and our daughter Sofia was born. I was keen, of course, for a son, but as the years went by, there was no second pregnancy. I quietly went for a test at the hospital in Iraklion to see if the problem was mine. I did not tell Anna. It was quite simple to do and the result was almost immediate. My sperm count meant that I was incapable of fathering a child. I could not be Sofia's father.

On that same day, I came home early and heard you and Anna in our marriage bed.

In one day, I experienced more humiliation, loss and damage to my pride than any man should. I managed to contain this for a while, but on that August night, as we drove into Plaka, Anna taunted me with her love for you and laughed in my face. It pushed me to fire the gun.

My conscience does not allow me to leave this world without revealing the truth of Sofia's paternity.
May God be with you.
Your cousin, Andreas

Markos Andreakis read the letter through again.

In his spare time, he was an avid reader of detective stories and enjoyed guessing who the murderer was, but this felt like he had skipped to the final chapter. He was slightly shocked by the honesty and bluntness of a real-life criminal. He folded the letter up and put it in his shirt pocket so that he could share it with his wife that night, and then went out into reception to deal with the mundane drama of yet another overbooking.

The manager's wife was equally intrigued by the letter but agreed that there was nothing they could do to ensure it got into the right hands. She put it behind a large clock on the dresser, feeling that it was not the kind of thing one should throw away. When the clock was eventually moved for repair, the envelope slipped down the back and was forgotten.

In more or less the time it had taken Pension Agathi to be transformed beyond recognition, Manolis, Agathi and Stavros had sailed across the world. They had stopped at a few places en route for sightseeing, including India and China, but their ship was now docking in Melbourne, and Agathi's cousin Pavlos and his wife were there to meet them.

They had left Piraeus in winter and arrived on the other side of the planet to find the summer. It was a beautiful day for their first encounter with this vibrant city. Pavlos drove them through its elegant streets, and they admired the lofty palm trees and gleaming modern buildings as they went. None of them had expected somewhere so affluent and sophisticated.

Pavlos had several apartments and had put one aside for Agathi to live in. He owned another close by where Manolis could stay.

He would not ask for any rent for the first six months, since Agathi was going to be his star singer at the *bouzoúkia*, and he immediately gave Manolis a job in his latest taverna. 'I can see you will be the perfect front man,' were almost his first words to this stranger.

Within a few days, Manolis was working at Zorba's. Restaurant work was less physical than the heavy manual labour he was used to. For now, his charm and his voice were the key assets for the job. The staff liked him and he revived his Cretan accent, which customers seemed to love. He even borrowed a lyra from one of the waiters and played for them. It made him smile to bring the authentic sound of Crete to this strange new version of Greece. It was years since he had felt the powerful vibration of strings beneath bow, and he lost himself in the sensation.

He also resolved to learn English, and spent his spare time with a grammar book and Pavlos's niece, Zoie, who was a language teacher.

Zoie was only notionally aware of her Greek roots. She had been born in Melbourne almost as soon as her parents arrived there, and had only seen images of Athens in picture books. She was blonde but with almost black eyes, and was always cheerful, with a disposition as sunny as the place she had grown up in. She had got her degree in Sydney but returned to Melbourne straight afterwards, and now in her late twenties, she worked in a language school specially for Greeks. Many of them who came off the boat did not speak a word of English and wanted to learn fast.

Agathi was not one of those. Her preoccupation in the first few weeks was to create a home. Her trunks duly arrived and Stavros deftly put up some shelves so that she could unpack her china figures. Miraculously, out of the several hundred, only Alice in Wonderland was slightly damaged. Stavros carefully glued her arm back on, impressing Agathi, who admitted that she could not see the join. He also built a cabinet for her record collection, and soon the apartment was more luxurious and comfortable than their old place in Piraeus. They had a generous balcony too, and discovered a passion for potted plants. In this sultry Melbourne climate, they planned to create a jungle of exotic creepers and cacti.

Manolis was in the taverna for most of his waking hours, so Agathi and Stavros offered to help furnish his apartment for him. Stavros built cupboards and put in a new kitchen, even though it seemed unlikely that Manolis would ever have time to use it. During his fifth lesson with Zoie, when they were naming parts of the house and items of furniture, it came up in conversation that Manolis had never bought even a single chair in his life. It led to the idea that he should have his next lesson in a shop. Together they selected a three-piece suite, a kitchen table and a bed. The following lesson was spent in a fabric store, ostensibly to learn colours and shapes, with Manolis happily accepting Zoie's advice on curtains and a bedspread.

'Perrpool,' he said, struggling.

'No, Manolis, *purple!*'

'Purble!' he said triumphantly.

Zoie's smile lit up her face.

They both laughed and laughed and found they could not stop. Manolis was unfamiliar with such a combination of beauty, kindness and good humour. He found Zoie both attractive and intoxicating, and only a short while later, they found themselves beneath the bedclothes they had chosen together.

A few months after they had arrived, Agathi performed at the *bouzoúkia*'s opening. She sang lustily from her favourite repertoire and the crowd cheered wildly and applauded between every song. It was a long night of music and *tsikoudiá*, and the place was entirely packed out by enthusiastic expatriate Greeks.

Stavros gazed at Roussa. The memory of that first time he had seen her in Piraeus was still vivid. Tonight he felt as if he was in a dream. All those thousands of kilometres away from where they had first met, he was listening to the woman he loved and she was singing just for him.

Manolis was a little late arriving, as he had to cash up at the taverna, but when he sat down, he found a case on the table. It had a label attached to the handle. Pavlos had heard about his lyra playing and thought he should have one of his own.

He looked around for the boss, as he was known, but Pavlos was busy with some customers. Manolis opened up the case and lightly plucked at the strings. It was already tuned.

When Agathi took a break, Manolis moved forward to the stage and began to play. The audience was hushed, enthralled by this pure Cretan sound. He continued for half an hour or more, and then began to sing too. All around him were smiles and eyes that welled with tears. When he finished, he found Pavlos standing by the side of the stage.

The two men embraced.

'I have no words,' said Manolis. 'It's a long time since I've received such a gift.'

He was still holding the exquisitely inlaid lyra in one hand, the bow in the other.

'The guys at Zorba's told me about your playing!'

'Ah . . .' responded Manolis modestly.

'If you like,' said Pavlos, 'you could hang it on the wall behind the bar, so it's there for you next time.'

Words failed him, but Manolis did manage a smile. Pavlos slapped him on the back and moved away to greet more customers.

Back at his table, Manolis found Zoie sitting there.

'That was perfect,' she said. 'I have never heard anything like that before. It was magical.'

'*Efcharistó*,' he said. 'Thank you.' He realised that her praise meant more to him than all the rest of the applause put together.

It was well beyond midnight now and even the soberest in the room were drunk. It was time for the noisier part of the evening.

It was obligatory now for the great *rebétiko* hits of the forties and fifties to be played. And when the musicians struck up the notes of the soulful *zeibékiko*, Manolis raised a glass with Stavros, Agathi and Zoie.

'*Stin yeia mas*,' they said in unison. 'To our health.'

In the minds of both men was the last occasion when Manolis had danced to this music. Tonight he felt no need. Finally his pain and loss had been left behind.

Afterword

IN THE SUMMER of 2001, I was on holiday with family and friends on the north coast of Crete, not far from Agios Nikolaos. We went on holiday to Greece most years, with the destination often randomly chosen.

That year we were staying in a rented apartment complex, with basic facilities and a swimming pool impractically shaped like the island of Crete. The pattern of our days was to spend the morning on the beach and then to visit a place of interest in the afternoon. By the end of the first week, we had visited all the archaeological sites scattered around the area, as well as every possible museum. These included an entire museum dedicated to the iris and its historic uses in the dyeing of thread and fabric. I loved them all, but unsurprisingly the children were less enthusiastic. They were ten and eight at the time and nagged to spend the whole day playing on the beach. I would have been the same at their age, but in spite of sympathising with them, I was determined to pursue the parental mission to educate them – even on a summer holiday. Greece for me, even then, was far more than a place for hedonistic pursuits.

On that particular July afternoon (I remember very clearly that it was excessively hot), there were complaints all round when I announced the day's outing. In the guidebook, I had found a small island that had once been a hospital for leprosy patients. It did not appeal to them. At all. But with the promise of a boat trip and ice creams, we set off along the winding road towards Elounda.

The drive took forty-five minutes or so, and eventually we arrived in the quiet village of Plaka (one small café, a few tavernas and no shop), where we were to take a boat across to Spinalonga. It was already after four o'clock, and we were just in time to catch the last one leaving for the island.

With ice creams in hand, we embarked. The boat journey was short, and for the first time that day, thanks to a welcome breeze, I remember feeling relief from the intense heat. Within a few minutes we were approaching the rounded walls of the imposing Venetian fortification and disembarking.

What had attracted me to that entry in the guidebook was a date: 1957. This was the year when an effective cure for leprosy was discovered and the entire population of the island departed. For me, this scarcely seemed like history. It was only two years before I was born and for this reason especially piqued my interest.

Like most people, I knew very little about leprosy, and what I did know turned out to be wrong. For a start, I thought the disease had been as contagious as the plague and that it could mutilate the sufferer beyond recognition within days. I also thought it was a disease of the biblical era and had not existed for millennia. It was only as we were getting close to the island that I realised none of this was true. One of my holiday companions was a doctor, a dermatologist, and he was quick to give me some of the key facts: leprosy is a dermatological disease; it can be very slow to develop; and in the late 1950s it became curable. He was also keen to tell me that it does not always result in the kind of disfigurement many of us imagine (as shown in the film *Ben Hur*, for instance).

The boat was tethered and the captain told us to be back within an hour. We quickly bought our tickets and walked through the dark tunnel that led to the interior of the island. There were no guides to take us around and no books on sale, leaving us free to wander and imagine. I realise now that this was key to my experience of Spinalonga that day.

I have a strong recollection of the moment when we passed from the darkness into the light and emerged into what is effectively the island's high street. It was a transformative moment in every way. I could not help putting myself into the shoes of someone who found themselves standing at the end of this road for the first time (sufferers were sent there from 1903). Most patients arrived knowing they would never leave.

Its beauty was a surprise. I had expected somewhere that looked more like a prison than a friendly Greek village. There were pots of geraniums, wild flowers, sunlight on warm stones. It had a real romanticism about it that I had not expected. There was even a cat. Restoration works were going on at the time, and I am sure the amiable tom was making himself useful by keeping the mouse population down. He definitely added a friendly touch.

I began to walk around. At that time, the buildings were in a greater state of disrepair than many of them are in now. I peered inside some of the small houses (built during the Ottoman period) and spotted signs of ordinary life that I had not expected: tiny shreds of curtain material still pinned to window frames; patches of bright blue paint on the walls; and shelving still in the recesses of interior walls. Occasionally a shutter creaked, moved by the wind.

The high street was just like that in every other Cretan village, complete with a little church, a bakery, shops and so on, and even this infrastructure surprised me. Venetian water tunnels were still in good condition, as useful in the twentieth century for collecting vital rainwater as they had been in the year of their construction three centuries earlier. High above, I spotted the large building used as a hospital, and at the top of the street saw a derelict apartment building where patients must have lived.

The island had a remarkably warm and happy atmosphere, and,

having anticipated a place of misery and despair, the environment seemed paradoxical. I realised that patients had gone there not just to die, but to live.

At that time, I was writing about travel for various major British newspapers and magazines. The obvious thing would have been to come up with a short article on Spinalonga with a title such as 'The forgotten leper colony of Crete'. I quickly dismissed the notion. With my mind bursting with ideas and inspiration, it seemed entirely inappropriate to encapsulate this remarkable place in a factual 800-word piece. There was something much more emotional and imaginative that I wanted to express, something that had no place in a piece of journalism.

The walk around the perimeter of the island took less than an hour, but it was enough to fill me with impressions and questions. As we arrived back at our starting point, I already had an idea in my head.

My dermatologist friend had already made it clear to me that leprosy did not destroy the face and body of every sufferer. And even when such a result did occur, it could take decades. So I had the beginning of a story in my mind even as we were walking around, and this scenario became the core of the novel I would go on to write.

The notion was this: suppose a female patient exiled on Spinalonga falls in love with the doctor who arrives with medicine for her incurable disease. And then he cures her. Such a situation would contain a central conflict. Treatment would bring her freedom from disease and captivity on the island, but would also bring her the heartbreak of losing the man she loves. This one central idea drove the story of the novel, but of course it needed to be expanded further.

We were back in Plaka by six o'clock, and we swam off the pebbly beach opposite the island. The waters there are astonishingly clear, and I remember feeling tingly and refreshed as I dried off. Later we met up with our friends again and ate in one of the tavernas, sharing a huge dish of lobster spaghetti. I remember it vividly, as if all the experiences and memories of that day had a particular poignancy. I also remember that my mind was elsewhere.

Nowadays, Spinalonga is sometimes lit up at night, but in those days, as the light faded and night fell, the island simply disappeared, vanishing into the blackness. As we enjoyed our dinner, my mind kept returning to this place and the impression it had made on me. I resolved to come back the following day when it was light; not to go across again, simply to see it once more from a distance.

Back in Elounda the next day, I bought two small guidebooks (the kind that are more photographic than textual) and read them as soon as I returned to the apartment. They told me very little, merely describing the buildings and the three different phases of Spinalonga's history: Venetian, Ottoman and then finally the twentieth century, when it was used to isolate the leprosy patients. I was slightly disappointed. I had hoped for more. But I think this was when and why my imagination began to take over.

The lack of facts available to me could have been an obstacle, but instead it spurred me to creativity. I hadn't intended to work on this holiday, so I did not have even a small notebook with me. All I had was an envelope that had contained some instructions from the owner of the apartment (how to operate the hot water system and the cooker, no toilet paper to be flushed, recommended tavernas, best beaches, etc.). I covered it with my scribbles. Over the remaining days of our holiday, I experienced a sense of contentment. I felt I had something. I couldn't determine what it was exactly, but I knew there was a story I wanted to tell. This excited me. I had not written a fictional story for more than thirty years (not since school, in fact). I had read and studied plenty of other people's, but I had not told one myself.

My first task was to talk to someone who knew about leprosy. A letter to the world expert based at the London School of Hygiene and Tropical Medicine was immediately and gratifyingly answered. Dr (now Professor) Diana Lockwood not only gave me her time, but also lent me some of her precious textbooks from the 1930s and 1950s. They gave an authentic voice not only to how people treated leprosy but also to how they thought of it in the period I wanted to write about. I read each line very carefully, locking these valuable and almost unique books away each night in a fireproof filing cabinet. I learned everything I needed to know about the disease.

The following spring, I went back to Plaka and rented a room opposite Spinalonga. I took my mother with me, and her presence allowed me to sit and while away the hours in cafés and tavernas. Being alone would have attracted attention, but this way we simply looked like the two women we were, enjoying our time in Crete. I spoke not a word of the language, which gave us a kind of valuable unapproachability. It also meant that I did not have the opportunity to ask questions of local people or find out anything about life in the village back in the days when Spinalonga was still functioning. I simply absorbed the atmosphere and observed people.

Each day while I was staying in Plaka I took the first boat across to Spinalonga. The boatman must have thought I was strange. He smiled as he sold me a ticket but asked no questions – and on several occasions did not even ask for any money. Perhaps they thought I had a long-lost relative who had been on the island. The lack of language was definitely an advantage here.

Each visit enriched my love for this unique place and furnished me with more characters and ideas about how the story would run. The proximity of Plaka never stopped making an impression on me, and the fact that you could see small figures moving about on the opposite shore gave the novel that was evolving in my mind an extra intensity.

I wrote a very detailed outline, having two key historical dates in my mind: the German invasion of Crete, and the eventual cure for leprosy. I also wanted to create two generations of sufferers in one family, along with a subsequent generation from whom the presence of leprosy in their past is hidden.

The synopsis was written, along with a sample chapter, and sent out to a number of British publishers. It was rejected by several. They liked the idea of a love story set on a Greek island, but leprosy was considered not only an unlikely subject but also an uncommercial one. By chance, the proposal then fell onto the desk of a young editor who immediately understood not just the content but the mood of the story. Flora Rees, who has since edited all the novels I have written, spent much of her childhood in Africa because her father was a doctor of tropical diseases. She vividly recalled the days when he went to visit leprosy patients, and the anxiety it still caused, in spite of the fact that this disease was curable. Flora, like many who had a close connection with leprosy, appreciated that people react strangely even to the mention of the disease.

Within a year or so, I had finished writing and the novel was published in the UK – and soon after that in Greece, Norway, Israel and eventually more than thirty-five countries. A year or so after publication in Greece came an offer from Mega Channel to turn it into a twenty-six-part television serial. There had already been many other approaches from producers and directors in various countries around the world, but I had declined all of them because of a lack of trust in their ability (and desire) to portray leprosy sufferers with the respect that I felt they deserved. I was afraid they might appear as monsters. However, Mega allowed me full involvement with the production and the two years it took to create the series were immensely exciting, with a result that was both beautiful and moving.

The local people gave the production their full support, and many of the older ones, who remembered the real stories of Spinalonga, found themselves playing roles in the fictional version. We even had the full involvement of one particularly special person. Eighty-six-year-old Manolis Foundoulakis, who had once suffered from leprosy himself and now lived in a village above Plaka, provided extraordinary insight, wisdom and friendship to everyone who worked on the production. He appeared in the final scene on Spinalonga itself, when all the patients are cured and leave the island. He was a man cured of leprosy, playing the role of a man cured of leprosy.

Victoria Hislop with Manolis Foundoulakis

Art and reality came together in a way that is almost impossible to describe. I believe this fusion of the two is what gave *To Nisi*, the serial, its magic, and is the reason the Greek public responded to it in the way they did. As well as leaving the streets eerily silent each Monday night at ten o'clock, the transmission time, it achieved the highest ratings for a television serial on record.

Writing the novel brought many new opportunities to me, not just as a writer. I became an ambassador for the charity Lepra, which works to relieve the suffering of leprosy patients around the world. Unbelievably, there are still more than 300,000 new cases each year, mostly in India and Bangladesh. I help Lepra raise funds for research and treatment.

More recently, a hugely exciting event took place in my life. In July 2020, I was awarded Honorary Greek Citizenship by the President of Greece. In the official announcement it stated that this was for promoting modern Greek history and culture, including the history of Spinalonga.

Novels sometimes have a life of their own, and readers interpret the meaning and content in their own way, bringing their personal hopes, fears and emotions with them as they read. Even as a writer, you are often left with the question 'What happened next?' So much in most novels is, and should be, open-ended. In *The Island*, there is a single devastating event on a night that is meant to be the occasion of a huge celebration. It changes the lives of several people for ever. The characters I have picked up on in particular are the three men connected with Anna, as well as her sister, Maria, who is faced with a huge dilemma at the end of *One August Night*.

Writing this new story has shown me that, unless there is a happy-ever-after ending to a story (or almost everyone is dead, like in a Greek tragedy), it is always exciting as a writer to open a door that has been closed for a while and to step through it once more . . .

A final note: my knowledge of Greek language and culture has deepened over the years since I wrote *The Island*, and the eagle-eyed among my readers will notice that for the sake of accuracy there are some subtle changes to the spelling of Greek names and words.

Victoria Hislop
October 2020

Note on Leprosy

Leprosy in the 21ˢᵗ Century

Leprosy is caused by the bacteria *Mycobacterium Leprae*. It can lie undetected and unnoticed for between one and twenty years before becoming apparent. Leprosy affects the nerves of the hands, feet and face and can reduce and remove the sensation of pain and the ability to move fingers, toes and eyelids. This results in many of those affected becoming prone to burns and injuries leading to serious infections and ultimately the loss of fingers, toes and eyesight. In addition, immunological leprosy reactions often cause severe pain and disability. These reactions can occur before, during and after treatment.

Although leprosy has been eradicated in Europe, it is still a major health problem in developing countries. Hundreds of thousands of cases continue to be diagnosed every year. Many of these are not officially recorded, as people affected by leprosy are subject to widespread prejudice and discrimination including from their own families and communities. This prejudice makes those affected fearful of coming forward for diagnosis, despite the available antibiotic treatment being free and effective. Unfortunately, the later the diagnosis the higher the chance of serious disability.

Victoria Hislop

Lepra

Victoria Hislop is an Ambassador for Lepra. Lepra is an international charity working to beat leprosy and the prejudice it draws. They work directly with those affected in Bangladesh, India, Mozambique and Zimbabwe, where all together two-thirds of the world's cases occur.

Lepra works to treat, rehabilitate and amplify the voices of people affected by leprosy and is one of the world's leading authorities on the subject.

They are a secular charity, open to every faith and those without faith.

Lepra introduced Dapsone, the first cure for leprosy, and since 1924 has campaigned to keep those affected by leprosy with their communities rather than in colonies or isolation.

Today, Lepra is needed more than ever. Their skills to diagnose, treat and support the disabilities of those with leprosy remain in high demand.

It costs just £20 to train one village doctor to recognise the symptoms of leprosy; vital to ensure accurate diagnosis and guarantee that people are given guidance and the correct treatment as soon as practicable.

Please donate £20 today to support Lepra by:
- *Making a donation online with a credit card, debit card, or PayPal at www.lepra.org.uk*
- *Calling us at 01206 216700*
- *Texting LEPRA followed by your donation amount to 70500*
- *Sending a cheque to Lepra, 28 Middleborough, Colchester, Essex, CO1 1TG*
- *Using a CAF account, or by donating directly via a bank transfer, please ask us for details*

www.lepra.org.uk 🐦 @LepraUK 📷 @leprauk 📘 @LepraUK

Patron: Her Majesty The Queen
Charity No. 213251 (England and Wales) SC039715 (Scotland)
Lepra is a company limited by guarantee,
registered in England and Wales.
Registered Number 324748

Acknowledgements

With thanks to:

Ian, Emily, Will, Miriam and Colin for all their love during lockdown

Mari Evans and team at Headline, my phenomenal and steadfast publisher, with special thanks to Flora Rees

Jonathan Lloyd and team at Curtis Brown, my lively and energetic literary agency

Emily Hislop and Fotini Pipi for their eagle eyes.